Anne Thackeray

To Esther

And Other Sketches

Anne Thackeray

To Esther
And Other Sketches.

ISBN/EAN: 9783337010706

Printed in Europe, USA, Canada, Australia, Japan

Cover: Foto ©Andreas Hilbeck / pixelio.de

More available books at **www.hansebooks.com**

THE WORKS

OF

MISS THACKERAY

VOLUME IV.

TO ESTHER and Other Sketches

LONDON

SMITH, ELDER, & CO., 15 WATERLOO PLACE

1876

TO ESTHER

And Other Sketches

BY

MISS THACKERAY

LONDON
SMITH, ELDER, & CO., 15 WATERLOO PLACE
1876

CONTENTS.

TO ESTHER

1859-60

TO ESTHER.

1859—60.

' 'Tis Rome-work, made to match.'

THE first time that I ever knew you was at Rome one winter's evening. I had walked through the silent streets—I see them now—dark with black shadows, lighted by the blazing stars overhead and by the lamps dimly flickering before the shrines at street corners. After crossing the Spanish-place I remember turning into a narrow alley and coming presently to a great black archway, which led to a glimmering court. A figure of the Virgin stood with outstretched arms above the door of your house, and the light burning at her feet dimly played upon the stone, worn and stained, of which the walls were built. Through the archway came a glimpse of the night sky above the court-yard shining wonderfully with splendid stars; and I also

B 2

caught the plashing sound of a fountain flowing in the darkness. I groped my way up the broad stone staircase, only lighted by the friendly star-shine, stumbling and knocking my shins against those ancient steps, up which two centuries of men and women had clambered; and at last, ringing at a curtained door, I found myself in a hall, and presently ushered through a dining-room, where the cloth was laid, and announced at the drawing-room door as Smith.

It was a long room with many windows, and cabinets and tables along the walls, with a tall carved mantel-piece, at which you were standing, and a Pompeian lamp burning on a table near you. Would you care to hear what manner of woman I saw; what impression I got from you as we met for the first time together? In after days, light, mood, circumstance, may modify this first image more or less, but the germ of life is in it—the identical presence—and I fancy it is rarely improved by keeping, by painting up, with love, or dislike, or long use, or weariness, as the case may be. Be this as it may, I think I knew you as well after the first five minutes' acquaintance as I do now. I saw an ugly woman, whose looks I liked somehow; thick brows, sallow face, a tall and straight-made figure, honest eyes that had no particular merit besides, dark hair, and a pleasant, cordial smile. And somehow, as I looked at you and heard your talk, I seemed to be aware of a frank spirit, uncertain, blind, wayward, tender, under this somewhat stern exterior; and so, I repeat, I liked you, and, making a bow, I said I was afraid I was before my time.

'I'm afraid it is my father who is after his,' you said. 'Mr. Halbert is coming, and he, too, is often late;' and so we went on talking for about ten minutes.

Yours is a kindly manner, a sad-toned voice; I know not if your life has been a happy one; you are well disposed towards every soul you come across; you love to be loved, and try with a sweet artless art to win and charm over each man or woman that you meet. I saw that you liked me, that you felt at your ease with me, that you held me not quite your equal, and might perhaps laugh at, as well as with me. But I did not care. My aim in life, Heaven knows, has not been to domineer, to lay down the law, and triumph over others, least of all over those I like.

The Colonel arrived presently, with his white hair trimly brushed and his white neckcloth neatly tied. He greeted me with great friendliness and cordiality. You have got his charm of manner; but with you, my dear, it is not manner only, for there is loyalty and heartiness

shining in your face, and sincerity ringing in every tone
of your voice.   As for the Colonel, your father, if I
mistake not, he is a little shrivelled-up old gentleman,
with a machine inside to keep him going, and outside
a well-cut coat and a well-bred air and a certain knowledge of the world, to get on through life with.   However, this is not the way to speak to a young lady about
her father; and besides it is you, and not he, in whom I
take the interest which prompts these maudlin pages.

Mr. Halbert and little Latham, the artist, were the
only other guests.   You did not look round when
Halbert was announced, but went on speaking to
Latham, with a strange flush in your face; until Halbert
had, with great *empressement*, made his way through the
chairs and tables, and had greeted, rather than been
greeted by, you.

So thinks I to myself, concerning certain vague
notions I had already begun to entertain, I am rather
late in the field, and the city is taken and has already
hoisted the conqueror's colours.   Perhaps those red,
flags might have been mine had I come a little sooner;
who knows?   *'De tout laurier un poison est l'essence,'*
says the Frenchman; and my brows may be as well
unwreathed.

'I came upstairs with the dinner,' Mr. Halbert was

saying. 'It reassured me as to my punctuality. I rather pique myself on my punctuality, Colonel.'

'And I'm afraid I have been accusing you of being always late,' you said, as if it were a confession.

'Have you thought so, Miss Olliver?' cried Halbert.

'Dinner, sir,' said Baker, opening the door.

All dinner-time Halbert, who has very high spirits, talked and laughed without ceasing. You, too, laughed, listened, looked very happy, and got up with a smile at last, leaving us to drink our wine. The Colonel presently proposed cigars.

'In that case I shall go and talk to your daughter in the drawing-room,' Halbert said. 'I'm promised to Lady Parker's to-night; it would never do to go there smelling all over of smoke. I must be off in half-an-hour,' he added, looking at his watch.

I, too, had been asked to the tea-party, and I was rather surprised that Halbert should be in such a desperate hurry to get there. · Talking to Miss Olliver in the next room, I could very well understand; but leaving her to rush off to Lady Parker's immediately, did not accord with the little theories I had been laying down. Could I have been mistaken? In this case it seemed to me this would be the very woman to suit me—(you see I am speaking without any reserve, and simply

describing the abrupt little events as they occurred)—
and I thought, who knows that there may not be a chance
for me yet? But, by the time my cigar had crumbled
into smoke and ashes, it struck me that my little castle
had also wreathed away and vanished. Going into the
drawing-room, where the lamps were swinging in the
dimness, and the night without streaming in through the
uncurtained windows, we found you in your white dress,
sitting alone at one of them. Mr. Halbert was gone,
you said; he went out by the other door. And then
you were silent again, staring out at the stars with
dreamy eyes. The Colonel rang for tea, and chirped
away very pleasantly to Latham by the fire. I looked
at you now and then, and could not help surprising
your thoughts somehow, and knowing that I had not
been mistaken after all. There you sat, making simple
schemes of future happiness; you could not, would not,
look beyond the present. You were very calm, happy,
full of peaceful reliance. Your world was alight with
shining stars, great big shining meteors, all flaring up
as they usually do before going out with a splutter at
the end of the entertainment. People who are in love
I have always found very much alike; and now, having
settled that you belonged to that crack-brained com-
munity, it was not difficult to guess at what was going on
in your mind.

I, too, as I have said, had been favoured with a card
for Lady Parker's rout; and as you were so absent and
ill-inclined to talk, and the Colonel was anxious to go off
and play whist at his club, I thought I might as well
follow in Halbert's traces, and gratify any little curiosity
I might feel as to his behaviour and way of going on in
your absence. I found that Latham was also going to
her ladyship's. As we went downstairs together Latham
said, ' It was too bad of Halbert to break up the party
and go off at that absurd hour. I didn't say I was going,
because I thought his rudeness might strike them.'

' But surely,' said I, ' Mr. Halbert seems at home there,
and may come and go as he likes?' Latham shrugged
his shoulders. ' I like the girl; I hope she is not taken in
by him. He has been very thick all the winter in other
quarters. Lady Parker's niece, Lady Fanny Fareham,
was going to marry him, they said; but I know very little
of him. He is much too great a swell to be on intimate
terms with a disreputable little painter like myself.
What a night it is !' As he spoke we came out into the
street again, our shadows falling on the stones; the Virgin
overhead still watching, the lamp burning faithfully, the
solemn night waning on. Lady Parker had lodgings in
the Corso. I felt almost ashamed of stepping from the
great entertainment without into the close racketing little

tea-party that was clattering on within. We came in, in the middle of a jangling tune, the company spinning round and round. Halbert, twirling like a Dervish, was almost the first person I saw; he was flushed, and looked exceedingly handsome, and his tall shoulders overtopped most of the other heads. As I watched him I thought with great complacency that if any woman cared for me, it would not be for my looks. No! no! what are mere good looks compared to those mental qualities which, &c. &c. Presently, not feeling quite easy in my mind about these said mental qualities, I again observed that it was still better to be liked for one's self than for one's mental qualities; by which time I turned my attention once more to Mr. Halbert. The youth was devoting himself most assiduously to a very beautiful, oldish young lady, in a green gauzy dress; and I now, with a mixture of satisfaction and vexation, recognised the very same looks and tones which had misled me at dinner.

I left him still at it and walked home, wondering at the great law of natural equality which seems to level all mankind to one standard, notwithstanding all those artificial ones which we ourselves have raised. Here was a successful youth, with good looks and good wits and position and fortune; and here was I, certainly no wonder, insignificant, and plain, and poor, and of commonplace intelligence, and as well satisfied with my own possessions, such as they were, as he, Halbert, could be with the treasures a prodigal fortune had showered upon him. Here was I, judging him, and taking his measure as accurately as he could take mine, were it worth his while to do so. Here was I, walking home under the stars, while he was flirting and whispering with Lady Fanny, and both our nights sped on. Constellations sinking slowly, the day approaching through the awful realms of space, hours waning, life going by for us both alike : both of us men waiting together amidst these awful sur- roundings.

You and I met often after this first meeting—in churches where tapers were lighting and heavy censers swinging—on the Pincio, in the narrow, deep-coloured streets : it was not always chance only which brought me so constantly into your presence. You yourself were the chance, at least, and I the blind follower of fortune.

All round about Rome there are ancient gardens lying basking in the sun. Gardens and villas built long since by dead cardinals and popes ; terraces, with glinting shadows, with honeysuckle clambering in desolate lux- uriance ; roses flowering and fading and falling in showers on the pathways ; and terraces and marble steps yellow

with age. Lonely fountains plash in their basins, statues
of fauns and slender nymphs stand out against the solemn
horizon of blue hills and crimson-streaked sky; of cypress
trees and cedars, with the sunset showing through their
stems. At home I lead a very busy, anxious life; the
beauty and peace of these Italian villas fill me with
inexpressible satisfaction and gratitude towards those
mouldering pontiffs, whose magnificent liberality has
secured such placid resting-places for generations of
weary men. Taking a long walk out of Rome one day in
the early spring, I came to the gates of one of these gardens. I remember seeing a carriage waiting in the shade of
some cedar-trees; hard by horses with drooping heads, and
servants smoking as they waited. This was no uncommon
sight; the English are for ever on their rounds; but
somehow, on this occasion, I thought I recognised one of
the men, and instead of passing by, as had been my
intention, I turned in at the half-opened gate, which the
angels with the flaming swords had left unguarded and
unlocked for once, and, after a few minutes' walk, I came
upon the Eve I looked for.

You were sitting on some time-worn steps; you wore a
green silk dress, and your brown hair, with the red tints
in it, was all ablaze with the light. You looked very
unhappy, I thought: got up with an effort, and smiled
a pitiful smile.

'Are you come here for a little quiet?' I asked. 'I am not going to disturb you.'

'I came here for pleasure, not quiet,' you said, 'with papa and some friends. I was tired, so they walked on and left me.'

'That is the way with one's friends,' said I. 'Who are the culprits, Miss Olliver?'

'I am the only culprit,' you said grimly. 'Lady Fanny and Mr. Halbert came with us to-day. Look, there they are at the end of that alley.'

And as you spoke, you raised one hand and pointed, and I made up my mind. It was a very long alley. The figures in the distance were advancing very slowly. When they reach that little temple, thought I, I will tell her what I think.

This was by no means so sudden a determination as it may appear to you, reading over these pages. It seems a singular reason to give; but I really think it was your hopeless fancy for that rosy youth which touched me and interested me so. I know I used to carry home sad words, spoken not to me, and glances that thrilled me with love, pity, and sympathy. What I said was, as you know, very simple and to the purpose. I knew quite well your fancy was elsewhere; mine was with you, perhaps as hopelessly placed. I didn't exactly see what good this confession was to do either of us, only there I was, ready to spend my life at your service.

When I had spoken there was a silent moment, and then you glowed up—your eyes melted, your mouth quivered. 'Oh, what can I say? Oh, I am so lonely. Oh, I have not one friend in the world; and now, suddenly, a helping hand is held out, and I can't— I *can't* push it away. Oh, don't despise. Oh, forgive me.'

Despise! scorn! . . . Poor child! I only liked you the more for your plaintive appeal; though I wondered at it.

'Take your time,' I said; 'I can wait, and I shall not fly away. Call me when you want me; send me away when I weary you. Here is your father; shall I speak to him? But no. Remember there is no single link between us, except what you yourself hold in your own hands.'

Here your father and Halbert and Lady Fanny came up. 'Well, Esther, are you rested?' says the Colonel cheerfully. 'Why, how do you do?' (to me). 'What have you been talking about so busily?'

You did not answer, but fixed your eyes on your father's face. I said something; I forget what. Halbert, looking interested, turned from one to the other. Lady Fanny,

who held a fragrant heap of roses, shook a few petals to
the ground, where they lay scattered after we had all
walked away.

If you remember, I did not go near you for a day
or two after this. But I wrote you a letter, in which I
repeated that you were entirely free to use me as you
liked: marry me—make a friend of me—I was in your
hands. One day, at last, I called; and I shall never
forget the sweetness and friendly gratefulness with which
you received me. A solitary man, dying of lonely thirst,
you meet me smiling with a cup of sparkling water: a
weary watcher through the night—suddenly I see the
dawn streaking the bright horizon. Those were very
pleasant times. I remember now, one afternoon in early
spring, open windows, sounds coming in from the city,
the drone of the *pifferari* buzzing drowsily in the sultry
streets. You sat at your window in some light-coloured
dress, laughing now and then, and talking your tender
little talk. The Colonel, from behind *The Times*, joined
in now and again: the pleasant half-hours slid by. We
were still basking there, when Halbert was announced,
and came in, looking very tall and handsome. The bag-
pipes droned on, the flies sailed in and out on the sunshine: you still sat tranquilly at the open casement; but
somehow the golden atmosphere of the hour was gone.

Your smiles were gone; your words were silenced; and that happy little hour was over for ever.

When I got up to come away Halbert rose too : he came downstairs with me, and suddenly looking me full in the face said, ' When is it to be?'

' You know much more about it than I do,' I answered.

' You don't mean to say that you are not very much smitten with our hostess?' said he.

' Certainly I am,' said I; ' I should be ready enough to marry her, if that is what you mean. I daresay I shan't get her. She is to me the most sympathetic woman I have ever known. You are too young, Mr. Halbert, to understand and feel her worth. Don't be offended,' I added, seeing him flush up. ' You young fellows can't be expected to see with the same eyes as we old ones. You will think as I do in another ten years.'

' How do you mean?' he asked.

' Isn't it the way with all of us?' said I: ' we begin by liking universally; as we go on we pick and choose, and weary of things which had only the charm of novelty to recommend them; only as our life narrows we cling more and more to the good things which remain, and feel their value ten times more keenly. And surely a sweet, honest-hearted young woman like Esther Olliver is a good thing.

'She is very nice,' Halbert said. 'She has such good manners. I have had more experience than you give me credit for, and I am very much of your way of thinking. They say that old courtly Colonel is dreadfully harsh to her—wants to marry her off his hands. I assure you you have a very good chance.'

'I mistrust that old Colonel,' said I, dictatorially; 'as I trust his daughter. Somehow she and I chime in tune together;' and, as I spoke, I began to understand why you once said wofully, that you had not one friend in the world; and my thoughts wandered away to the garden where I had found you waiting on the steps of the terrace.

'What do you say to the serenade Lady Fanny and I have been performing lately?' Halbert was saying meanwhile, very confidentially. 'Sometimes I cannot help fancying that the Colonel wants to take a part in the performance, and a cracked old tenor part, too. In that case I shall cry off, and give up my engagements.' And then, nodding good-by, he left me.

I remember the evening of that day, a sudden wind had risen driving the clouds across the city; the soft wild gust came with a wail and a splashing of rain dashing against my uncurtained window. The city lights were flaring and extinguished. The woman of the house had piled up a wood fire on the stone hearth, and the logs

c

were smouldering in a bed of white ashes. I had not gone out as usual, but I had stayed at home reading a book which had been sent out to me from England. It was the *Idylls of the King*, I remember, which had lately come out. About nine o'clock someone came ringing at the door, and old Octavia brought me a note in a writing I recognised. 'The Signorina's cook had left it on his way home,' said Octavia. 'He lodges close by.'

Poor little note! it was wet with rain-drops. I have it now.

'*Via della Croce:* Friday.

'DEAR MR. SMITH' (I read)—'I have just seen my father and heard some news which has surprised and bewildered me. He is engaged to be married to Lady Fanny Fareham. Will you come and see me to-morrow? Goodnight, dear kind friend.

'ESTHER.'

That was all. Poor little Esther.

I met Halbert in the Babuino the very next day. He came straight up to me, saying, 'Going to the Ollivers', eh? Will you take a message for me, and tell the Colonel I mean to look in there this evening? That old fox the Colonel—you have heard that he *is* actually going to marry Lady Fanny. She told me so herself, yesterday.'

'I think her choice is a prudent one,' I answered. 'I suppose Colonel Olliver is three times as rich as yourself? You must expect a woman of thirty to be prudent. I am not fond of that virtue in very young people, but it is not unbecoming with years.'

Halbert flushed up. 'I suppose from that you mean she was very near marrying me? I'm not sorry she has taken up with the Colonel after all. You see, my mother was always writing, and my sisters at home; and they used to tell me . . . and I myself thought she——, you know what I mean. But, of course, they have been reassured on that point.'

'Do you mean to say,' I asked, in a great panic, 'that you would marry any woman who happened to fall in love with you?'

'I don't know what I might have done a year ago,' said he, laughing; 'but just now, you see, I have had a warning, and, besides, it is my turn to make the advances.'

I was immensely relieved at this, for I didn't know what I was not going to say.

Here, as we turned a street-corner, we came upon a black-robed monk, standing, veiled and motionless, with a skull in one bony hand. This cheerful object changed the current of our talk, and we parted presently at a fountain. Women with black twists of hair were standing round

about, waiting in careless attitudes, while the limpid water
flowed.

When I reached your door, I found the carriage waiting, and you and your father under the archway.   'Come
with us,' said he, and I gladly accepted.   And so we drove
out at one of the gates of the city, out into the Campagna,
over which melting waves of colour were rolling.   Here
and there we passed ancient ruins crumbling in the sun ;
the roadsides streamed with colour and fragrance from
violets and wild hyacinths and sweet-smelling flowers.
After some time we came suddenly to some green hills,
and leaving the carriage climbed up the slopes.   Then we
found ourselves looking down into a green glowing valley,
with an intense heaven above, all melting into light.   You,
with a little transient gasp of happiness, fell down kneeling
in the grass.   I shall always see the picture I had before
me then—the light figure against the bright green, the
black hat, and long falling feather ; the eager face looking
out at the world.   May it be for ever green and pleasant
to you as it was then, O eager face !

As we were parting in the twilight, I at last remembered to give Halbert's message.   It did not greatly affect
your father ; but how was it ?   Was it because I knew you
so well that I instinctively guessed you were moved by it ?
When I shook hands with you and said good-night, your
hand trembled in mine.

' W on't you look in too ? ' said the Colonel.

But I shook my head. 'Not to-night—no, thank you.'
And so we parted.

My lodgings were in the Gregoriana ; the windows
looked out over gardens and cupolas; from one of them I
could see the Pincio. From that window, next morning,
as I sat drinking my coffee, I suddenly saw you, walking
slowly along by the parapet, with your dog running by
your side. You went to one of those outlying terraces
which flank the road, and, leaning over the stone-work,
looked out at the great panorama lying at your feet:—
Rome, with her purple mantle of mist, regally spreading,
her towers, her domes, and great St. Peter's rising over the
house-tops, her seven hills changing and deepening with
noblest colour, her golden crown of sunlight streaming
and melting with the mist. Somehow I, too, saw all this
presently when I reached the place where you were still
standing.

And now I have almost come to the end of my story,
that is, of those few days of my life of which you, Esther,
were the story. You stood there waiting, and I hastened
towards you, and fate (I fancied you were my Fate) went
on its course quite unmoved by my hopes or your fears.
I thought that you looked almost handsome for once.
You certainly seemed more happy. Your face flushed and

faded, your eyes brightened and darkened. As you turned
and saw me, a radiant quiver, a piteous smile came to
greet me somewhat strangely. You seemed trying to
speak, but the words died away on your lips—to keep
silence, at least, but the faltering accents broke forth.

'What is it, my dear?' said I at last, with a queer
sinking of the heart, and I held out my hand.

You caught it softly between both yours. 'Oh!' you
said, with sparkling eyes, 'I am a mean, wretched girl—
oh! don't think too ill of me. He, Mr. Halbert, came to
see me last night, and—and, he says . . . Oh! I don't
deserve it. Oh! forgive me, for I am so happy;' and
you burst into tears. 'You have been so good to me,' you
whispered on. 'I hardly know how good. He says he only
thought of me when you spoke of me to him, when—when
he saw you did not dislike me. I am behaving shamefully—
yes, shamefully, but it is because I know you are too kind
not to forgive—not to forgive. What can I do? You know
how it has always been. You don't know what it would
be to marry one person, caring for another. Ah! you
don't know what it would be to have it otherwise than as
it is' (this clasping your hands). 'But you don't ask it.
Ah! forgive me, and say you don't ask it.' Then standing
straight and looking down with a certain sweet dignity,
you went on—'Heaven has sent me a great and unex-

pected happiness, but there is, indeed, a bitter, bitter cup to drink as well. Though I throw you over, though I behave so selfishly, don't think that I am utterly conscienceless, that I do not suffer a cruel pang indeed. When I think how you must look at me, when I remember what return I am making for all your forbearance and generosity, when I think of myself, I am ashamed and humiliated; when I think of him——' Here you suddenly broke off, and turned away your face.

. Ah me! turned away your face for ever from me. The morning mists faded away; the mid-day sun streamed over hills and towers and valley. The bell of the Trinità hard by began to toll.

I said, 'Good-by, and Heaven keep you, my dear. I would not have had you do otherwise.' And so I went back to my lodging. .

1866.

After Seven Years.

'I leaned a little and overlooked my prize,
  By the low railing round the fountain-source
  Close to the statue, where a step descends.'

'*Bosost:* August 20.

'Do you remember the story I wrote you in 1860, when I came back from Rome? To complain was a consolation, when it was to you I complained. I was lonely enough and disappointed, and yet I have been more unhappy since. Then I thought that at least you were happy, but later they said it was not so, and bitterness and regret overpowered me for a time. But this was after I had written to you.

'I scarcely remember what I said now, it is so long ago, but I know every word had a meaning since you were to see it, and the Esther I wrote to, the Esther whose image was for ever before me, seemed mine sometimes though we were for ever parted. I have often thought that the Esther I loved loved me though the other one married Halbert. Perhaps you were only her semblance, and she was waiting for me elsewhere in a different form. But the familiar face with the sallow cheeks and dark brows, and all the sudden light in it, comes before me as I write even now. I have seen it a thousand thousand times since we parted by the Trinità; do you remember when the bell was ringing for matins? Only as years have gone by the lines have faded a little, the eyes look deep and tender, but they have lost their colour; though I know how the lights and the smiles still come and still go, I cannot see them so plainly. The woman herself I can conjure across the years and the distance, but the face does not start clear-set before me as in those days when I only lived to follow your footsteps, to loiter among the shadows in your way, and in the sunshine through which you seemed to move; to drink up the sweet tones of your voice, to watch you when you sat at your window, when you lingered in the silent Italian gardens, or moved with a gentle footfall along echoing galleries, with dim golden pictures, and harmonies of glowing colour all about you.

'What sea-miles and land-miles, what flying years and lagging hours, what sorrows and joys lie between us—and joys separate more surely than sorrows do. People scale prison walls, they wade through rivers, they climb over arid mountains, to rejoin those whom they love, but

the great barriers of happiness and content, who has surmounted them?

'I say this, and yet success has been mine since I saw
you. Many good things have come to me for which I
did not greatly care, but though the spring tides and
bright summers and the bitter winter winds and autumnal
mists were fated to part us year after year, yet it also
seemed destined that I should love you faithfully through
all—that even forgetfulness should not prevent it, that
disappointment should not embitter, that indifference
should not chill. What I have borne from you I could not
have endured from any other. Once, long before I knew
you, a woman spoke to me hastily, and I left her, and
could not forgive her for years, and sometimes I ask myself
is my ill-luck a judgment upon me?

'I, who was so impatient once and hard of heart, make
no merit of my long affection for you, Esther: it was
simply fate, and I could not resist it. Changing, unchanging, faithful, unfaithful, who can account for his
experiences? Does mistrust bring about of itself that
which it imagines? is *everything* there that we fancy we
see in people? Often I think that fallen as we are,
and wearied and soiled by the wayside dust and mud,
and the many cares of life, some gleam of the divine
radiance is ours still, and to those who love us best it is

given to see it. That the sweetness and goodness and brightness we had fancied are no fancies, but truth. True though clouds and darkness come between us, and the mortal parts cannot always apprehend the divine.

'Love is blind; indifference sees more clearly, people say, and I wonder if this can be true; for my part I think it is the other way. I have sometimes asked about you from one and from another, and people have spoken of you as if you were to me only what they are, what I am to them, or they to you. I seem to be writing riddles and ringing the changes upon the words which you will not see. Whether you see them or not what does it matter? you would not understand their meaning, their sorrowful fidelity, nor do I wish that you should.

'For, as I have said, years have passed, other thoughts and ties and interests have come to me; I am sometimes even vexed and wearied by my own unchanging nature, and I am tired of the very things from which I cannot tear myself away. I don't think I care for you now, though I still love the woman who jilted me years ago upon the Pincio. It might be that, seeing you again, all the old tender emotion of feeling would revive towards you. It might be that you would wound me a second time by destroying my dreams, my ideal remembrance. Very sad, very sweet, very womanly and trustful my remembrance is. I should imagine you must have hardened—improved as people call it—since then, and been moulded into some different person. Six years spent with Halbert must have altered you, I think, and marred the sweet imperfections of your nature. At any rate you are as far removed from me as if poor Halbert were alive still to torment you.

'This morning at Luchon my courier brought me a letter which interested me oddly enough, and brought back all the old fancies and associations. It came from my cousin's wife, Lady Mary. There were but a few lines, but your name was written thrice in it; and like an old half-remembered tune, all the way riding along the rough road I have been haunted by a refrain—'Meet Esther again, shall it be, can it be?'—fitting to a sort of rhythm, which is sing-songing in my head at this instant.

'For want of a companion to speak to, I have written this nonsense at length. I cannot talk to my courier except to swear at the roads. They narrowed and roughened as we got into Spain, after we had crossed a bridge with a black river rushing beneath it. High up in the mountains, the villages perched like eagles' nests; the streams were dashing over the rocks in the clefts below. This is not a golden and sun-painted land like the country we have been used to. Italy seems like summer as I

think of it, and this is like autumn to me. The colours
have sombre tints; there are strange browns and yellows,
faded greens with deep blue shades in them. Stones roll
from the pathway and fall crashing into the ravines below.
No roads lead to the villages where the people live for a
lifetime, tilling their land, weaving their clothes, tending
their cattle; many of them never coming down into the
valley all their lives long, sufficing to themselves and
ignoring the world at their feet. So my guides have told
me, at least, and it was their business to know. . . .'

    *   *   *   *   *

All this had been written on the rail of a balcony to
the jangling of a church-bell and the sympathetic droning
of a guitar with one note. It was played by a doleful-
looking soldier in tight regimentals, sitting upright on a
chair on the landing-place, and never moving a muscle,
while the flies buzzed about his head. A motionless companion sat near listening to the melody. Presently, in
the midst of his writing, Geoffry Smith, who had scarcely
heeded the guitar or the bell, suddenly heard a great
chattering and commotion in the street below, and looking
over the rail, he saw a crowd of little gipsy children
swarming in front of the house. They were trying to
climb up into the balcony, getting on one another's backs,
clapping their hands, screaming and beckoning to him :—

'Mossoo! Mossoo!—tit sou—allons donc!' with an en· couraging gesture. 'Tit sou—'lons donc!—vite, *Mossoo!*' and the brown faces grinned beneath their little Moorish-looking turbans—yellow, green, scarlet handkerchiefs; and all the brown bare legs went capering. The narrow street was crowded with people hurrying to the call of the church-bell. Women came out of the low doorways of their houses, adjusting their mantillas. Rosina tripped by with the duenna. Don Basilio strode past with flapping skirts, pantomime-like cocked hat, cotton umbrella and all. Smith looked at them all from over his balcony, like from a box at the opera. At the other end of the Place—Plaza de la Constitucion its name was—the French Consul, leaning over his eagle, was sleepily smoking a cigar and watching the church-goers pass by. Strum-tumty, strum-tumty—tumty-strum, went the guitar, and presently—still like a scene at the play—the light darkened, the people looked up at the sky, and there came an artificial clap of thunder from the hill-top over the town, with a sudden storm of hail and lightning. Rosina set off scampering with her duenna. So did the priests; the young men with their bright red caps, lounging at the corner of the street; the old man with his donkey; and the little grinning beggar-children.

Smith thought he, too, should like to see the inside of

the church, which seemed to be looked upon as a safe
refuge : everybody was rushing in the same direction. He
had not very far to go : up a short street, and along the
Plaza, and then, after crossing a little wooden drawbridge,
Smith found himself at the church-door. He stooped
and went in through a low Moorish-looking arch, and
descended a short flight of black-marble steps which led
down into the aisle.

It seemed quite dark at first, except that the tapers
were flaring at the altar, where three unprepossessing-
looking priests were officiating. By degrees Smith found
that he was standing in a beautiful old Templar church,
with arches, with red silk hangings, and a chequered
marble floor, and a dark carved gallery from which some
heads were peeping. The women were sitting and squat-
ting on the floor with their shoes neatly ranged at their
sides, and their babies dandling in their arms. The men
were behind, nearer the door; and in the front row of
all, grinning, showing their teeth, and plucking at his
legs as he went by, Smith discovered the little company
of persecuting boys and girls, pretending to bury their
faces in their hands when he looked at them, and peeping
at him through their wiry little fingers with shining
malicious eyes.

The service came to an end; the storm passed away.

Smith left the church with the children swarming at his
heels, and found his guide waiting with the horses ready
harnessed. They had no time to lose, the man said—the
bill was paid. Smith sprang into the saddle, flung a
handful of half-pence to the Moorish little bandits, and
rode off as hard as he could go along the rough bridle-
path.

It was very late before he got back. He dined by
himself about ten o'clock, with a tired, shirt-sleeved waiter
to attend upon him, and then he went and sat under the
trees on the Cours, listening to the music and trying to
make up his mind. Should he go to Bigorre? Yes; no;
un peu; beaucoup; pas du tout. He changed his plans
over and over again. About midnight, when the music
and the lights were still alive, the people still drinking their
coffee and lemonade in the soft starlit night, and chatting
and humming all round about, Smith determined at last
that he would stay for a day or two longer, and then go to
Tarbes and on to Marseilles and to Italy. Having made
out this scheme, he called a voiturier with a whip and
jack-boots who happened to be passing, and asked him if
he was engaged and what was his fare to St. Bertrand.
Smith had a fancy to see the old place, which lies on the
road to Tarbes. It also lies on the road to Bigorre, but
Smith thought that he did not remember this. The guide

was a Bigorre man and anxious to get there. He was willing enough to go to St. Bertrand. After that he should like to get home, he said. His horses wanted a rest. Smith came to a compromise with him at last. The tired horses were to take him to St. Bertrand, and then they were to make further arrangements.

Two roads cross the country which divides Luchon from Bigorre. One runs direct in noble undulations over hill-tops and mountain ranges. It goes bursting over the great Col d'Aspin, from whence you may see the world like a sea, tossing and heaving at your feet, and trembling with the light upon a thousand hills; and then the highway plunges down into deep valleys, where the air is scented with pine-wood.

The other road winds by the plain and follows the course of a flowing river, past villages sun-decked and vine-wreathed, but silent and deserted in their whiteness. A sad-faced woman looks from her cottage-door; a dark-headed boy comes skimming over the stones with his naked feet, and holds up his hand for alms; a traveller, resting on a heap by the dusty roadside, nods his head in token of weary fellowship. At last, as you still follow the road in the valley, with the low range on either side, you suddenly reach a great hill with the towers of a strong city rising from its summit. It dominates the land-

.waves, which seem flowing down from the mountains, and the great flat marshes which stretch away to the sea.

Smith chose the plain to return by, wishing, as I have said, to see St. Bertrand: ho had crossed the mountain before, in the course of his travels. He went rolling along through the fresh morning air, with his head full of old sights and thoughts—very far away, hankerings and fancies which he had imagined safely buried in the Campagna or mouldering with the relics of his old Italian sight-seeing times. Along the banks of the river, crossing and recrossing many times from one side to another, through plains and sunny villages, they had come at last to St. Bertrand, the city on the hill. The driver, a surly fellow, hissed and cursed as the horses went stumbling up the steep ascent, straining and slipping in the blazing sun over bleached white stones. There were four bony horses, ornamented with bells and loaded with heavy harness. Smith reclined at his ease among the fusty cushions of the carriage ; his courier clung nervously to the narrow railing on the box; Pierre, the driver, cracked his long whip, muttered horrible oaths between his teeth, gulped, choked, shrieked, with hideous jerks and sounds. They slowly climb the hill of St. Bertrand. Everything seems to grow whiter and brighter as they mount. They reach the town at last : there is an utter silence and look of abandonment :

flowers are hanging over the walls and gables and postern-
gates. They pass fountains of marble, stone casements,
and turrets and balconies, all white, blazing, deserted,
with geraniums hanging and flowering. They pass under
an archway with carvings and emblazonments throwing
deep shadows, by strange gables and corners and turrets,
up a fantastic street. It was like a goblin city, so dreary,
silent, deserted, with such strange conceits and ornaments
at every corner.

The hotel was empty, too; one demure, sour visage
came to the door to receive them. Yes, there was food
prepared; the horses could be put up in the stables. A
human voice seemed to break the enchantment, for I
think until then Smith had almost expected to find a
sleeping princess upon a bed, a king, a queen, a court, all
dreaming and dozing inside this ancient palace : for the
inn had been a palace, at some time or other perhaps
inhabited by the ancient bishops of St. Bertrand, or by
some of the nobles whose escutcheons still hang on the
gates of the city. There were two tables, both laid and
spread in readiness, in the solemn old dining-room, with
its white painted panels and carved chimney. Smith was
amused to see a Murray lying on the white cloth nearest
the window. Even here, in this forgotten end of the
world, the wandering tribes of Britain had hoisted the

national standard and hastened to secure the best place at
the feast. There were three plates, three forks, three
knives. Smith, dimly pursuing his morning fancy, and
bewitched by the unreality and silence of all about him,
thought that this was the place in which he should like to
meet Esther again—if he was ever to meet her. Here, in
this white, blinding silence, she might come like an
apparition out of his dreams—come up the steep me-
diæval street, past the fountain—with her long dress,—
how well he remembered it, rippling over the stones, her
slim straight figure standing in relief against the blazing
sky. . . . 'Cutlets—yes; and a chicken; and a bottle
of St. Julien.' . . . This was to the waiting-woman,
who asked him what he would like.

Geoffry walked out into the garden to wait until his
cutlets should be ready, and he found an unkept wilder-
ness, tangled and sweet with autumnal roses, and a carved
stone terrace or loggia, facing a great beautiful landscape.
As he leaned against the marble parapet, Smith, who
still thought he was only admiring the view, imagined
Esther walking up the street, coming nearer and nearer,
approaching along the tangled walk through the rose-
trees, and standing beside him at last on the terrace. It
was a fancy, nothing more; it was not even a presentiment; all the beautiful world below shimmered and

melted into greater and greater loveliness; an insect went flying and buzzing over the parapet and out into the clear atmosphere; a rose fell to pieces, and as the leaves tumbled to the ground one or two floated on to the yellow time-worn ledge against which Smith was leaning. No, he would not go to Bigorre, he said to himself, he would turn his horses' heads, or travel beyond Bigorre, to some one of the other mountains—to Luz or St. Sauveur, or farther still, to Eaux Bonnes, in the heart of the Pyrenees. He pulled out his letter and read it again; this was all it said, in Lady Mary's cramped little hand :—

' B. de Bigorre.

' DEAR GEOFFRY—Someone has seen you somewhere in the Pyrenees ; will you not take Bigorré on your way, and come and spend a few days with us? It would cheer my husband up to see you; his cough is troublesome still, though he is greatly better than when we left the rectory. There are one or two nice people in the place. I am sure you would spend a few pleasant days. We have the three Vulliameys, Mr. and Mrs. Penton, and Olga Halbert;— that poor Mrs. Halbert, too, is with them ; her children make great friends with ours. Mrs. Halbert tells us she knows you. She is very much altered and shaken by her husband's death, though one cannot but feel that it must be more a shock than a sorrow to her, poor woman. The Pentons and Mrs. Halbert are at the hotel. She says they find it comfortable. I know you like being independent best, otherwise we have a nice little room for you, and should much prefer having you with us while you stay. The children are flourishing, and I expect my sister Lucy to join us in a few days. *Do* try and come, and give us all a great deal of pleasure.

'Affectionately yours,

MARY SMITH.

'P.S.—I shall send this to St. James's Place on the chance that it may be forwarded back again to you with your other letters.'

Smith read the letter and tore it up absently, and threw it on the ground. He would not go to Bigorre; he was past the age of sentiment; he would never marry; he did not want to see Esther again and destroy his remembrance of her, or make a fool of himself perhaps, and be bound to a woman hardened by misfortune, by long contact with worldly minds, by devotion to an unworthy object. 'How could she prefer Halbert to me?' Smith thought, with an amused self-consciousness.

Esther was a clever woman : she had thought for herself : she needed a certain intellectual calibre of companionship. Halbert cultivated his whiskers : his best aspirations were after Lady X and Y and Z and their tea-parties ; and then Smith wandered away from poor Halbert, who was gone now, to the lovely sight before him.

It was not so much the view as the beautiful fires which were lighting it up. If colour were like music— if one could write it down, and possess for good—the gleams of sudden sweetness, the modulation, the great bursting symphonies of light thrilling from a million notes at once into one great triumphal harmony : if the passion of loveliness—I know no better word—which seems all about us at times, could be written down, one would need words that should change and deepen and sweeten with the reader's mood, and shift for ever into combinations lovely and yet more lovely.

Smith was looking still with a heart full of gratitude and admiration, when he heard a step upon the gravel walk. He turned round to see who was coming. Was this an enchanted city he had come to? A tall slim figure of a woman in black robes was advancing along the gravel walk and coming to the overhanging terrace where he was standing. Alas! it was no enchantment. The genii had not brought his princess on their wings.

It was no one he had ever seen before—no sallow face with the sweet bright look in it; it was only a hansdome-looking young woman, one of the thousands there are in the world, with peach-red cheeks and bright keen eyes, who glanced at him suspiciously. Two great black feathers were hanging from her hat; her long silk gown rippled in the sunshine and her black silk cloak was fastened round her neck by a silver clasp.

It was a very charming apparition, Smith thought, though it was not the one he had hoped for—there was nothing gracious about this well-grown young lady. This was no Esther—this was not a woman who would change her mind a dozen times a day, who would be weak and foolish and trustful always. Geoffry was half repelled, half attracted by the keen determined face, the firm-moulded lines. He might not have thought twice about her at another time; but in this golden solitude and Garden of Eden it almost seemed as if a companion was wanted. He had been contented enough until now with a shadowy friend of his own exorcising. The lady in black, after looking at the view for a second, turned round and walked away again as deliberately as she had come, and he presently followed her example for want of something better to do. The hills were still melting, roses were flushing and scenting the air, insects floating as before; but Smith, whose train of thought had been disturbed, turned his back upon all their loveliness and strolled into the house to ask if his breakfast was ready.

Prim-face, who was busy at a great carved cupboard, seemed amazed at the question. 'You have not seen the cathedral yet: travellers always go over the cathedral before the *déjeûner*. We have had to catch and kill the fowl,' in an aggrieved tone. ' Encore vingt minutes n'est-ce pas, Auguste!' shrieks the woman suddenly, without budging from her place.

' Vingt minutes,' repeats a deep voice from somewhere or other behind the great cupboard, and there was no more to be said on the subject.

Smith spent the twenty minutes during which his chicken was grilling and his potatoes frizzling, in a great lofty cathedral. It stands on the very summit of the hill, high above the town and the surrounding plains; wide flights lead to the great entrance, the walls and roof are bare, but of beautiful and generous proportions; lofty arches vault high overhead. The sunshine, which seems weird and goblin in the city, falls here with a more solemn light; slant gleams flit across the marble pavement as the great door swings on its hinges and footfalls echo in the distance. Smith seemed to recognise the place somehow—it looked familiar: the rough beautiful arches, the vastness, the desertion: no priests, no one praying, no glimmer of shrines and candles; only space, silence, light from the large window, only a solemn figure of an abbot lying upon his marble bed with a date of three hundred years ago.

Smith remembered dreaming of such a place in his old home years and years before, when he was a boy, and had never even heard Esther's name. The abbot on his marble bed seemed familiar, the placid face, the patient hands, the dog crouching at his feet. A great gleam of sun from a window overhead streaked and lighted the marble. Smith sat down on the step of the tomb and looked up at the great window. A white pigeon with a beautiful breast shining in the sun was sitting upon the mullion. It sat for a time, and then it flew away with a sudden rush across the violet blue sky. Smith did not move, but waited in a tranquil, gentle frame of mind, like that of a person who is dreaming beautiful dreams, nor had waited very long when he seemed to be conscious of people approaching, voices and footsteps coming nearer and nearer, until at last they were somewhere close at hand, and he overheard the following uninteresting conversation between two voices:

' Why don't they do it up with chintz if they are so poor? chintz costs next to nothing. I am sure that lily of the valley and ribbon pattern in my dressing-room seems as if it never would wear out. I was saying to Hudson only the other day, " Really, Hudson, I think while we are away you must get some new covers for my dressing-room." '

Here a second voice interrupted with—' Charles, do you remember any allusion to St. Bertrand in *Jamieson's Lives of the Saints?* I read the book very carefully, but I cannot feel quite certain.'

To which the first voice rejoined—' Why, Olga, I do wonder you don't remember. I think Charles has a very bad memory indeed. And so have I ; but *you* read so much.'

Charles now spoke. ' Here, Mira, look at this a-hm —a-interesting monument.—To the right, Mira, to the right. You are walking away from it.'

' Dear me, Charles! what a droll creature. He puts me in mind of uncle John.'

' I cannot help thinking,' Charles said impressively, ' that this is the place Lady Kidderminster was describing at Axminster House. I am almost convinced of it.'

Then Smith heard Charles saying rapidly and speaking his words all in a string as it were :—

' Lady-Kidderminster-a-été-beaucoup-frappée-par-une-

Cathédrale-dans-les-Pyrénées. Est-ce-qu'elle-a-passé-par-ici? . . . I am sure—I—a-beg your pardon.—I had not perceived—' and a stout consequential-looking gentleman, who was in the middle of his sentence, stumbled over ·Smith's umbrella, while Smith, half amused, half pro-voked, rose from his seat and seemed to the speaker to ·emerge suddenly, red beard and all, from the tomb. Mira gave a little scream, Olga looked amused.

'I trust I have not seriously injured—a-hm—any-thing,' said the gentleman; 'we were examining this—a—relic, and had not observed—' Smith made a little bow, and another to the beautiful apparition on the terrace, whom he recognised. Next to her stood another very handsome youngish lady, stout, fair, and grandly dressed, who graciously acknowledged his greeting, while Olga slightly tossed her head, as was her way when she thought herself particularly irresistible. Behind them the curé was waiting—a sad, heavy-featured man, in thick country shoes, whose shabby gown flapped against his legs as he walked with his head wearily bent. He only shrugged his shoulders at the many questions which were put to him. Such as, Why didn't they put in stained-glass windows? wasn't it very cold in winter? was he sure he didn't remember Lady Kidderminster? Leading the way, he opened a side-door, through which Smith saw a beautiful old cloister, with a range of violet hills gleaming through the arches. It was unexpected, and gave him a sudden thrill of pleasure.

' What a delightful place you have here,' he said to the guide. ' I think I should like to stay altogether.'

' Not many people care to pass by this way now,' said the curé. ' It is out of the road; they do not like to bring their horses up the steep ascent. Yes, it is a pretty *point de vue*. I come here of an evening sometimes.'

' Extremely so,' said Mira. ' Olga, do you know I am so tired? I am convinced that I want bracing. I wish we had gone to Brighton instead of coming to this hot place.—Charles, do you think the "déjeûner" is ready? I am quite exhausted,' she went on, in the same breath.

' Would *ces dames* care to see the vestments?' the curate asked, a little wistfully, seeing them prepare to go.

' Oh-a-merci, we are rather pressed for time,' Charles was beginning, when Smith saw that the man looked disappointed, and said he should like to see them. Olga, as they called her, shook out her draperies, and told Charles they might as well go through with the farce, and Mira meekly towered after her husband and sister. These are odious people, poor Smith thought. The ladies are handsome enough, but they are like About's description of his two heroines: ' L'une était une statue, l'autre une poupée.' This statue seemed always complacently contemplating its own pedestal. In the *sacristie* there were only one or two relics and vestments to be seen, and a large book open upon a desk.

' People sometimes,' said the curé, humbly shuffling and looking shyly up, 'inscribe their names in this book, with some slight donation towards the repairs of the church.'

' I thought as much,' said Olga, while Charles pompously produced his purse and began fumbling about. Smith was touched by the wistful looks of the guide. This church was his child, his companion, and it was starving for want of food. He wrote his name— ' Mr. Geoffry Smith,"—and put down a couple of napoleons on the book, where the last entry was three months old, of two francs which someone had contributed. The others opened their eyes as they saw what had happened. The curé's gratitude and delight amply repaid Geoffry, who had more napoleons to spend than he could well get through. The pompous gentleman now advanced, and in a large, aristocratic hand inscribed,—' Mr. and Mrs. Penton, of Penton ; ' ' Miss Halbert.' And at the same time Mr. Penton glanced at the name over his own, and suddenly gleamed into life, in that way which is peculiar to people who unexpectedly recognise a desirable ac- quaintance.

' Mr. Smith ! I have often heard your name. You —a—knew my poor brother-in-law, Frank Halbert, I believe.—Mrs. Penton—Miss Halbert.—A most cu- rious and fortunate chance—hm-a !—falling in with one another in this out-of-the-way portion of the globe. Per- haps we may be travelling in the same direction ? we are on our way to Bigorre, where we rejoin our sister-in-law, Mrs. Frank Halbert.'

Geoffry felt as if it was the finger of Fate interfering. He followed them mechanically out into the street.

' How hot the sun strikes upon one's head. Do you dislike it ?—I 'do,' said Mrs. Penton, graciously, as they walked back to the hotel together. . . .

People say that as they live on, they find answers in life to the problems and secrets which have haunted and vexed their youth. Is it so ? It seems as if some questions were never to be answered, some doubts never to be solved. Right and wrong seem to change and blend as life goes on, as do the alternate hours of light and darkness. Perhaps some folks know right from wrong always and at all times. But there are others weak and inconsistent, who seem to live only to regret. They ask themselves with dismay, looking back at the past —Was that me myself? Could that have been me? That person going about with the hard and angry heart; that person uttering cruel and unforgiving words; that person thinking thoughts that my soul abhors? Poor Esther! Often and often of late her own ghost had come to haunt her, as it had haunted Smith—sometimes in a girlish guise, tender, impetuous, unworn and unsoiled, by the wayside wear, the thorns and the dust of life. At other times—so she could remember herself at one time of her life—foolish, infatuated, mad, and blind— oh, how blind! Her dream had not lasted very long; she awoke from it soon. It was not much of a story. She was a woman now. She was a girl when she first knew her husband, and another who she once thought would have been her husband. She had but to choose between them. That was all her story; and she took in her hand and then put away the leaden casket with the treasure inside, while she kept the glittering silver and gold for her portion.

> 'Some there be that shadows kiss;
> Some but have a shadow's bliss.'

Poor Esther! her shadows soon fled, parted, deepened into night; and long sad years succeeded one another; trouble and pain and hardness of heart, and bitter, bitter pangs of regret; remorse of passionate effort after right, after peace, and cruel failures and humiliations. No one ever knew the life that Esther Halbert led for the six years after she married. Once in an agony of grief and humiliation she escaped to her stepmother with her little girl. Lady Fanny pitied her, gave her some luncheon, talked good sense. Old Colonel Olliver sneered, as was his way, and told his daughter to go home in a cab. He could not advise her remaining with him, and, in short, it was impossible.

'You married Frank with your eyes open,' he said. 'You knew well enough what you were about when you threw over that poor fellow Smith, as if he had been an old shoe; and now you must make the best of what you have. I am not going to have a scandal in the family, and a daughter without a husband constantly about the house. I'll talk to Halbert and see if matters can't be mended; but you will be disgraced if you leave him, and you are in a very good position as you are. Injured wife, patient endurance—that sort of thing—nothing could be better.'

Esther, with steady eyes and quivering lips, slowly

turned away as her father spoke. Lady Fanny, her stepmother, was the kindest of the two, and talked to her about her children's welfare, and said she would drive her back in her brougham. Poor Esther, dazed, sick at heart; she thought that if it were not for her Jack and her Prissa she would go away and never come back again. Ah! what a life it was; what a weary delusion, even for the happiest—even for those who obtained their heart's desire! She had a great burst of crying, and then she was better, and said meekly, Yes, she would go home, and devote herself to her little ones, and try to bear with Frank. And she made a vow that she would complain no more, since this was all that came to her when she told her troubles to those who might have been a little sorry. Esther kept her vow. Was it her good angel that prompted her to make it? Halbert fell, out hunting, and was brought home senseless only a few days after, and Esther nursed him tenderly and faithfully: when he moaned, she forgave and forgot every pain he had ever inflicted upon her, every cruel word or doubt or suspicion. He never rallied; and the doctors looked graver and graver, until at last Frank Halbert died, holding his wife's hand in his.

The few first weeks of their married life, these last sad days of pain and suffering, seemed to her all that she had

left to her; all the terrible time between she blotted out
and forgot as best she could, for she, would clutch her
children suddenly in her arms when sickening memories
overpowered her, and so forget and forgive at once. For
some time Esther was shocked, shaken, nervous, starting
at every word and every sound, but by degrees she gained
strength and new courage. When she came to Bigorre
she was looking better than she had done for years; and
no wonder: her life was peaceful now, and silent; cruel
sneers and utterances had passed out of it. The indig-
nities, all the miseries of her past years, were over for
ever; only their best blessings, Jack and Prissa, remained
to her; and she prayed with all her tender mother's heart
that they might grow up different from either of their
parents, good and strong and wise and upright—unlike
her, unlike their father.

The Pentons, who were good-natured people in their
way, had asked her to come; and Esther, who was too
lazy to say no, had agreed, and was grateful to them for
persuading her to accompany them. She liked the place.
The bells sounding at all the hours with their sudden
musical cadence, the cheery stir, the cavalcades arriving
from the mountains, the harnesses jingling, the country-
folks passing and repassing, the convents tinkling, Carmes
close at hand, Carmelites a little farther down the street,

---the streams, the pretty shady walks among the hills, the pastoral valley where the goats and the cattle were browsing,—it was all bright and sunshine and charming. Little Prissa in her big sun-bonnet, and Jack helping to push the perambulator, went up every morning to the Salut, along a road with shady trees growing on either side, which led to some baths in the mountain. One day the children came home in much excitement, to say they had seen a horse in a chequed cotton dressing-gown, and with two pair of trowsers on. But their greatest delight of all was the Spaniard of Bigorre with his pack. Esther soon grew very tired of seeing him parading about in a dress something between a brigand and a circus-rider; but Prissa and Jack never wearied, and the dream of their outgoing and incoming was to meet him. Prissa's other dream of perfect happiness was drinking tea on the terrace at the Châlet with little Geoffry and Lucy and Lena Smith, where they all worshipped the Spaniard together, and told one another stories about the funny horse and the little pig that tried to eat out of Lena's hand. Their one trouble was that Mademoiselle Bouchon made them tell their adventures in French. At all events they could *laugh* in English, and she never found it out. Lady Mary would come out smiling while the tea was going on, and nod her kind cap-ribbons at them all. She was a portly and good-

humoured person, who did foolish things sometimes, and
was fond of interfering and trying to make people happy
her own way.   She had taken a fancy to Esther, and one
day—ingenious Lady Mary—she said to herself, ' I am
sure this would do for poor Geoffry : he ought to marry.
This is the very thing.   Dear me, I wish he would come
here for a day or two,' and she went back into her room
and actually wrote to him to come.

The two ladies went to the service of the Carmes that
evening.   It was the fashion to go and listen for the voice
of one of the monks.   There was a bustle of company
rustling in; smart people were coming up through the
darkening streets ; old French ladies protected by their
little maids, arriving with their ' Heures ' in their hands;
lights gleamed in the windows here and there, and in the
chapel of the convent a blaze of wax and wick, and
artificial flowers, and triumphant music.   It was a lovely
voice, thrilling beyond the others, pathetic, with beautiful
tones of subdued passionate expression.   The Carme who
sang to them was a handsome young man, very pale, with
a black crisp beard : his head overlooked the others as
they came and went with their flaming tapers in mystic
processions.   Was it something in the man's voice, some
pathetic cadence which recalled other tones to which
Esther had listened once in her life, and that of late years

she had scarcely dared to remember? Was it chance, was it fate, was it some strange presentiment of his approach, which made Esther begin to think of Rome, and of Geoffry, and of the days when she first knew him, and of the time before she married? As she thought of old days she seemed to see Smith's kind blue eyes looking at her, and to hear his voice sounding through the music. How often she had longed to see him—how well she remembered him—the true heart, the good friend of her youth.

Esther's heart stirred with remembrances of things far far away from the convent and its prayers and fastings and penances. Penance and fastings and vigils—such things should be her portion, she thought, by rights; and it was with a pang of shame, of remorse, of bitter regret, and of fresh remorse for the pang itself, that she rose from her knees—the service over, the music silent, and wax-lights extinguished—and came out into the night with her friend. As they were walking up the street, Lady Mary said quietly and unconsciously enough, though Esther started guiltily, and asked herself if she had been speaking her thoughts aloud—

'Mrs. Halbert, did you ever meet my husband's cousin, Jeff Smith? I hear he is in the Pyrenees; I am writing to him to come and stay with us, he is such a good fellow

Esther, if she had learnt nothing else since the old Roman days, had learnt at least to control herself and to speak quietly and indifferently, though her eyes suddenly filled with tears and there came a strange choking in her throat. Her companions noticed nothing as Mrs. Halbert said, ' Yes, she had known him at Rome, but that she had not seen him for years.'

' Ah, then, you must renew your acquaintance,' Lady Mary said; adding, abruptly, ' Do you know, I hear a Carmelite is going to make her profession next week?— we must go. These things are horrible, and yet they fascinate me somehow.'

' What a touching voice that was,' said Esther. ' It affected me quite curiously.' To which Lady Mary replied,—

' I remember that man last year : he has not had time to emaciate himself to a mummy. He sat next me at the table-d'hôte, and we all remarked him for being so handsome and pleasant, and for the quantities of champagne he drank. There was a little quiet dark man, his companion. They used to go out riding together, and sit listening to the music at the Thermes. There was a ball there one night, and I remember seeing the young fellow dancing with a beautiful Russian princess.'

' Well ? ' said Esther, listening and not listening.

' Well, one day he didn't come to dinner, and the little dark man sat next me alone. I asked after my neighbour; heard he had left the place, but Marguérite—you know the handsome chamber-maid—told me, under breath, that Jean had been desired to take the handsome gentleman's portmanteau down on a truck to the convent of the Carmes; a monk had received it at the garden-door, and that was all she knew. I am sure I recognised my friend to-night. He looked as if he knew me when he came round with the purse.'

' Poor thing,' said Mrs. Halbert, sighing. Esther came home to the hotel, flushed, with shining eyes, looking like she used to look ten years ago. She found Mrs. Penton asleep in the sitting-room, resting her portly person upon the sofa. Olga was nodding solemnly over a dubious French novel. Mr. Penton was taking a nap behind his *Galignani*—the lamp was low. It all looked inexpressibly dull and commonplace after the glimpses of other lives which she had had that night. She seemed lifted above herself somehow by the strains of solemn music, by memories of tenderest love and hopeless separation, by dreams of what might have been, what had been before now, of the devotion which had triumphed over all the natural longings and aspirations of life. Could it be that these placid sleepy people were of the same race and make as herself and others of whom she had heard? Esther crept away to the room where her children were sleeping in their little cots, with faithful old Spicer stitching by the light of a candle. As the mother knelt down by the girl's little bed, a great burst of silent tears seemed to relieve her heart, and she cried and cried, she scarcely dared tell herself why.

Have you ever seen a picture painted in black and in gold? Black-robed saints, St. Dominic and others, on a golden glory, are the only instances I can call to mind, except an Italian painter's fancy of a golden-haired woman in her yellow damask robe, with a mysterious black background behind her. She had a look of my heroine, though Esther Halbert is an ugly woman, and the picture is the likeness of one of those beautiful fair-haired Venetians whose beauty (while people are still saying that beauty fades away and perishes) is ours after all the centuries, and has been the munificent gift of Titian and his compeers, who first discerned it, to the unknown generations that were yet to be born and to admire. As one looks at the tender face, it seems alive, even now, and one wonders if there is light anywhere for the yellow lady. Can she see into that gloom of paint more clearly than into the long gallery where the people are pacing and the painters are working at their easels?

—or is she as blind as the rest of us? Does she gaze
unconscious of all that surrounds her? Does she fancy
herself only minute particles of oil and yellow ochre
and colouring matter, never guessing that she is a whole,
beautiful with sentiment, alive with feeling and harmony?

I daresay she is blind like the rest of us, as Esther
was that Friday in July when she came hurrying
through the midday sunshine, with her little son
scampering beside her, hiding his head from the burning rays among the long folds of her black widow's dress.

At Bigorre, in the Pyrenees, there is one little spot
where the sun's rays seem to burn with intenser heat—
a yellow blaze of light amid black and sudden shade.
It is a little *Place* leading to the Thermes. In it a
black marble fountain flows, with a clear limpid stream,
and a Roman inscription still renders grace for benefits
received to the nymph of the healing waters. Arched
gates with marble corner-stones, windows closed and shuttered, form three sides of the little square; on the
fourth there is a garden behind an iron railing, where
tall hollyhocks nod their heads, catalpas flower and
scent the air, and great beds of marguérites and sad
autumnal flowers lead to the flight of black-marble
steps in front of the house.

Esther, hurrying along, did not stop to look or to

notice. She was too busy shielding and helping little blinded Jack to skurry across the burning desert, as he called it. They reached the shady street at last. Jack emerged from his mother's skirts, and Esther stopped, hesitated, and looked back across the place from which they had just come. The sun was blinding and burning, great dazzling patches were in her eyes, and yet—— It was absurd; but she could not help thinking that she had seen someone as she crossed: a figure that she now seemed to *remember* seeing coming down the black marble steps of the house in the garden—a figure under an umbrella, which put her in mind of someone she had known. It was absurd: it was a fancy, an imagination; it came to her from the foolish thoughts she had indulged in of late. And yet she looked to make sure that such was the case; and, turning her head, she perceived in the distance a man dressed in white, as people dress in the Pyrenees, walking under a big umbrella down the opposite street, which leads to the Baths. Esther smiled at her own fancies. An umbrella! why should not an umbrella awaken associations?

'Come along, mamma,' said Jack, who had seen nothing but the folds of his mother's dress, and who was not haunted by associations as yet. 'Come along, mamma, don't stop and think.'

Esther took Jack's little outstretched paw into her long slim fingers, but as she walked along the shady side of the street—past the Moorish shop-fronts arched with black marble, with old women gossiping in the interiors, and while Jack started at the passers-by, at a monk plodding by with sandalled feet, at a bath-woman balancing an enormous machine on her head, or longed as he gazed at the beautiful peaches and knitted wool-work piled on the shop-ledges, Esther went dreaming back to ten years before, wishing, as grown-up people wish, not for the good things spread before them, but for those of years long gone by —for the fruit long since eaten, or rotten, or planted in the ground.

'Mammy, there's the Spaniard. Oh! look at his legs,' said Jack, 'they are all over ribbons.' And Esther, to please him, smiled and glanced at a bandy-legged mountebank disposing of bargains to two credulous Britons.

'Why, there's uncle Penton come back,' Jack cried in great excitement; 'he is buying muffetees. Mammy, come and see what he has got,' cried Jack, trying to tug away his hand.

'Not now, dear,' said Esther. The slim fingers closed upon Jack's little hand with too firm a grasp for him to escape, and he trudged on perforce.

They had almost reached the hotel where they lived by this time. The great clock-tower round which it is built serves as a landmark and beacon. The place was all alive—jangling and jingling; voices were calling to one another, people passing and repassing along the wooden galleries, horses clamping in the courtyard. A riding party had just arrived; yellow, pink, red-capped serving-women were hurrying about, showing guests to their chambers or escorting them across the road to the dependencies of the house.

As Esther and her little boy were walking along the wooden gallery which led to her rooms, they met Hudson, Mrs. Penton's maid, who told them with a sniff that her mistress was in the drawing-room.

' Was Mrs. Penton tired after her journey last night?' Esther asked. ' I was sorry not to be at home to receive her, but I did not expect you till to-day.'

' No wonder she's exhausted,' said Hudson; 'not a cup of tea have we 'ad since we left on Tuesday-week. They wanted me to take some of their siroppy things. *I* shan't be sorry to see Heaton Place again.'

Hudson was evidently much put out, and Esther hurried to the sitting-room, where she found Mrs. Penton lying down as usual, and Olga, in a state of excitement, altering the feathers in her hat.

'How d'ye do, dear?' said Mrs. Penton. 'We are come back again.'

'We have had a most interesting excursion,' said Olga, coming up to kiss her sister-in-law. 'I wish you had cared to leave the children, Esther. You might have visited the Lac d'Oo, and that most remarkable ruin, St. Bertrand de Comminges. In *Jamieson's Lives of*——'

'We met such a nice person,' interrupted Mrs. Penton. 'He came to Bigorre with us in another carriage, but by the same road. He knows you, Esther, and he and Olga made great friends. They got on capitally over the cathedral, and he kindly fetched the Murray for us. We had left it on the table in the *salle-à-manger*, and were really afraid we had lost it.' And Mrs. Penton rambled on for a whole half-hour, unconscious that no one was listening to her.

Esther had turned quickly to Olga, and asked who this was who knew her.

'Oh, I daresay you don't remember the name,' said Olga, rather consciously. 'Smith — Mr. Smith of Garstein. He told me he had known you at Rome, before he came into his property.'

'Did he say that?' said Esther, flushing a little.

'Or before you married, I really don't remember,'

said Olga. 'We had a great deal of conversation, and persuaded him to come back to Bigorre.'

'It's so hot at twelve o'clock,' Mrs. Penton was going on; 'and parasols are quite insufficient. Are you fond of extreme heat, Esther? Charles says that Lady Kidderminster, summer and winter, always carries a fan in her pocket. They are very convenient when they double up, and take less——'

'What sort of looking person is Mr. Smith?' Esther asked, with a little effort.

'Distinguished-looking, certainly: a long red beard, not very tall, but broadly built, and a very pleasant gentlemanlike manner. You shall see him at the table-d'hôte to-day; he promised to join us. In fact,' said Olga, 'he proposed it himself.'

'I heard him,' said Mrs. Penton, placidly. 'Olga, I think you have made another conquest. I remember,' &c.

Poor Esther could not wait any longer to hear Mrs. Penton's reminiscences, or Olga's self-congratulations; she went away quickly with Jack to her own room, and got her little Prissa into her lap, and made her put her two soft arms round her neck and love her. 'Mamma, why are you crying?' said Jack; 'we are both quite well, and we have been very good indeed, lately. Madame Bouchon

says I am her *petty marry*. I shan't marry her though.
I shall marry Lena when I am a man.'

Esther dressed for dinner in her black gauze gown,
and followed the others to her usual place at the long,
crowded table. Her hands were cold, and she clasped
them together, reminding herself by a gentle pressure
that she must be quiet and composed, and give no sign
that she remembered the past. She no longer wore her
widow's cap, only a little piece of lace in her hair, in
which good old Spicer took a pride as she pinned up the
thick braids. Esther's grey eyes were looking up and
down a little frightened and anxiously: but there was
no one she had ever seen before, and she sat down with
a sigh of relief; only in another minute, somehow, there
was a little stir, and Olga said,—' Esther, would you
make room?' and popped down beside her; and then
Mrs. Halbert saw that her sister-in-law was signing to
someone to come into the seat next beyond her.

Esther had been nervous and excited, but she was
suddenly quite herself again. And as Smith took his
place, he bent forward, and their eyes met, and then
he put out his hand,—' Is it my old Esther?' he
thought, with a thrill of secret delight; while Esther, as
she gave him her slim fingers, said to herself,—' Is this
my old friend?'—and she looked wistfully to see whether

she could read his kind, loyal heart, stamped in his face as of yore. They were both quite young people again for five minutes; Olga attributed the laughter and high spirits of her neighbour to the charms of her own conversation. Esther said not one word, did not eat, did not drink, but was in a sort of dream.

After dinner they all got up, and went and stood in one of the wooden galleries, watching the lilac and gold as it rippled over the mountains, the Bedat, the Pic du Midi.

And so this was all, and the long-looked-for meeting was over. Esther thought it was so simple, so natural, she could hardly believe that this was what she had hoped for and dreaded so long. There was Smith, scarcely changed,—a little altered in manner perhaps, with a beard which improved him, but that was all. All the little tricks of voice and of manner, so familiar once, were there : it was himself. She was glad, and yet it was not all gladness. Why did he not come up to his old friend? Why did he not notice or speak to her ? Why did he seem so indifferent ? Why did he talk so much to the others, so little to her? Mrs. Halbert was confused, disappointed, and grieved. And yet it was no wonder. She thought that of all people she had least right to expect much from him. She was leaning over the side of the gallery, Olga

with a pathetic pleasant tune,—'Si tu savais,' its name was. She gave it with charming expression, and when she had finished, they were all silent for a moment or two, until Lady Mary began to bustle about and to pour out the tea.

'Take this to Mrs. Halbert, Geoffry,' she said, 'and tell her about my scheme for to-morrow, and persuade her to come.'

Smith brought the tea as he was bid.

'We all want to go over to Grippe, if you will come too,' he said.

He looked down kindly at her as he spoke, and the poor foolish woman flushed up with pleasure as she agreed to join them. She was sorry afterwards when she, and Olga, and Mr. Penton walked home together through the dark streets.

'I wonder whether Mr. Smith means to join all our excursions,' said Miss Halbert. 'I just mentioned my wish to see Grippe, and he jumped at it directly.'

Esther felt a chill somehow as Mr. Penton answered,—

'Certainly, I—a—remarked it, Olga; you-a are not—perhaps aware that you have attractions—to a—no common degree. Mr. Smith has certainly—a—discovered them.'

Poor Esther! it seemed hard to meet her old friend at

last, only to see how little he remembered her; and yet she thought, 'All is as it should be; and with my Jacky and my Prissa to love, I am not to be pitied.' Only, there was a strange new ache in her heart next morning, when they all assembled after the early breakfast; she could not feel cheery and unconscious like Lady Mary, or conscious and flattered like Olga. The children in their clean cotton frocks were in raptures, and so far Esther was happy.

The road to Grippe is along a beautiful mossy valley, with a dashing stream foaming over the pebbles, and with little farms and homesteads dotting the smooth green slopes. Olga and Smith were on horseback; Penton was also bumping majestically along upon a huge bay mare; Esther and Lady Mary, and the Smith children and her own, were packed away into a big carriage with Mdlle. Bouchon, and little Geoffry Smith on the box. The children were in a state of friskiness which seriously alarmed the two mammas. They seemed to have at least a dozen little legs apiece. Their screams of laughter reached the equestrians, who were keeping up a somewhat solemn conversation upon the beauties of nature, and the cultivation of Indian corn: Geoffry wondered what all the fun might be, and Olga remarked that the children were very noisy, and that Esther certainly spoilt little Jack.

'Lady Kidderminster strongly advises his being sent to a preparatory school,' said Penton, with a jog between each word; while Smith looked up at the blue sky, then down into the green valley, and forgot all about his two companions, trying to catch the tones of the woman he had loved.

The châlet was a little rough unfinished place at the foot of the Pic, where people come to drink milk out of clean wooden bowls: the excursionists got down, and the horses were put up. The whole party crowded round the wood fire, and peeped at the rough workmen and shepherds who were playing cards in the next compartment—room it could not be called, for the walls were only made of bars of wood at a certain distance from each other. The children's delight at seeing all over the house at once was unbounded. Jacky slipped his hand between the wooden bars, and insisted on shaking hands with a great rough road-maker in a sheepskin, who smiled kindly at the little fellow's advances.

Lady Mary was very much disappointed and perplexed to see the small result of her kindly schemes. It was unbelievable that Geoffry should prefer that great, uninteresting, self-conscious Miss Halbert, to her gentle and tender little widow; and yet it was only too evident. What could be the reason of it? She looked from one to

the other. Esther was sitting by the fire on a low wooden
stool. She seemed a little sad, a little drooping. The
children were laughing about her as usual; and she was
holding a big wooden bowl full of milk, from which they
sipped when they felt inclined. The firelight just caught
the golden tints in her brown thick hair; her hat was on'
the floor at her feet; little Prissa—like her, and not like
her—was peeping over her shoulder. It was a pretty
picture: the flame, the rough and quaint simplicity of the
place, seemed to give it a sort of idyllic grace. As for
Smith, he was standing at the paneless window looking
out at the view: all the light was streaming through his
red beard. It was a straight and well-set figure, Lady
Mary thought; he looked well able to take care of himself, and of her poor gentle Esther too. He was abstracted
—evidently thinking of something besides the green
valleys and pastures—could it, could it be that odious
affected woman stuck up in an attitude in the middle of
the room who was the object of his dreams?

An odd jumble of past, present, and future was running
through Geoffry's mind, as he looked out of the hole in
the wall, and speculated on what was going to happen to
him here in this green pasture-land by the side of the
cool waters. Were they waters of comfort—was happiness
his own at last? somewhat sadly he thought to himself

that it was not now what it would have been ten years ago. He could look at the happiest future with calmness. It did not dazzle and transport him as it would have done in former times—he was older, more indifferent: he had seen so many things cease and finish, so many fancies change, he had awakened from so many vivid dreams, that now perhaps he was still dreaming; life had only become a light sleep, as it were, from which he often started and seemed to awaken. Even Esther . . . . what did it all mean? did he love her less now that he had seen her, and found her unchanged, sweeter if possible—and he could not help thinking it—not indifferent? Would the charm vanish with the difficulties, as the beauty of a landscape ends where the flat and prosperous plains begin? He did not think so—he thought so—he loved her—he mistrusted her; he talked to Olga, and yet he could not keep his eyes from following Esther as she came and went. All she said, all she did, seemed to him like some sort of music which modulates and changes from one harmonious thing to another. A solemn serenity, a sentiment of wordless emotion was hers, and withal, the tender waywardness and gentle womanliness which had always seemed to be part of her. She was not handsome now, any more than she had ever been—the plain lines—the heavy hair —the deep-set eyes were the same—the same as those

eyes Smith could remember in Roman gardens, in palaces
with long echoing galleries, looking at him through imploring tears on the Pincian Hill. They had haunted
him for seven years since he first caught the trick of
watching to see them brighten. Now, they brightened
when the two little dark-headed children came running to
her knee. Raphael could find no subject that pleased
him better. Smith was no Raphael, but he, too, thought
that among all the beautiful pictures of daily life there is
no combination so simple, so touching as that of children
who are clinging about their mother. And these pictures
are to be seen everywhere and in every clime and place;
no galleries are needed, no price need be paid; the background is of endless variety, the sun shines, and the
mother's face brightens, and all over the world, perhaps,
the children come running into her arms. White arms or
dusky, bangled or braceleted, or scarred with labour, they
open, and the little ones, clasped within loving walls, feel
they are safe.

Quite oblivious of some observation of Miss Halbert's,
Smith suddenly left his window and walked across
to the fire, and warmed his hands, and said some little
word to Esther, who was still sitting on her low seat. She
was hurt and annoyed by his strange constraint and
distance of manner. She answered coldly, and got up by

a sudden impulse, and walked away to where Lady Mary was standing cutting bread-and-butter for the children. ' Decidedly,' thought the elder lady, 'things are going wrong. I will ask Geoffry to-night what he thinks of my widow.' 'I am a fool for my pains,' Geoffry thought, standing by the fire, ' and she is only a hard-hearted flirt after all.'

He was sulky and out of temper all the way back. In vain did Olga ransack her brain, and produce all her choicest platitudes for his entertainment. In vain Penton recalled his genteelest reminiscences. Smith answered civilly, it is true, but briefly and constrainedly. He was a fool to have come, to have fancied that such devotion as his could be appreciated or understood by a woman who had shown herself once already faithless, fickle, unworthy. Smith forgot, in his odd humility and mistrust of himself, that he, too, had held back, made no advance, kept aloof, and waited to be summoned.

Geoffry had the good habit of rising early, and setting out for long walks across the hills before the great heat came to scorch up all activity. The water seemed to sparkle more brightly than later in the day. The flowers glistened with fresh dew. Opal morning lights, with refractions of loveliest colour, painted the hills and brooks, the water-plants, the fields where the women were working already, and the slippery mountain-sides where the pine-trees grow, and the flocks and goats with their tinkling bells were grazing. It was a charming medley of pastoral sights and scent and fresh air : shadows trembling and quivering, birds fluttering among green, the clear-cut ridges of the hills, the waters bubbling among reeds and creeping plants and hanging ferns, among which beautiful dragon-flies were darting. Smith had been up to the top of the Bedat, and was coming down into civilised life again, when he stopped for an instant to look at the bubbling brook which was rushing along its self-made ravine, some four or five feet below the winding path ; a field lay beyond it, and farther still, skirting the side of a hill, the pretty lime-tree walk which leads to the baths in the mountain. Smith, who had been thinking matters over as he stumbled down the steep pathway, and settling that it was too late—she did not care for him—he had ceased caring for her—best go, and leave things as they were—suddenly came upon a group which touched and interested him, and made him wonder whether, after all, prudence and good sense were always the wisest and the most prudent of things. In the middle of the stream, some thousand years ago, a great rock had rolled down from the heights above, and sunk into the bed of the stream, with the water rushing and bubbling all round it,

and the water-lilies floating among the ripples. . . .
Perched on the rock, like the naïad of the stream, was
Esther, with Jacky and Prissa clinging close to her, and
sticking long reeds and water-leaves into her hair. The
riverkin rushed away, twisting and twirling and disappearing into green. The leaves and water-plants swayed
with the ripples, the children wriggled on their narrow
perch, while Esther, with a book in her hand, and a great
green umbrella, looked bright, and kind, and happy.

'Cousin Jeff, cousin Jeff!' cried little Jack, in imitation of the little Smiths, 'come into the steamer, there's
lots of room.'

'How d'ye do?' said his mother, still laughing.

'How d'ye do, Mrs. Undine?' said Smith, brightening
and coming to the water's edge.

As Smith walked back to his breakfast, he thought to
himself—'If she would but give me one little sign
that she liked me, I think—I think I could not help
speaking.'

And Lady Mary, who had her little talk out with her
cousin after breakfast, discovered, to her great surprise,
that what she had thought of as a vague possibility some
day, very far off, was not impossible, and might be near
at hand after all. She did not say much to Smith, and
he did not guess how much she knew of all that was passing

in his mind. ' He will go away, he will never come forward unless Esther meets him half-way,' the elder lady thought to herself, as he left the room; and she longed to· speak to Esther, but she could not summon courage, though opportunity was not wanting.

They were all standing in the balcony of the châlet that very afternoon, watching the people go by: but first one· child went aw&y, then another, and at last Lady Mary and' Esther were left alone. 'Look at that team of oxen dragging· the great trunks of the trees,' said Lady Mary; 'how picturesque the peasant people are in their mountain dress!'

' The men look so well in their *bérets*,' Esther said; ' that is a fine-looking young fellow who is leading the cart. There is Mr. Smith crossing the street—he would look very well in a *béret*, with his long red beard.'

' Certainly he would,' said Lady Mary; and then she suddenly added, ' Esther, would you do me a favour?' You have been talking of going to the fair at Tarbes tomorrow. I shall be obliged to stay at home with my husband and Lucy. Would you bring Geoffry a *béret*, and give it to him, and make him wear it? I know you will if I ask you.'

' A red, or a blue one?' said Esther, smiling.

' The nicest you can get,' said Lady Mary. ' Thank you very much indeed.'

Lady Kidderminster, who must have employed her time well while she was in the Pyrenees, 'had been very much struck by Tarbes,' Mr. Penton declared. 'It is pleasantly situated,' Murray says, 'on the clear Adour, in the midst of a fertile plain in full view of the Pyrenees. Public walks contribute to the public health and recreation. The market-people, in their various costumes, are worth seeing.'

Geoffry Smith received a short note from Mrs. Penton two mornings after the Grippe expedition. It ran as follows :—

'DEAR MR. SMITH,—Mr. Penton is planning an excursion to Tarbes to-day. We start at two, so that we may not miss our lunch, as it is not safe to trust to chance for it, and we should be much pleased for you to join us after, but in case of rain we should give it up. Unfortunately, there appears no chance of anything so refreshing.

'Sincerely yours,

'MIRA PENTON.'

To which Smith, who was rather bewildered, briefly answered that he should be delighted to join them at the station at two. The station was all alive with country-folks, in their quaint pretty dresses, *bérets*, red caps and blue brown hoods, and snooded gay-coloured kerchiefs, and red cloaks like ladies' opera cloaks. The faces underneath all these bright trappings were sad enough, with brown wistful eyes, and pinched worn cheeks. Ruskin has written of mountain gloom and mountain glory, and in truth the dwellers among the hills seem to us, who live upon the plain, sad and somewhat oppressed.

Smith looked here and there for his party, and discovered, rather to his dismay, only Olga, her sister and her brother-in-law, sitting on a bench together. Then Esther had not come after all? He felt inclined to escape and go back to the town, but Olga caught sight of him, and graciously beckoned.

'Mrs. Halbert is not coming, I am afraid?' said Smith, shaking hands.

'Esther, do you mean?' asked Mrs. Penton. 'She was here a minute ago. Jacky took her to look at a pig.—Was it a pig or a goat, Olga? I didn't notice.'

Mrs. Penton's naïve remarks gave Smith a little trouble sometimes, and he could not always suppress a faint amusement. Fortunately Esther came up at this moment, and he could smile without giving offence.

Esther at one time had not meant to come, but she could not resist the children's entreaties, or trust them to the Pentons alone. She was weary and dispirited; she had passed a wakeful, feverish night. How or when or where it began, she did not know, but she was conscious now that in her heart of hearts she had looked to meet Geoffry again some day, and hoped and believed that he would be unchanged. But she now saw that it was not so —he liked her only as he liked other people, with that kindly heart of his—no thought of what had been, occurred to him. He might be a friend, a pleasant acquaintance, but the friend of old, never, never again. How foolish she had been, how unwomanly, how forward. Even at seven-and-twenty Esther could blush like a girl to think how she had thought of Geoffry. She whose heart should be her children's only; she who had rejected his affection when it might have been hers; she who had been faithless and selfish and remorseful so long—she was glad almost to suffer now, in her self-anger and vexation. In future she thought she would try to be brave and more simple; she would love her darlings and live for them only; and perhaps some day it might be in her power to do something for him—to do him some service—and when they were very old people she might tell him one day how truly she had been his friend all her life.

The sun was blazing and burning up everything. The train stopped at a bridge, and they all got down from their carriages, and set off walking towards the market. Squeak, chatter, jingle of bells, screaming of babies, pigs and pigs and pigs; pretty grey oxen with carts yoked to their horns, priests, a crowd assembled round an old woman with a sort of tripod, upon which you placed your foot for her to blacken and smarten your shoes; mantillas, green and red umbrellas, rows of patient-looking women, with sad eyes, holding their wares in their hands, scraggy fowls, small little pears, a cabbage, perhaps brought from over the mountain, a few potatoes in a shabby basket;—the scarcity and barrenness struck Smith very sadly. Esther was quite affected; she was emptying her purse and putting little pieces right and left into the small thin hands of the children. They passed one stall where a more prosperous-looking couple—*commerçants* from Toulouse— were disposing of piles of blue and red Pyrenean caps. Esther stopped and called Jack to her, and tried a small red *béret* on his dark curly head, and kissed her little son as she did so. She had not seen Smith, who was close behind her with Olga, and who smiled as he watched her performance. Miss Halbert, soon after leaving the rail-way-carriage, had complained of fatigue, and taken poor Geoffry firmly but gently by the arm, with a grasp that it was impossible to elude. Esther scarcely noticed them: she walked on with her children as usual, and her motherly

G

heart was melting over the little wan babies, whose own
mothers found it so hard a struggle to support them. They
were lying in the vegetable baskets on the ground, or slung
on to their mothers' backs, and staring with their dark
round eyes. Some of the most flourishing among them
had little smart caps, with artificial flowers, tied under
their chins. After buying Jack's *béret*, Mrs. Halbert
seemed to hesitate, and then making up her mind she
asked for another somewhat larger, which she paid for,
and she turned to Smith with one of her old bright looks
and gave it him, saying,—

'I think you would look very well in a *béret*, Mr.
Smith—don't you like a blue one best?'

Smith wore his *béret* all day; but Olga the inevitable
held him, and would not let him go. Esther thought
it a little hard, only she was determined *not* to think
about it. They wandered for hours through the bare
burning streets. There seemed to be no shade: the
brooks sparkled, bright blazing flowers grew in gardens,
the houses were close shuttered, scarcely anyone was to
be seen; little bright-plumaged birds came and drank at
the streams, and flew away stirring the dust. The
children got tired and cross, and weary; the elders' spirits
sank. Someone, standing at a doorway, told them of a
park, which sounded shady and refreshing, and where

they thought they would wait for their train. The road
lay along a white lane with a white wall on either side,
and dusty poplars planted at regular intervals. Esther
tried to cheer the children, and to tell them stories as well .
as she could in the clouds of dust. Mrs. Penton clung to
her husband, Olga hung heavily upon Geoffry's aching
arm. . . . They reached the gates of the park at last. It
was an utter desolation enclosed behind iron railings—so
it seemed, at least to the poor mother: ragged shrubs,
burning sun, weeds and rank grass growing along the
neglected gravel walks. There was a great white museum
or observatory in the middle to which all these gravel
paths converged; and there was—yes, at last! there was
a gloomy-looking clump of laurel and fir trees, where she
thought she might perhaps find some shade for Jack and
for Prissa. As she reached the place, it was all she could
do not to burst out crying, she was so tired, so troubled,
and every minute the dull aching at her heart seemed to
grow worse and worse. Poor Esther! The others came
up and asked her if she would not like to see the view
from the observatory; but she shook her head, and said
she was tired, and should stay where she was with Prissa,
and they all went away and left her. One French lady
went by in her slippers, with a faded Indian scarf and an

old Leghorn hat, discoursing as she went to some neglected-looking children :—

'Savez-vous, ma fille, que vous faites des grimaces; ce n'est pas joli, mon enfant, il faut vous surveiller, mon Hélène. Les grimaces ne se font pas dans la bonne société. . . . Le parc est vaste,' she continued, changing the subject; her voice dwindled away into the arid, burning distance, and the desolation seemed greater than ever. . . . It seemed to Esther as if hours and hours had passed since the others had left her. . . . Prissa was languidly listening to the story poor Esther was still trying to tell.

'Why don't you make it more funny, mamma ?. You say the same things over and over. I don't like this story at all,' said Prissa.

'I have some good news for you,' said Smith, cheerfully, appearing from behind the laurels. 'Mrs. Halbert, we have only just time to catch the train. Come, Jack, I'm going to be your horse; get up on my back,' and Geoffry set off running with the delighted Jack, just as Olga appeared in search of him.

Esther and Prissa set off running too, and the Pentons followed as best they could.

The little station was again all alive and crowded by peasants and countrywomen, Spanish bandits with their packs, three English tourists in knickerbockers. Smith

met them with Jack capering at his side, and swinging
by his new friend's hand,—

'I have taken the tickets,' he said. 'Thank goodness,
we have done with Tarbes. What a horrible hole it is.'

'I am surprised,' Penton remarked, 'that Lady
Kidderminster should have had such a high opinion of
this—a—position. She particularly mentioned an amphitheatre, of which I can gain no information.'

'Oh, dear! we shall never get in in time for the table-
d'hôte,' faintly gasped Mrs. Penton, sinking into a seat,
'and the dinner will be over.'

The benches were full, and they were all obliged to
disperse here and there as they could find places. Esther
perched herself upon a packing-case once more, with
little Prissa half asleep on her knee. What a dreary day
she had spent—she gave a sigh of relief to think it was
over.

'Have you room here for Jack?' said Geoffry, coming
up. 'He won't own he is tired.'

'Come, my son,' said Esther, putting her arm round
the boy, and pulling him up beside her. 'You have been
very good to Jack, Mr. Smith,' she said, with an upward
look of her clear eyes.

Smith looked at her.

'It seems very strange,' he said, with a sudden emotion, 'to meet you again like this. I sometimes wonder whether we are indeed you and me, or quite different people.'

'.I thought,' said Esther, 'you had forgotten that we had ever been friends, Mr. Smith.'

'I thought *you* had forgotten it,' said Smith, very crossly. There was a jar in his voice—there was a mist before her eyes. She was tired, vexed, over-done. Poor Esther suddenly burst into tears.

'My dear, my dear, don't cry,' said Smith. 'What can I say to beg your pardon? you should have known me better—you . . .'

'I cannot understand about that amphitheatre,' said Mr. Penton, coming up. 'Murray, you see, does not allude to it.'

'Why don't you go and ask the man at the ticket-office?' said Smith authoritatively, and Penton, rather bewildered, obeyed.

'I was a little afraid of you,' said Smith, 'when I first saw you. I tried to keep away, but I could not help myself and came. I should have gone to the end of the world if you had been there. I have never changed —never forgotten. I love you as I have always loved you. Dear Esther, say something to me; put me out of this horrible suspense——'

'What a fearful crowd; how it does crush one,' said Mrs. Penton, suddenly appearing. 'Can you tell me where Charles has hidden himself? He put my eau-de-Cologne in his pocket, and really in this crowd . . . .'

Esther could not answer. She was bending over Prissa, and trying to hide her tears. Smith politely pointed out the ticket-office to Mrs. Penton, and then, with great gravity, turned his back upon the lady, and took Esther's hand, and said with his kind voice, 'Dear Esther, once you used not to be afraid of telling me what you thought. Won't you speak to me now? Indeed I am the same as I was then.'

'And I am not the same?' said Esther, smiling, with her sweet face still wet with tears; and with a tender Esther-like impulse she took her children's two little hands and put them into Geoffry's broad palm.

Geoffry understood her, though he did not know all she meant. The Pentons joined them again, and the train came up, and the others wearily sank into their places, but Mrs. Halbert's fatigue was gone. All the way back neither Smith nor Esther spoke one word to each other. The sun was setting: all the land was streaming with light; the stars were beginning to shine behind the hills when they got back to Bigorre.

'Shall you be too tired to come for a walk after

dinner?' said Smith, as he left Esther at the door of
the inn; and in the evening he came for her; and,
though Olga looked puzzled and not over-pleased, Esther
put on her hat, and said,—

' I am ready, Mr. Smith.' And they went out together without any explanation.

They went up the pretty lime-tree walk which leads
to the baths of the Salut. People were sitting in the dark
on the benches talking in low evening whispers. Priests
were taking their recreation, and pacing up and down in
groups. From the valley below came an occasional tinkle
of goats' bells, a fresh smell of wild thyme, a quizzing
of crickets. The wain was moving over the hill-side,
the lights twinkled from the houses in the town; and
Smith and Esther talked and talked, counting over the
fears, the doubts, and the perplexities of the last few
days. Now, for the first time, Esther felt a comfort and
security which had never been hers before—not even in the
first early days of her marriage; not since the time when
she bade Smith farewell on the Pincio. It seemed to her
now as if all care for the future, all bewilderment and
uncertainty, were over. It was all real to her—vivid,
overwhelming. Here was the faithful friend once more
ready to do battle for her with the difficulties of life:
ready to shield, and to serve, and encourage to decide—

to tell her what was right; and poor Esther had long felt that to her decision was like a great pain and im-- possibility. But here was Smith to advise, and it seemed to her as if troubles and difficulties became like strong places now that he was there. His manner of looking at life was unlike that of the people among whom she had been living : he seemed to see things from a different level, and yet she felt as if he only saw clearly, and that everything he said was right and true. Some people, as I have said, seem by intuition to see only truth and right; others must needs work out their faith by failing and sorrow. They realise truth by the pain of what is false, honour through dishonour, right by wrongs repented of with bitter pangs. And Esther had long felt that this was her fate. She did not realise all that she understood later-- only she felt it somehow ; she drifted into a peaceful calm ; she seemed suddenly and unawares to be gliding through still waters after the tempest, and a thankful song of praise went up from her heart.

When she awoke in the morning she knew that he was near at hand ; she heard his kind voice, and the children's prattle down in the courtyard below. Later in the day he would come up to see her, and they talked over old days, and the new days seemed to shine with a sudden gleam now that he had come into them ; the dull hours went more swiftly, the sky seemed brighter; evening came full of sweet tones, mysterious lights, and peace and perfume; people passing by seemed strolling, too, in a golden beatitude. They too, Esther fancied, surely must feel the sweetness and depth of the twilight. The morning came with a bright flash, not dawning with a great weight of pain and listlessness as before. In the hot blaze of the mid-day sun Geoffry would enter the shaded room where the women were sitting at work by the window.

To Esther it was very real—to Geoffry it was still like a memory of old times, to be sitting with Esther at an open window, with the shadows of the orange-trees lying on the floor where the shade of the awning did not reach. Jack liked playing with the shadows, putting his little leg out into the sunshine, and pulling it back, to try and cheat the light and carry some away; but Prissa (her grown-up name was to be Priscilla) liked best sitting quietly on her mother's knee, and, as it were, staring at the stories she told her with great round eyes. The story broke off abruptly when Smith came in, and another tale began. It seemed like a dream to Geoffry to find himself sitting there, with Esther, at an open window, with the sounds and the sunshine without, sounds of horses at the water, of the water rushing, of voices calling to each other, of sudden bursts of bells from the steeples of Bagnères de Bigorre. It was as if all the years were not, and he was his old self again. Can you fancy what it was to him after his long waiting, long resignation, long hopelessness, to find himself with his heart's desire there before him and within his grasp? Can you wonder that for a little while he almost doubted his own happiness, and lived on in the past instead of the present? Death, indifference, distance, other men and women, years, forgetfulness, chance, and human frailty, had all come between them and divided them, and now, all these things surmounted, like a miracle these two seemed to be brought together again, only divided by a remembrance.

· Some things are so familiar, so natural, that while they last they seem almost eternal, and as if they had been and would be for ever. They suit us, and harmonise and form part of ourselves and of our nature, and so far in truth they are eternal if we ourselves are eternal, with our wondering and hopes and faithful love.

OUT OF THE WORLD

OUT OF THE WORLD.

I.

'Why should we faint and fear to live alone,
Since all alone so Heaven has willed we die?
Not e'en the tenderest heart and next our own
Knows half the reasons why we smile and sigh.'

ONE afternoon Dr. Rich rode up as usual to the door of
Dumbleton House; he passed in through the iron gates,
came up the sweep along which the lilac-trees were
beginning to scatter their leaves, and then he dismounted
at the stone steps under the portico (it was a red brick
house with a Grecian portico), rang at the bell, and asked
if Miss Berners was at home.

He was shown into the drawing-room—a pleasant,
long, ground-floor room, full of comfortable chairs and
sofas, with windows through which you saw the garden,
the autumn flowers all a-glow, the sun setting behind the
trees. One or two tall pictures of Dumbletons who had
once lived in the long drawing-room, and walked in the

garden, hung upon the walls. There was a pleasant perfume of hot-house flowers and burning wood. The room
was hot, be-chintzed, be-perfumed; Horatia, dressed in a
black velvet gown, was sitting by the fire.

She got up to welcome the doctor. He thought that
this black-velvet lady, with the glowing window behind
her, was like a picture he had seen somewhere; or had he
read about it? or had he dreamt it? Somehow, he
knew she was going to say, 'We are going away; good-
by!' And Horatia gave him her hand, and said,—

'Oh, Doctor Rich!—I am so sorry—my aunt tells me
we are going away!'

'Well,' he said, wondering a little at this odd realisa-
tion, 'I am sorry to lose my patient. Though, in truth,
I had meant to tell you to-day that you yourself can best
cure yourself. All you want is regular exercise and
living, and occupation. And this is physic I cannot tell
the chemist to put up in a bottle and send you.'

'What makes you think I want occupation?' said
Horatia, a little angry, and not over-pleased.

'Don't most women?' said the doctor, smiling. 'Don't
I find you all like prisoners locked up between four
walls, with all sorts of wretched make-shift employments,
to pass away time? Why, this room is a very pretty
prison, but a great deal too hot to be a wholesome one.'

'You are right; I am a prisoner,' said Horatia, in her velvet gown; 'but I assure you I work very hard.' The doctor looked doubtful. 'Shall I tell you what I do?' she went on. 'This is not the first time you speak in this way.'

'It is an old observation of mine,' Dr. Rich said, 'and I cannot help repeating, that women in your class of life have not enough to do.'

'That is because you do not know: take my life, for instance; I never have a moment to myself. I have to keep up, correspond, make appointments, dine, drive, drink tea, with three or four hundred people all as busy and over-tired as I am. I go out to dinner, to a party, to a ball almost every night in the season. All the morning I shop and write letters; all the afternoon I drive about here and there, and drink five-o'clock tea. I am never alone; I must for ever be talking, doing, attending, coming, going. Is not this work for ten women instead of one poor, unhappy, tired-out creature like myself?' cried she, strangely excited.

Dr. Rich was a soft-hearted man, especially so when he thought of Horatia, and he said kindly, 'That does, indeed, seem a dreadful life to me. Can't I help you? Can't I prescribe some more rational scheme of existence?'

'No, no; nobody, nothing can save me,' said Miss Berners. 'I am utterly jaded, battered, wearied out. I owe everything to my aunt. I must go her ways and lead her life; there is no help for me.'

'But you might, perhaps,' said the doctor, hesitating —'perhaps——'

'No!' cried Horatia, with some emotion, 'I shall never marry! if that is what you mean. Ten or fifteen years ago it might have been; but now—now I am ashamed to look people in the face when she tries . . . . What dreadful things I am saying!—but, all the same, I must go on, and on, and on. There is no rest for me except where the weary go in time. Where— where——' She finished her sentence by bursting out crying.

Dr. Rich thought there was some excuse for her. He went up to one of the windows, and, pushing aside the flower-stand, opened it wide, and looked out into the garden. Then he walked up and down the room once or twice, and then he came back to the fire. It was a tall old chimney-piece, round which the Dumbletons (the masters of the house) had assembled for two centuries and more. A lady let into the wall, with a pearl necklace and powdered hair, seemed to look him full in the face, and nod her head once or twice.

Horatia had sunk down on a low sort of couch, and was wiping her tears away. The fresh gust of air which had blown in through the open window cheered and revived her more than any consoling remarks or talking. When she had wiped her tears she looked up, and he saw all the lines that care had written under those dark eyes, and he was suddenly filled with immense sympathy, pity, liking. For a moment he was silent, and then he made a great resolve, and he said, in a low voice—

'I think I could help you, if you would let me. Instead of being a straw in a whirlpool, how would you like to come and stagnate in a pond? How would you like to be a country doctor's wife?'

Horatia blushed up, started with amazement, and then leant back among her cushions to hide her agitation; while Dr. Rich went on to say, with extra deliberation, that social differences had never impressed him greatly —that he could not see why a fine lady should not take a turn at everyday life; 'for it is at best only a very commonplace, everyday life that I have to offer you,' he said smiling.

He was apt to be a little didactic; but he had soon finished his speech, and he waited for Horatia to begin hers.

'I am so surprised,' she said, trying to speak steadily. 'I——I don't—you don't know me, Dr. Rich.'

The doctor answered, still at his ease, that he had wished to marry for some time past; that he did not expect his sister, who had been his housekeeper, to remain with him always; that he had never fancied anybody in the neighbourhood; and it seemed to him that this arrangement might make them both more happy than they had either of them been hitherto. He spoke so quietly and deliberately (it was his way when he was excited) that Horatia never guessed that this was an ardent, loving heart, full of chivalrous impulse, of passionate feeling; a treasure which he was offering her —that this homely country doctor was as much her superior in every tender, feminine quality as in manly strength, and power, and vigour.

She was looking at him intently with flushed cheeks. She saw a middle-sized, thick-set man, with a kind face, with what seemed to her trustworthy and keen eyes, instead of sleepy ones like her own, with a very sweet voice, whose tones she seemed to hear after he had ceased speaking.

She pictured to herself his ivy-grown house. She had once driven past it with her cousin, Mrs. Dumbleton. She tried to imagine the daily round of life, the quiet little haven, the silence after all these years of noise and racket, the stillness after all this coming and going—one good friend instead of a hundred more or less indifferent. A man with every worldly advantage would not have tempted her so greatly just at that moment. She thought to herself that she wished she had the courage to say 'yes.'

When she found courage at last to speak at all, she said—not the 'no,' she imagined she was going to say—but, 'I can't—I can't give you any answer now. I will send—I will write. I will talk to them. *Please* go, before they come in.'

So Dr. Rich made her a little grave bow, and walked away. His plebeian breeding stood him in good service. He was quite composed and quiet, and at his ease, and here she was trembling, and agitated, and scarcely able to control herself. When he was gone she went upstairs, slowly crossing the hall, and passing along the gallery which led to her room. There was nobody else coming or going, there were only gathering shadows and shut oaken doors, and more Dumbletons hanging from the walls, and windows set with carved panels, looking out over the country and the tree-tops, and the sunset.

She stopped and looked out. She saw the high-road gleaming white between the dark woods on either side; she saw a horseman riding away; past the gate, and

the haycock, and the little row of cottages; past the break
in the trees, and then the road turned, and she could see
him no longer.   She looked out for some ten minutes,
without much heeding all that was going on.   Great
purple clouds heaving out of the horizon, blending and
breaking; winds rising; leaves fluttering in the evening
breeze; birds wheeling in the air, and rooks cawing from
their nests; the great Day removing in glory, and speed-
ing in solemn state to other countries; the Night arriving,
with her pompous, shining train—all these great changes
of dynasties and states of living did not affect her; only
as she watched the sun disappear behind the trees, Horatia
found, to her great surprise, that she had almost made up
her mind—that what had seemed at first so impossible,
and so little to be thought of; that what had appeared to
her only a day ago unattainable, and far beyond her reach,
was hers now, if she had but the resolution to open her
hand and to take it—to accept that tranquil existence,
that calm happiness, which she had told herself a thousand
thousand times was never to be hers.   Suddenly the poor
battered barque had drifted into a calm little haven; the
ocean was roaring still; the winds and the waves beating
and tossing all about; but here, sheltered, protected,
safely anchored, she might stay if she would.   And yes,
she would stay.   If she had scarcely the courage to re-

main, she had still less to face the ocean again. She would stay, come what might. Perhaps Horatia exaggerated to herself the past storms and troubles of her life, but it is certain (and so she kept saying to herself) that at two-and-thirty she was old enough to be her own mistress. She was not ungrateful to her aunt for years of kindness, but she could surely best judge for herself. ·And so, telling herself that she was not ungrateful, she began to wonder how she could send a note to the doctor ; how she could best break the dreadful news to Lady Whiston, who was her aunt, to Mrs. Dumbleton, who was her cousin and Lady Whiston's daughter. It is a way that people have ; they tell themselves that they are not ungrateful, and they go and do the very thing which does not prove their gratitude.

II.

The ladies came in very late, and went to their rooms at once to make ready for dinner. Horatia, who had dressed with nervous haste, and who was too much excited to be still, went wandering up and down the drawing-room in her white dinner-dress, trying to find words and courage to tell them of what had occurred.

The housemaids came in to put the room to rights, to straighten cushions and chairs, to sweep the hearth, and make up the fire. The Dumbletons were chilly people, and fires burned on their hearth almost all the year round. The housemaids departed, leaving a cheerful blaze behind them, comfortable furniture in orderly array, lights with green shades, evening papers folded on the table. The place might have looked tranquil and homelike enough but for the restless Horatia pacing backwards and forwards. She hardly noticed Mr. Dumbleton, the master of the house, who came in quietly and sank down in a big chair, and watched her as she flitted to and fro. This constant coming and going worried him. He was a good-looking, kindly, shrewd, reserved young man. He was usually silent, but he would answer if he was spoken to. Sometimes he spoke of his own accord.

To-night he spoke, and said, 'What is the matter, Horatia? What are you going into training for?' and Horatia stopped suddenly, and turned round, and looked at him for a minute without speaking. An hour ago her mind had been made up, and now again she was hesitating, shrinking, and thinking that she had almost rather change her mind than tell it, it seemed so terrible a task. But here was an opening. Henry Dumbleton was good-natured, perhaps he might help her; at all events, he would give her good advice. She stopped short in her walk, stood straight and still in her white dress, with a drooping head. 'You can help me,' she said, at last looking up; 'I am trying to decide for myself for once, and I do not know how to do it.'

'You surprise me—and so you actually don't know your own mind?' said Dumbleton, smiling.

'Tell me,' said Horatia, suddenly, 'would you think a woman foolish who—suppose you were a woman over thirty, Henry?'—

'I shouldn't own to it,' says Mr. Dumbleton.

'Henry, listen to me,' said Horatia. 'Suppose the case of some one whose life is passing on, who has no settled home, who has not known for years and years the blessings and privilege of being much considered, or much loved. Don't think me heartless—Aunt Car has been kindness itself—I shall always, always be grateful; but——'

'All the gratitude in the world would not induce me to live with her, if that is what you mean,' said Dumbleton.

'Oh, Henry!' said Horatia, coming and standing in front of him: 'should you think very badly of me if, if—can *anything* be a *mésalliance* for a woman in my position?' The tears came into her eyes as she spoke, and Dumbleton saw that her hands were trembling. I think it was for this foolish reason, as much as for any she could give him, that he determined to help her through the ordeal if he could.

'Who is it?' he asked, a little alarmed as to what the answer might be.

The answer came, and Horatia, blushing, and looking twenty again, said—'Dr. Rich.'

'So that is what he came for?' says Henry, opening his eyes.

'Don't you like him?' implored Horatia.

'I think Rich is a capital good fellow,' said Dumbleton, hesitating. 'I don't think he is doing a very wise thing. You will have to turn over a new leaf, Ratia, and tuck up your sleeves, and all that sort of thing; but I suppose you are prepared?'

'You do like him?' said Horatia. 'Oh, Henry, I think you are very, very kind! I did not expect to find one single person to listen to me so patiently.' And Horatia was, in truth, a little surprised that Henry did not insist more upon the inequality of the match. To her, brought up as she had been, in the semi-fashionable world, the difference seemed greater than it really was. She seemed to be performing some heroic feat; she had a sort of feeling that she was a princess stepping down from her throne; that her resolution did her extraordinary credit; that the favour she was conferring was immense; that Dr. Rich's gratitude must be at least equal to her condescension......

And now I must confess that the doctor only spoke a truth when he had said that social differences did not greatly impress him. For Horatia herself he had the tenderest regard and admiration; for her position as the niece of a baroness, and the cousin of one or two Honourables, he did not greatly care; he might have thought more of it if he had been more in the world. As it was, the subject scarcely occurred to him. He was at that moment close at home, riding along a dark lane, hedged with black-looking trees, with the stars coming out overhead in a sky swept by drifting clouds. The wind was rising and shaking the branches, but the doctor was absorbed as he rode along, and as he thought with tenderest affection of the gracious and beautiful woman whom he had enshrined in the temple of his honest heart. It was for herself that he loved her, and not for her surroundings. He would have married her out of a hovel, if she had happened to be born there; whereas she, I fear, took him more for what he had to give her than for what he was. She wanted to marry him, not because he was upright and tender and wise; not because she could hope to make him happy and be a good wife to him—but because she told herself he could make *her* happy. She was by way of giving up everything for him, but in truth, if she gave anything up, it was for her own sake, and because she was tired of it.

Lady Whiston and her daughter came down as the dinner was announced. Mr. Dumbleton offered his arm to his mother-in-law, the other two followed across the hall. The dinner-table dazzled them for a moment with its lights and shining silver and flowers, but their eyes soon became accustomed, and they sat down and took their places. Lady Whiston was a shrivelled and rather flighty old lady; Mrs. Dumbleton, a kind little fat woman, who chirped and chattered and responded to her mother's constant flow of talk. Mr. Dumbleton, as usual, carved, and did not mix much in the conversation. Horatia could hardly rouse herself to attend to what was going on. Why are people always expected to rouse themselves and to talk of the things they are not thinking about?

'I am quite worn out,' Lady Whiston was saying. 'Henry, you know how far from strong I am. I drove to town this morning. I was shopping for two hours. I lunched at the De Beauvilles'. There I met Jane Beverley, who insisted upon taking me all over the South

Kensington Museum, and from there to Marochetti's studio. We then went back to Chapel Street, and paid a number of visits. We got to Lady Ferrars' about half-past five, and had only time to drink a cup of tea. I found the carriage with Augusta in it waiting at the door. Henry, you ought to get Lady Jane to come down and stay with you. There is no one like her.'

Mr. Dumbleton smiled rather grimly, and Mrs. Dumbleton hastily changed the conversation, and said,—

'Well, dear Ratia, what have you been about all day?'

Horatia looked at her plate, Mr. Dumbleton looked at Horatia.

'Did Dr. Rich call again?' said Lady Whiston.

'Yes,' Horatia said.

'Those people are really unconscionable,' cried the old lady. 'Horatia, I hope you made him understand that we are going away, and all that, and shall not require his attendance any more. I don't know what he will not charge. He is not an M.D. though he calls himself a doctor. Now, Mr. Bonsey, a married man with a large family, never asked more than 3s. 6d. a visit. Those sort of people must be kept down.'

Horatia was blushing pinker and pinker, Henry

Dumbleton was more and more amused, and so the
desultory conversation went on, all at cross purposes.
There seemed to be some fatality in the way in which
doctors kept popping up with every course, and from
under every dish-cover. Dr. Rich, and Mr. Caton his
partner, went round with the *entrées* ; with the roast
Mr. Bonsey was served over again, and all the London
physicians. And then, with the dessert, arrived a series
of horrible illnesses, which had attacked various ladies
of high rank, symptoms following each other in alarming
succession. Horatia heard nothing. She was sitting in
a sort of dream, only she listened when they spoke of
Dr. Rich. Was it indeed fated? Was this new distant
country awaiting her? Was she an alien already
doomed to go away and leave them all, and live the
unknown life he had offered her? It seemed unreal
and shadowy, like the night all round about. When
the ladies got up from table, Horatia followed. But
Dumbleton got up, too, contrary to his usual custom,
and said, '*I* will tell my lady,' in an undertone, as she
passed him.

So Horatia, with a beating heart, stayed in the hall,
and went and gazed out through the glass door at the
black landscape, at the murky, wind-blown sky. It had
been raining, but the clouds were breaking; the crescent

moon rose palely and faintly from behind the black trees, the veils of vapour wreathed and curled in the sky, the wind blew in soft sudden gusts over the country, and across the grass and the fields. A lamp was burning, hanging from the pillars in the hall. It looked like a sort of temple, and Horatia in her white robes might have passed for a priestess, looking out at the heavens and trying to read her fate—her fate, which other people after all were settling and arranging at their fancy; for Lady Whiston, discomposed, astonished, indignant, on the drawing-room sofa, was condemning her to live her present life to the very end of her days. Mr. Dumbleton, in the arm-chair, was mildly but firmly marrying her to the doctor. Mrs. Dumbleton was sympathising with her mother and husband alternately, and Horatia herself, who had most at stake, waiting outside, was watching the clouds and the moon. At last Mr. Dumbleton got up with a yawn, and sauntered out of the room. He came out into the hall with the lamp and the flowers, and the white-robed lady staring out at the sky. She started as he called her.

'I am going to send down to the station,' he said. 'The man can take a note if you like to put poor Rich out of suspense. There is a pen and ink in my room.' He lit a cigar as he spoke, and went out and stood on the wet steps under the portico. And Horatia, doing as he told her, went into the study. It was all lighted up, for Dumbleton often sat there of an evening. She sat down at his table, and slowly took up a pen, and then hid her face in her hands for a moment, and then wrote, hardly seeing the words as she formed them :—

'You must help me to bear my aunt's displeasure. I have determined to come to you—I know I can rely upon you.

'HORATIA.'

She folded up the piece of paper and sealed it, and came out again, carrying it in her hand. Dumbleton, who was still waiting outside talking to one of his grooms, took it without asking any questions. He merely nodded, 'Thank you,' and gave it to the man, saying, 'You can leave this at the doctor's on your way, and call and see if there is any answer coming back.'

And then Horatia knew that the die was cast, and with her own hand she had signed and sealed her fate.

III.

It is very puzzling to define the extraordinary difference, so small and yet so great, which exists between a
number of people living in the same place, talking the
same tongue, feeling the same emotions. There are, let
us say, first, the great people, a number of whom make
up what is called the great world. Then, people of the
world; then, people out of the world; and, lastly, the
people—*le peuple*, properly speaking. Dr. Rich and his
sister Roberta, and Mr. Caton, his partner, were people
out of the world, who had been very happy notwithstanding. Horatia was a small person of the world, who
had been very unhappy in it, and yet who had learned
unconsciously certain ways and habits there which made
her unlike Roberta Rich, and superior to her as far as
mere outward manner was concerned. As for the doctor,
he was forty years old and more. He had been a surgeon
on board ship, he had been to India and back, he had
knocked about for fifteen years, he had been at death's
door once or twice (the last time was when he nearly
died of small-pox, before Roberta came to live with him
—some one, to whom she was not as grateful as she

I

might have been, had nursed him through it all). If
years and experience; if rubbing up against people of
every degree, from savages without any clothes at all,
to lords and ladies in silken gear; if a good heart, if
good wit, and good education do not make a gentleman
after twoscore years, it is hard to say what will. Poor
Mr. Caton had not enjoyed all these advantages—only
the good heart was his. That very morning the doctor
and his sister had had a little discussion out in the
garden about the young surgeon's merits. Roberta
liked him and she didn't like him; she almost loved
him when he was sad, silent, subdued; she almost hated
him if, finding her perchance more kind, he became gay,
confident, talkative, and funny. Even George owned
sometimes it was a pity that Caton had so noisy a scorn
for social observance.

If Berta had declared that she fancied him, very
likely her brother might have regretted her fancy, and
thought she was throwing herself away; as she seemed
to care little for him—shook her head, laughed, blushed,
would have nothing to say when she saw him—George,
out of some strange contradiction, had all the more
sympathy for Caton because his sister showed so little;
asked him to the house, praised him continually, and
told Berta at last that she was fine and foolish not to

be able to appreciate a kind and honourable man when he came in her way.

'I may be foolish, George; you know I am not fine— I hate fine ladies,' said Berta, with whom it was a sore subject.

They had just done breakfast on the morning of this eventful day, the doctor had come out for a stroll with *The Times* and his cigar, Berta walked beside him with a basketful of roses. The garden was on a slope—a long, narrow, and somewhat neglected strip, with grass, with rose-beds, with elm-trees, with all London and its domes and spires for a background. There lay the city in the valley stretching farther and farther away beyond the morning mist. Long lines of railway viaducts and arches, lonely church towers, domiciles nestling amidst trees, chinking workshops, fields, roads, and gardens, children's voices shouting, cattle lowing, sheep, and the sound of cocks and hens— all this life lay between the doctor's quiet garden and the great misty city. A great silent city it seemed to be as it glistened in the gentle morning rays; for its roar could scarcely reach the two standing on their distant hill-top. Every now and then came the shrill whistle of a train dashing across the landscape and gone in a moment, only a little smoke remained curling, drifting, breaking, shining with sunlight, vanishing away. All the late summer roses were smelling sweet and were heavy with drops of dew, all the birds in the trees were chirping and fluttering, and Berta, in her pink cotton dress, fresh, slim, and smiling, looked up into her brother's face and said,—

'You know I am not fine—I hate fine ladies.'

Dr. George winced, and puffed his cigar.

'They have never done you any harm. Why should you hate people you know nothing about?' said her brother.

Roberta looked up a little surprised, a little hurt; she could not understand how it was possible that George should speak in such a tone. 'They have never done me any *real* harm,' she said, in a voice not quite her own. 'They have made me feel very uncomfortable.'

'Nonsense, my dear Berta,' said George, hastily turning away; 'that was your fault, not theirs. I can't talk to you now; order a good dinner at all events, for poor Caton is coming, and don't starve him and snub him too.' And he walked across the lawn, at the glass door, and Berta heard the hall-door shut with a bang as he rode off to his fate.

Roberta was a born housewife, a domestic woman

—she was gentle and deliberate—she was placid and happy—she was contented with small interests. A calm summer's evening, a kind word from George, a novel sometimes, a friend to talk to, an occasional jaunt to London—these were her chiefest pleasures. Her troubles lay in her store-room, her kitchen, in the meshes of her needlework, in the cottages of the poor people round about; and now and then, it must be confessed, in occasional and frightful ordeals gone through at her brother's desire, when she called at Dumbleton House, and such like ogres' castles, once in six months. Berta's thoughts were all of objects, of things almost always the most pleasant and the most simple. She had no mental experience in particular : crises of morbid dissatisfaction were undreamt of by her ; hankerings after what she could not get, aspirations after other duties than the simple one which fell to her share, passionate self-reproach and abasement, fervent resolutions, presently to be forgotten—all these things were unknown, unrealised, unimagined by the girl as she came and went about her little busy domain, while Horatia was fuming, fussing, railing at herself and her cruel fate elsewhere.

Berta was not clever. She had not half Miss Berners' powers ; she performed her simple duties simply, and without an effort. Horatia did not always do her duty, but sometimes she went through prodigies of self-reproach, control, denial, culture, inspection, condemnation, or whatever it might happen to be.

Roberta's life was a tranquil progress from one day to another. Her steps paced across the grass-plot, tarried at every rose-tree in turn, led her along the walks to her favourite seat in the arbour, into the house again, moving from one room to another, arranging, straightening, ordering.

And so at six o'clock Berta had put out some of her roses upon the dinner-table, dressed herself in her muslin dress, looked into the kitchen to see that all was satisfactory. At five minutes past six Mr. Caton arrived, and found Berta sitting in the window at work.

As the time went by they both began to think that George would never come back. Caton did not like to say what was in his mind when she told him that the doctor was at Dumbleton House : she was so perfectly unconscious. What was the use of setting her against the inevitable fate ? Her brother could best tell her, if anything was to be told.

Only that morning, with the strange knowledge of another person's feelings which we all possess, Caton had known more than Berta, or Dr. Rich, or Horatia; but meanwhile the day had sped on its course, causes had produced effects, one destiny had evolved out of another, the world rolled into the appointed space in the firmament, and, after ceaselessly travelling hither and thither upon its face for forty years and more, Dr. Rich rode up that afternoon as usual to the door of Dumbleton House, came up the sweep along which the lilacs were beginning to scatter their leaves, and asked if Miss Berners was at home? . . . .

When the tramp of a horse's hoofs came, some two hours later, thudding along the quiet glimmering lane which led back to the doctor's own house, the doctor's sister, who had grown very weary of a long *tête-à-tête*, ran out to the door to meet her brother, and Mr. Caton followed more leisurely. As George dismounted, agitated, wearied, excited, the kindly welcome seemed inexpressibly soothing and pleasant.

For home opened its wide door to him, he thought, and seemed to say, 'Come in; here you have a right to enter, a right to be loved; whatever befalls you without, come in; forget your anxiety, your suspense, put away your fears for to-night. Welcome, welcome!' Home said all this as Berta kissed him, and Caton his partner cried,—

'I say, George Rich, you ask me to dinner at six, and it is near eight before you come in.'

'I—I couldn't come; I was detained,' said Dr. Rich; 'order dinner, Berta.'

And in a few minutes they also were sitting down to dinner, at a table with roses, with candles, and over-roasted mutton; with Betty in desultory attendance: it was a silent repast, chill, belated, and yet pleasant and friendly enough.

After the sun had set, as I have said, the purple clouds turned to grey, and to black, and the wreathing mist began to fall down in occasional showers pattering against the window. Berta could not go out into the garden for her evening stroll, and she had to return into the darkling little sitting-room after dinner, while the gentlemen sat over their wine.

She got out one of her long seams to sew, and as she stitched she faintly wondered what was to be the end of these silent *téte-à-tétes* and long seams. She heard the voices rising and mumbling in the dining room; she could distinguish George's soft tones from Caton's harsh treble; she asked herself whether it was possible that she could one day like the harsh voice as well as she loved the other; she broke her thread, and stitched—no, never, never; nobody could be to her what her brother was—whom else did she want? she would live for him always.

And now, while Berta is still sewing at her seam, some

one passes the window through the rain; there is a ring at the bell, a brief colloquy, and Betty comes in with a letter which she puts upon the table. Berta, busy speculating, wondering to find herself so silly—she always counted silliness and sentiment together—with an effort turns her well-regulated little mind from a dim involuntary mystic dream, and wakes up to every day.

It was time to make the tea, to fold up her work. Should she be able to find her way in the dark to the cupboard upon the landing? Poor little Roberta, she did not guess what was at hand, and in what manner she would find her way there. For she looked up with a smile when the door opened, and George and Caton came in.

Caton glanced at the table and the letter lying there, and then walked across and sat down beside Berta, and began to tell her that he and her brother had been having a discussion; and meanwhile George took up the letter, a candle, and walked away out of the room.

About five minutes passed, and then Berta heard his voice calling—'Roberta!' She ran out to him.

He was standing in the study, with the letter still in his hand: he looked bright, round-eyed, strange, unlike himself. 'Berta,' he said, 'something has made me very happy,' and he put out his hand.

She looked up, with her sweet anxious face wondering, as she took it. 'Some one has promised to be your sister, whom you must love for my sake,' he went on, smiling. He did not see that Berta was trembling and quaking, as she gasped, 'Who is it, George?'

'You know her, dear. You have seen her at Mrs. Dumbleton's,' the doctor went on. 'You must love her, and help me to make her happy.'

Berta's grasp loosened, and her heart sank with dismay. She had seen a beautiful fashionable lady at Mrs. Dumbleton's, who had made her feel all elbows when she talked to her; a fine lady—did not she hate fine ladies? a terrible alarming London beauty. What had he done— what foolish thing had he done? She was clinging to her brother again, with her arms round his neck.

'Oh, how I hope you will be happy! oh, how I hope she will make you happy! Why didn't you tell me? Why have you never said a word?'

'I only made up my mind and spoke to her this afternoon,' said her brother, pulling her gently away. 'I have only had her answer this moment.'

Berta looked at him once again, with her fond doubting eyes. She felt somehow as if it was the last time, and as if Horatia's husband would not be the same man as her brother George. And then she went gently out of the room, still carrying her work, for she felt that tears were coming into her eyes, and she did not want him to see them. She turned and went upstairs, and then, walking along the familiar dark passage, she felt for the key, and opened the great cupboard door, and put down her work upon the shelf with the lavender. Only as she did so, suddenly a great sorrowful pang came over her, and, with a choking sob, she laid her head upon the shelf, feeling all alone in the dark, with her bitter bitter grief. She had not thought, as she sat below sewing her seam, in what a sad fashion it was fated she should put it away. After this night, Roberta could never smell lavender without thinking of darkness and trouble. The rain had ceased by this time, and, as the clouds broke, a faint pale moonlight came creeping coldly along the passage.

IV.

While Berta was crying in the cupboard, Horatia was sitting with her cousin, Mrs. Dumbleton, and saying, 'Augusta, you must stand by me and help me. I assure you I shall be happy. You know I have always wished for a quiet country life, and hoped to marry a clergy-man.'

' But you have not always wished to marry a country doctor,' said Mrs. Dumbleton.

' He will do quite as well,' said Horatia, eagerly. ' I shall occupy myself with the poor people, with the schools. I shall escape from the hateful monotonous round of dismal gaiety.'

' But this will be still more dull in a little while,' said Mrs. Dumbleton.

' No,' said Miss Berners, decisively; ' because it is a natural and wholesome existence; the other is un-natural, and morbid, and exhausting. Augusta, you must help me, and persuade Aunt Car to forgive me. For it is too late to prevent it any more, and—and—Henry sent off a note when the groom went to the station.'

' Is it all settled?' cried Mrs. Dumbleton, very much relieved. She was always delighted when people decided things without her. ' Then, of course, mamma must forgive you;' and the good-natured little woman went off, and knocked at Lady Whiston's door, and there was a great long long conference, and at last Horatia was summoned. And when she came out she was pale and exhausted, but triumphant. She and

Mrs. Dumbleton had talked over the old lady between them. 'Of course, you are going to do exactly as you like,' says Lady Whiston, 'but I suppose you know you have forfeited your place in society. I shall come and see you now and then, when I am not too busy. My consent is all nonsense. I must say I had hoped differently.'

'But you will forgive her in time, mamma?' pleaded Augusta.

'I cannot discharge Mr. Bonsey, if that is what she wants. Horatia! what could you want when you made this ridiculous arrangement?'

'Good-night, dearest, kindest Aunt Car,' said Horatia, suddenly clasping the little old woman in her arms. 'I can't tell you what I wanted, but I must keep to my decision. Good-night, Augusta.'

What had she desired? Happiness, rest, quiet, a tranquil home, sympathy: and now all this was hers at last. She caught a glimpse of her glowing cheeks in the glass. She could hardly believe that bright and brilliant face was her own—her own old face, whose wan glances had met her for so many years. . . .

One day, not long after the day I have been describing, Mrs. Dumbleton's little carriage was travelling along the road which leads from Dumbleton to Wandsworth; Augusta was driving the ponies, and Horatia was going in state to visit her new dominions. They roll on across the country roads, and lanes, and commons; through the western sunshine, through the warm sweet September air, with a great dazzling vault overhead, a shining world all round about them. Horatia leans back too languid, too happy, too excited to talk. She lazily watches the crisp shadows that advance alongside—the nodding heads of the ponies, the trees and houses in the distance, the children and wayfarers who look up to see them pass. It is like a fairy tale, Horatia thinks—a princess driving along the road. And what will be the end of the story? They come to a cross-road at last, and then Augusta turns the ponies' heads, and they trot up a lane full of flickering shadow and sunshine. They stop suddenly at an iron gate in front of a Queen Anne brick house, with all the windows open, and growing ivy wreaths. And Horatia, with a start, says to herself, 'So this is my home?' while Augusta points and says, 'Here we are; doesn't it look nice?'

Behind the iron gate is a little garden, full of red and blue, margarites and geraniums; then three worn steps lead to the door with the old-fashioned cornice, over which a rose-tree is nailed. When Betty opened the door, they could see into the passage, and into the garden beyond, green and sunlight there as here in the lane.

Dr. Rich was not at home ; Miss Rich was in the garden : Betty proposed to go and tell her ; but Horatia quickly said, ' No, we will go to her.'

: So the ladies got down. As Horatia crossed · the threshold, she suddenly thought, with a thrill, how this was her new life, her future into which she was stepping. It had all lain concealed behind the door but a moment ago, and now it was revealed to her. It had begun from that minute when Betty admitted the strangers. The ladies swept through the little hall in their silk gowns, glanced with interest at the doctor's hats hanging upon their hooks, peeped into the little sitting-rooms on either side : the drawing-room with the horsehair sofa and mahogany chairs, the cottage piano, the worsted works of art, the three choristers hanging up on the wall, the funny old china cups and bowls on the chimney, the check tablecloth, some flowers in a vulgar little vase on the table, a folding-door half open into an inner room.

' Is that another drawing-room ?' Horatia asked.

' It ain't used much,' says Betty. ' It 'ave been Miss Rich's play-room. She does the lining there now, and keeps the preserves and groceries.'

Horatia peeped in. There was no carpet; there was a wooden press, there was a glass door leading into the garden. It was not much of a place; but she thought how she would have chintz curtains, tripod tables, gilt gimcracks; and how pretty she could make it! Mrs. Dumbleton was quite enthusiastic.

'These are very nice rooms, Horatia, all except the furniture; with a few alterations they might be made quite pretty.'

But she was so used to her own trim lawns and hot-houses that she could find no praise for the garden. How-ever, there was all Fulham beyond for her to expatiate on. 'The view is too lovely,' said Augusta; 'it would be too, too beautiful, if you could only help looking at the railways and the houses. . . . I should advise you to build a high wall, Ratia.'

'It will do very well when the garden is put in order,' said Horatia, drawing a deep breath.

'It is a pity the garden is so neglected,' Augusta went on, looking up and down, and round about. Cabbages and roses were growing in friendly confusion; honey-suckle straggled up the old brick walls; parsley, mint, saffron, herbs of every sort, grew along the beds. Joe, the odd man, kept it in a certain trim; and the doctor sometimes ordered in a barrowful of flowers. It was not much of a place. Three straight walks led up to the low ivy wall at the end, where a little arbour had been put up, and where the ivy, and spiders'-webs, and honeysuckle, and various pretty creeping plants, tangled, and sprouted, and hung luxuriantly, as you see them at the end of a long summer. The entertainment is nearly over, and they lavishly fling out all their treasures, their garlands, their sweetness.

Under this pleasant, triumphal, autumnal arch, Berta, in a broad hat and blue ribbons, was sitting with a novel; and looking up as she heard steps, she saw a tall woman coming towards her with a long silk trailing gown which swept the mint and parsley borders; and then she guessed in a moment that this was the future mistress of the little domain. What a beautiful lady! the heroine of the novel she had just been reading was not to be compared to her. What dark eyes! what bright glowing cheeks! What a charming smile!

Roberta, who had only seen her once before, and who had thought her very alarming, and said herself that she hated fine ladies, was vanquished utterly for a moment. No wonder George was in love with this gracious creature, who was ready to give up all her state for him. She jumped up to meet her.

K

'I have come to see my new home,' said Horatia, holding out her hand in a royal sort of way.

And Berta, blushing, took it timidly, and said,—

'George told me. How I hope you will both be happy. Isn't it a dear old house?'

The old cistern at the back, the familiar chimney-stacks, the odd windows, the water-spout with the bird's nest, the worn steps where she had played when she was a child, the mouldy little arbour, had all dear old charms for Roberta, which naturally enough Horatia could not appreciate.

'I am afraid it is more for the sake of your brother, than for the merits of the house, that I mean to come and live here,' said Horatia, smiling. 'I want you to show me over the house, and to give us some tea. We came on purpose, when we thought he would be out. I think you know Mrs. Dumbleton.'

'We peeped into your store-room as we came along,' said Mrs. Dumbleton, shaking hands, 'and we want to see some more. I see you do not care much for your garden.'

'I am so glad to have found you,' continued Horatia; 'but we meant to come in anyhow.'

Roberta was rather bewildered by all this conversation, but most of all by the demand for tea. Betty was apt to be ill-tempered if anything was expected that did not come naturally in the course of every twenty-four hours. She began to feel as if her future sister-in-law was a fine lady again. Her heart sank within her. What had George done? What foolish thing had he done? However, she put the doubt away, and said, smiling, that she would be delighted to show them everything. There was not much to see. She pointed out St. Paul's, and the Abbey, and the Tower, and the new railway bridge close at hand; and then tripped back into the house before them, opened doors, showed them the surgery, the study, the drawing-room over again, the dining-room (there were some old carved chairs in the dining-room the ladies were pleased to approve of); she pointed out the convenient cupboards, but she felt a little awkward and sad as she led them here and there; she could not help feeling that their praises and dispraises were alike distasteful to her.

'What an old-fashioned paper!' said Mrs. Dumbleton. 'Horatia, you ought to have white and gold, and matting on the floor, with Persian rugs. Yes; and we must do up this room.'

'What a funny, dismal little room,' said Horatia, stepping in, and indeed almost entirely filling it with her voluminous skirts.

They had turned poor Roberta's store-room into a

boudoir; they had built a bow-window, they had sacrificed all the dear old chairs and tables, and now this was George's study that they were invading. It was very hard to bear. Berta only came in on great occasions—when she wanted money, when she said good-bye, and when she dusted his books. It seemed almost sacred to her, and Betty the clumsy was never allowed to dust or to touch George's possessions. There was a little inner closet with a window, where her brother used to let her sit when she was a child, as a great great treat, while he was at work. In the looking-glass over the chimney, she had, in former years, standing on tiptoe, looked at herself with a sort of guilty feeling of profanation; and now, instead of Roberta's demure, respectful peeping face, it reflected two flounced ladies poking about, staring at the shabby old furniture, turning over the books, talking and laughing.

'What a bachelor's house it is!' said Horatia to Berta, without a notion of the wounds she and good-natured little Mrs. Dumbleton, who would not wilfully have pained any living creature, were inflicting; but women of thirty and upwards have a knack of snubbing and ruffling very young girls, and Berta was very young for twenty summers. She slipped away to the kitchen to order the tea, and to recover her temper.

'Please, Betty, put it out in the dining-room; Dr.

Rich would particularly wish it if he were at home,' Berta said.

'Well, this is the fust time *I* ever heard of tea before dinner !' says Betty, with a bang of the tray upon the table ; and Berta fled at the sound, and came back to find her guests upstairs on the bed-room landing, opening doors, and talking and laughing still.

' That is my brother's room—that is the spare room,' Berta said.

' This one would make a nice boudoir,' chirped Mrs. Dumbleton, thoughtlessly, looking into a pleasant chamber full of western sun-rays, with a window full of flowers.

' That is my room,' said Berta, shortly, blushing up ; ' it has always been mine ever since I came to live with George.'

' How pretty you have made it !' said Horatia, who saw that she was vexed. ' Shall we go down again ? '

Berta made way for them to pass, and they sallied down into the drawing-room again.

But no tea was to be seen ; so, at Berta's request, they went across the passage once more into the dining-room, and sure enough there it was. Betty had not vouchsafed a cloth, but had put out three cups on the red table-cover, three very small old-fashioned willow-patterned plates, knives and forks, a dish of thick bread and scraped butter, a plate of hard biscuits, a teapot, and a glass milk-jug. Three chairs were set, at which they took their places; and while Berta was busy pouring out the tea, Betty arrived with a huge black kitchen-kettle to fill up the pot.

'Shall you want any more bread and butter cut, Miss Roberta?' she said; and poor Berta could not help seeing that Mrs. Dumbleton and Horatia glanced at each other, somewhat amused. They did not hear Berta's sigh as she sent Betty away. Berta sighed indeed, but then she forced herself to smile; and when George Rich rode up, a minute or two later, he came in to find a dream of old days realised at last—a little happy family group in the old house, a beautiful woman looking up with bright gladness to greet him; Berta, evidently happy too, already adopted as a sister. He had not thought as he came slowly along the lane that it was to this that he was coming. He was touched to be able at last to welcome Horatia under his roof; and as he glanced at her beautiful face, as he realised the charm of her refinement, her soft breeding, he asked himself more than once if that was indeed his wife? His welcome was charming, his tender kindness melted and delighted Horatia, who had not experienced over-much in her life. She was grateful, gentle, and happy, and cordial. When they drove off, the doctor was standing at the gate, as happy and as certain of coming happiness as she was herself.

I wonder would it have been different if Dr. Rich could have known that evening what was to come as days went by? It was yet time. If he could have been told the story of the next two years, would he have hesitated—have held back? I think not. He was a man so brave and so incautious that I imagine he would not have heeded the warning. I am sure he could have borne to know the end of it all—and could have heard of trouble to come, with that same courage with which he endured it when it fell upon him.

V.

Horatia had determined to marry her husband against all warnings: except Mr. and Mrs. Dumbleton there was no one in favour of the match. But she would not listen to any objections. Her aunt's laments, angry retractions, exclamations of horror, shakes of the head, nods, groans, sighs, grand and agitated relations who drove up from town to put a stop to the match, and to crush the presumptuous doctor under their horses' hoofs, if need be—, nothing could prevent her from doing as she liked.

'I am beginning to see that this is not at all a good match for you,' the doctor said one day. 'Horatia, do you understand that you will have to be really a woman of the working classes? You will have to do as Berta does—for instance, sew and stitch, and make a pudding on occasions, and I don't know what else.'

'I am older than Berta, and have been brought up differently,' said Horatia, smiling. 'I assure you it is a popular fallacy to think that households do not go on very well with a little judicious supervision. The mistress is not necessarily always in and out of the kitchen.—Where are you going to?' she went on, glad to change the subject, which was one she hated.

'I am going to see a very sick man, who lives three miles off. Caton is attending him, and he has sent for me.'

'I do not much fancy that Mr. Caton,' said Horatia. 'I wish you would beg your friends not to congratulate me without knowing me.'

'Caton is a very good young fellow—he is a rough diamond,' said the doctor. 'He saved my life once when I had the small-pox, so you must forgive him for that and other reasons, Horatia.' And he nodded, and went away more in love than ever.

When Mr. Caton, whom he met presently, began talking over the marriage, with as many misgivings as the grandest of Horatia's great aunts, George Rich stopped him almost angrily.

'What do you mean about keeping in one's own class of life? I suppose a gentleman is the equal of any lady; and if she does not object to marry me, I cannot see what concern it is of yours. Men or women are none the worse, in any station of life for a good education, and for having some idea of what is happening out of one particular narrow sphere.'

'Look at your sister,' began Mr. Caton.

'My sister will be all the better for learning a little more of the world,' said Dr. Rich; 'she is too fond of housekeeping.' But he knew very well what Mr. Caton thought of Roberta.

Six weeks went by—very happily for George and Horatia, very slowly for poor Berta, who all the while fought an heroic little battle which nobody suspected: she was fighting with herself, poor child! and got *all* the blows.

Andrew Caton, indeed, may have guessed that she was not happy; and one day he came up to condole with her, but he had put on such a very long sympathetic face for the occasion that Berta burst out laughing, and would not say a word on the subject. Much less would she understand when he tried to speak of what was much nearer his

heart. The little maiden gently parried and avoided all
sentiment. At the very bottom of *her* heart I think she
liked him, and meant some day to make him happy; but at
twenty life is long, the horizon stretches away far, far into
the distance. There is plenty of time to love, to live, to
hate, to come, to go. Older people are more impatient,
and hurry things on. Young folks don't mind waiting;
at least, so it has seemed to me. Roberta did not mind
much, only sometimes, when a sort of jealous loneliness
came wearily weighing upon her. She could not help
feeling that she was changed somehow, that life was not
the placid progress she had always imagined; wishes,
terrors, fancies, were crowding round her more and
more thickly every day. She began to see what was
going on all about her, to understand what was passing in
other people's minds, as she had never done in her life
before.

As the day approached which was settled for George's
marriage, Berta became more sad. Her wistful eyes
constantly crossed his; she took to following him about;
she would come out to meet him on his return, and creep
gently into his room when he was smoking, or at work.
The night before his marriage she whispered a little
sobbing blessing in his ear.

'My dearest Berta,' he said, 'let us pray that we may

all be happy—don't cry, you silly child,—you do not think that anyone or anything can ever change my love for you.'

George was not demonstrative; he had never said so much before, and Berta slept sounder than she had slept for weeks.

Dr. Rich˙and Miss Berners were married at Putney Church early one wintry morning. Mr. and Mrs. Dumbleton went to the wedding, and Roberta, in a pretty white bonnet. There was scarcely anyone else. After it was all over, Roberta walked home, packed up her things, and went back by the train to the country village where her stepfather was vicar, and where her mother, who was not George's mother, but his late father's wife, was busy from morning to night with little boys and girls at home and abroad; with soup-kitchens, training-schools; with a very tiresome, fidgety second husband, who could do nothing himself, but was very particular about everybody else's doings. He loved his own children, but was not over fond of his stepdaughter; and I think that is why Mrs. Baron was glad that Berta, her dearest and favourite child, should be almost constantly away. But, all the same, it was a delight to have her at home, and Roberta came to the garden-gate to be clasped in kind motherly arms, while all the stepbrothers and sisters streamed out in a little procession to welcome her. It was Christmas Holiday time—the boys were at home. Ricarda (Mrs. Baron had a fancy for inventing names) was grown up quite a young woman; Tina had broken her front tooth; Stephana was naughty, but she should come down from her room after tea; Will, and Nick, and Harry, were hovering about, long-legged, and kindly, and glad. It seemed impossible to Berta that she was only an hour or two away from the struggle of love and jealousy, of tenderness and anxiety, she had been going through for the last few weeks—only two hours distant from the last tears she had dropped, as with Betty's assistance she packed up her boxes and came away; only an hour away from George's last kind words and thoughtful care. And so she settled down quietly in this other home.

She cut out frocks for the children, set to work at the choir, and for three whole days she and her sisters were busy dressing up the old church with ivy, and holly, and red berries.

Months went by. She heard from George; she had one or two letters from Horatia, in the beautiful handwriting. They were back long ago, and settled down quite comfortably, Darby and Joan-wise. They hoped she would come soon, and stay as long as ever she liked one day. George added, 'Caton says he would like to come down and pay you a visit. I daresay you may see him before long.' Poor Mrs. Baron was very much excited, but also rather alarmed by this piece of intelligence. She did not know how her husband might take this attention of the young doctor's. I think, as a rule, women are more hospitable than men, and more glad to see their friends at more hours of the day, but I must confess that it was not only hospitality which made her so anxious on this occasion to play hostess. Mr. Caton was ten years younger than George, was very well to do, and certainly was not coming all this way to see her and the ungracious vicar only. She was right. When Mr. Caton arrived, he asked for Berta eagerly, and Berta appeared. But so unwilling, so little glad to see him, so silent, so anxious to get out of his way, that he determined to go back again without saying anything of what he had meant to say, and had come all this long way to tell her.

'How is George getting on?' Mrs. Baron asked, by way of making some sort of talk.

Mr. Caton shrugged his broad shoulders. 'I hardly ever go there now. Mrs. Rich gives herself no end of airs, but I cannot drop him altogether; he looks ill enough, poor fellow, and I think he begins already to repent of his bargain.'

'These unsuitable marriages rarely answer,' said Mrs.
Baron, with a sigh.

'That is just what he was so angry with me for
saying,' said the young man. '*I* like a woman who is
not above her station, who minds her house, and takes
care of her husband, and that is what Mrs. R. *doesn't do.*
Why, it was as different in Miss Berta's time. . . . . Now,
the house is all topsy-turvy. She's got a lady's-maid,
they tell me, but the dinner is disgraceful. I assure you,
I am not particular—you know I'm not, Miss Berta—but
I couldn't eat what was on my plate. I give you my
honour I couldn't.'

Berta hoped that this might be a prejudiced report,
but she could not help feeling sad and anxious as the
time came near for her to go back to them again.

Alas! the prejudiced report happened to be the true
one.

If Horatia had married younger it might have been
different, but it is almost impossible suddenly, in middle
life, to become a new woman altogether; and from being
lazy, nervous, languid, and unhandy, suddenly to grow
brisk, orderly, thoughtful, and hard-working.

Berta paid them one very short visit, during which
all went smoothly, and yet she went home for another
six months, very doubtful as to how things might turn.

Her brother was not repenting, as Mr. Caton had told them, but it seemed to her that Horatia might begin to get tired of this new life, as she had wearied of the old one.

When George and Horatia married, they both pictured to themselves the lives they were going to lead; and the two pictures were not in the least like one another, or like the reality even. George's picture was of Horatia, a happy woman, a good wife, beautiful, sympathetic, interested in his schemes, contented with her destiny, cheerful, and devoted. He saw her busy in a thousand ways, working among the poor with more energy than Roberta had ever shown, understanding his plans far better, better able to advise, helping him, encouraging him in all good, the best friend, the most faithful companion. 'These instincts are unfailing,' he said to himself. 'I know her as well as I know myself; by what strange, happy intuition is one led to these discoveries?'

Horatia's picture was also of herself. Elegantly but simply dressed, gracefully entertaining her relations, leading a sort of Petit Trianon existence. Giving delicious but inexpensive little dinners, with croquet on the lawn, perhaps; afterwards returning among her old companions; gracious, unpresuming, independent, much made of; she was, especially at first, well satisfied with herself and with what she had done, and with her husband. He might be a little rough and abrupt, but *that* she should be able to change. He was kind and clever and full of consideration; and, with her connections, it would be indeed strange if he did not get on, and become—who knows?—a prosperous man in time. Then, of course, he would have to make some radical change in his way of life. I do not know when it began, but by degrees she began to think the calm haven was perhaps a little too calm after all—if it was to continue only broken by the vagaries of Betty and the cook. Horatia had now and then lost all patience with them, as well as with other peculiarities of her husband's house. She detested a racket, but she was not accustomed to this utter seclusion, or, what was even worse, this strange company: young ladies who called her dear, and who were surprised at everything; homely matrons, with funny husbands; and that intolerable young man, Mr. Caton, who was worst of all. Fortunately she had still her own relations to go to.

And meanwhile George went on prosing to himself— nearly a year since he married! Long happy evenings: Horatia playing on the piano while he sat and smoked (as he was doing now) on the lawn. The whole house brightened by her coming—a stir of life, pleasant talk, where there had only been silence before, or poor Roberta's gentle commonplaces. Dear Berta! It would be as happy a change for her as for himself. He could hardly believe that all this treasure of happiness was his, that he had a wife in the drawing-room, and that wife Horatia; and he put down his cigar, and went and looked in at the window to assure himself that it was not all a fancy brought about by the smoke, the faint perfume of roses, the sweet bewildering air of a summer's day. And in a minute he came back, and began to puff tobacco, not castles in the air any more. For Horatia was there certainly, but so was Lady Whiston; so was Mrs. Dumbleton. Voices, flounces, big carriage at the garden-gate. It was no fancy; and as he did not want to face them all, he went back to his seat in the arbour.

'George!' Horatia calls, opening the window and looking out.

George looks round and shakes his head.

Horatia, surprised, comes out across the grass. 'Won't you come and see Aunt Car?'

'I am busy,' says the doctor.

'They want us to dine there,' says Horatia, putting her hand on his shoulder. 'They expect Lord Holloway.

'We dined there yesterday—there is that breakfast next week; make some excuse.'

L

'But in your profession it is of great consequence that you should improve your acquaintance,' says Horatia, blushing up. 'They were just saying so. Lord Holloway has dreadful attacks of the gout.'

'That is what I shall have if I dine there any more. You can go, you know. You can make up to Lord Holloway all the better if I am not there.'

'How can you say such disagreeable things? Of course I must go without you, if you will not come. It will look very odd; I don't like it at all.'

'Then why don't you stay?' says the doctor in his kind voice, smiling as she frowns.

'Aunt Car will be hurt as it is,' says Horatia, looking round. 'I suppose I had better go back and tell her. It is most unpleasant.'

George glanced a quick, doubtful look as she walked away unconscious, slim, tall, graceful, with her violet dress trailing over the grass and the daisies. She stoops her head at the window, and passes in under the clustering roses. After all why she should not like to go? George asks himself, and though he might have answered the question, perhaps he took care not to do so. How many such questions are there which are best unasked and unanswered? Truth, indeed, is greater than silence, and if we could always tell what was true, it would be well to speak always. But silence is often better than the half-truths we utter; silence to ourselves and of ourselves, as well as to others.

Horatia came home about one o'clock in the morning, and found her husband still up, sitting in the little study, and Mr. Caton with him. The window was open, a candle was flaring on the table, and she thought there was a strange aromatic smell in the room. But it was hard to find Mr. Caton always there, even at that hour of the night. She was not safe, and she looked her displeasure.

He got up with such a grave face as he made her a little stiff bow, that she was still more indignant. George too was grave, though he smiled and put out his hand.

Horatia wrapped her white cloak round her, and turned her back upon Caton.

'What have you been concocting, George? why do you sit with the window open? I wish you had been with me. Lord Holloway is perfectly charming, and——'

'Well, good-night,' said Caton, suddenly. 'Good-evening, Mrs. Rich,' and he walked off. As the door shut Horatia began indignantly, 'That man is insup——' but her husband stopped her languidly, and said he was not up to fighting his friend's battles that night, He was tired. 'Is this the way he speaks to me?' Horatia thought.

The next day the doctor went up to town and came back to dinner very silent and much out of spirits. And Mr. Caton, as usual, looked in in the evening, and they were closeted together for some time. Horatia had taken a nervous dislike to the poor young man; his presence was almost unendurable to her. Rich looked hurt and vexed when she said so one day.

'Why have you taken this aversion to my old companion?' he asked.

'Because he is familiar and interfering,' cries Horatia.

'What do you say to Lady Whiston, then?' says the doctor, provoked.

Horatia was still more provoked, and the little discussion ended in her going off alone, as usual, to the Dumbleton fête.

But she looked so bright and so handsome in her white dress, as she wished him good-bye, that George secretly relented, and thought he should like to see her admired, and determined, if he could, to come for her after all.

VI.

Horatia was not sorry to go by herself. She felt more at her ease when her husband was not there. Old friends came up to greet her. Two old adorers asked her to dance. Mr. Dumbleton gave her his arm, and took her into the conservatory for an ice. Here they all were, making much of her, welcoming her. Horatia could not help contrasting all this with her husband's grave looks and unconcerned manner.

'How does the housekeeping go on?' said Mr. Dumbleton.

'Don't talk about it,' cried Horatia. 'Everything is so different. My genius does not lie in that direction; and yet—would you believe it? my doctor grumbles at times. What a pretty effect!'

They were in a long conservatory, full of trees and shrubs, and flowers and Chinese lanterns. The sound of distant music, the perfume of the plants, the soft glimmer of the lights, filled the whole place, and the stars came twinkling through the glass domes. Horatia was enchanted instead of being bored as in old times. It was an Arabian Night's Entertainment. One of her cousins, who had been an old admirer of hers, came up and scarcely recognised her, she looked so wonderfully handsome and happy; he asked her to dance, and Horatia consented, and went off laughing and radiant, but Henry Dumbleton looked after her a little doubtful as to the entire success of his match-making.

Horatia, meanwhile, twirled and twisted, the musicians played one of those charming waltzes that seem to be singing and sighing with one breath. The music surged and sank again; it was like the sea flowing upon a shore; breathless, excited, Horatia danced on in cadence to the tune, and thought this moment ought to last for ever; she and her partner went to one of the windows to refresh themselves, and stood out upon a low balcony, close to the ground, and began to talk of old days, as people do when they suddenly grow confidential with time and place, and then they talked down to later days, and the cousin, whose name was Charles Whiston, reproached her for having left them as she had done: 'Did she never regret it? Had she quite given up old friends for new?'

'No, no, no!' cried Horatia; 'unequal marriages are foolish things, Charles. It is not until you find yourself lonely and misunderstood in the midst of people who have been brought up to see things *en-dessous*, instead of *en-dessus*, that you begin to discover how real and how insurmountable certain differences are. Things with which I have been familiar all my life seem strange and unfamiliar to them. 'There is a sort of suspicious defiance I cannot describe—a sort of meanness, of familiarity, of low jocularity.'

'But how could you ever marry him?' cried Charles

Whiston, much concerned, 'This is terrible. You must come away; you must come to us, we are always——'

Someone who had been sitting under the window started up at that moment, and got up and walked away.

'I am not speaking of my husband,' said Horatia, blushing, and starting, and a little ashamed of herself. 'I was thinking of—of friends—persons who come to the house whom I cannot be rid of. There is his step-mother, for instance—who came a short time ago, and interfered in the most unwarrantable manner. There is a certain dreadful Dr. Caton whom George is for ever asking. Can you fancy that man daring to call me Mrs. Gallipots?—don't laugh—such vulgar insults are no laughing matter.'

'Poor Horatia,' said her companion, sentimentally. 'I assure you I do not feel inclined to laugh.'

The musicians began to play a new measure, and the dancers set off with fresh spirit. The people outside were still pacing and talking in low voices, the trees were hung with brilliant jewels of fire, no breath stirred the branches, the white dresses gleamed mysteriously through the darkness, the light steps loitered, the low voices sank. Horatia stood immovable, with her head against her hand: her companion was sitting on the low stone parapet, and leaning lazily over the side of the balcony, when suddenly he started up, and stood listening.

'Did you hear that?' he said. And once more distinctly sounding through the still night came a plaintive cry out of the wood.

'Oh! go and see,' said Horatia; 'what can it be?'

In a moment all the silent enchantment of the hour seemed broken and dispelled. That forlorn cry had shaken and dispersed the dreams, the illusions, the harmonies of the summer's night. It was like a pebble falling into still waters. But it was only for a moment: by degrees the silence, the music, the starlight, reassured the startled people; they forgot once more that pain existed in the world, that trouble could approach them. Horatia had almost forgotten her alarm when her cousin rejoined her.

'It was nothing,' he said. 'Someone fainted—a woman was frightened, and screamed. Dr. Rich was there, and another doctor.'

'My husband!' said Horatia, surprised.

'Someone told me he had gone home with the patient,' said Charles Whiston. 'Shall we have another waltz?' Tum—tum-te-tum, te-tum—the music plays, and off they go.

When Horatia got home she found a little note hurriedly scrawled. 'Don't expect me to-night, I am detained.—Yours, G. R.'

He came home next day, looking pale and exhausted, as if he had been up all night.

'Who was ill?' Horatia asked. 'Who fainted?'

'I cannot tell you who it was,' said the doctor. 'Caton attended him. I have been very busy, and I am not well myself, Horatia. I shall go and lie down.'

'You went up to the hall last night, then?' persisted Horatia.

George did not answer, but looked at her once in an odd sort of way, and then went out of the room.

Horatia never knew exactly what had happened that night. It seemed to her somehow that her husband was never quite the same again after that unlucky fête. She actually began to wish for Berta to come back again.

Roberta's mother had brought her the first time, and left her and gone away, after managing to give great offence to George, as well as to his wife, by one or two awkward speeches. And when Berta came back to the old trouble once more—the old battle and disappointment —she determined to be warned by her mother's example. She would gladly have stayed on at home, but George kept writing for her to come, and the bugbear of a stepfather growled out, 'Why didn't she go, since they were so anxious to have her?' and besides, there was a natural yearning after George in her heart, which would have brought her from the end of the world, if he wished it.

So now that Horatia was mistress of his house, Berta did not like to interfere in the household disarrangements —for it was nothing else: she found Horatia evidently discontented and unsatisfied—George looking worn and out of spirits—the dinner unsatisfactory, the furniture dim and neglected, maids careless and unpunctual. Horatia had theories about everything, but did not possess the gift of putting them in practice. Every human being had its rights, she used to say, and those of servants were constantly infringed. The consequence was, that though Betty had time to read the paper and a course of history judiciously selected by her mistress, she had not time to dust and scrub and scour, as in days of yore, when the poor doctor's rights only were considered.

Roberta found that it was almost more than she could do, not to speak, not to interfere. She was ready to cry sometimes when her brother came in, tired and exhausted, and had to wait an hour for his dinner. She thought him looking ill, indeed, and changed. By degrees she almost got to hate Horatia, and did not do her justice for those good qualities she certainly possessed. Horatia's temper was perfect; she bore Berta's irrepressible glances and loud reproaches admirably. She saw that her husband loved his sister; she would not pain him by blaming her. She often wondered that he should seem more at home with Roberta than with herself. She thought herself infinitely superior, cleverer, handsomer, better bred; but she had not Berta's rare gift of home-making, her sweet repose of manner, her unselfish devotion to those for whom she cared. Horatia rarely forgot herself. Berta was like her brother, and almost lived in the people she loved.

And so Horatia's beautiful black eyes did not see all the many things that were amiss; her soft white hands did not work for her husband's comfort; days went by; little estrangements went by; the geese cackled on the common; sick people died or got well; well people fell sick; George went his rounds, and sighed sometimes as he looked at his beautiful wife. It had not answered, somehow.

Every day little stories are told: sometimes about great things, sometimes about nothing at all. This one was about nothing at all, and yet the story was there to read, and I am trying to write it down.

The people who tell the stories are generally too interested and unhappy, or happy, or anxious, or vexed, to look at their daily lives from another person's point of view; and sometimes even other people standing by have not the gift of seeing what is passing before their eyes. Horatia, who was quick about other people, was blind to her own faults. Dr. Rich was the person in that household who could best read the disappointing little history that was telling out, day by day, under his roof, and the struggle of his daily life was to be blind, and not to read the open page. Horatia had no such scruples, and always said what she thought, and thought what she liked, and spoke openly to George, to the Dumbletons, of her fancies, disappointments, dislikes, particularly of her dislike to Mr. Caton. Now that Berta was there, he was always coming, and Horatia did not at all fancy such a brother-in-law; and so she told the girl, who laughed, and blushed, and acquiesced. Horatia said as much to George one day: he answered, somewhat absently, 'Caton is a very clever, good fellow. I am afraid Roberta will have nothing to say to him; but he comes to see me, Horatia.' And that evening, after dinner, coming out into the garden, she saw, much to her disgust, Mr. Caton's red whiskers and a cloud of tobacco under the arbour, where her husband was also sitting, apparently deep in conversation with his friend.

Another grievance she had, which was this: she inherited a few hundred pounds unexpectedly about this time, which she wanted to lay out in doing up the house and the garden, and in more Persian mats, and a brougham. Dr. Rich insisted on her leaving the whole sum untouched at the banker's. 'You shall have it in due time,' he said.. 'Horatia, can't you believe that I have some good reason for not spending money just now?' She could not understand this strange fancy for saving. He would go nowhere; he would insist on economising in every way; he would not willingly ask even her cousins to dinner.. Wearied, disappointed, provoked, she began to tell herself that her marriage had been a mistake—she began to long to get away, to sigh for and to dream of liberty. She did not know how far these dreams had carried her, once she had given way to them. She had wished for Berta, but when Berta came she grew jealous of her. Life was a miserable delusion, Horatia often thought.

Berta could not help seeing there was something wrong, and put it all to poor Horatia's score. It seemed to her that Mr. Caton knew more than he chose to tell; for sometimes she would catch a half-pitying, hesitating glance; and once, when she met him on the common, he stopped short and said, 'Miss Roberta, I want to speak to you;' but she walked on rapidly and pretended not to hear, and then he changed his mind and turned away abruptly. She did not dare to ask what it was, for she thought that after all it might only be the old story that she did not want to listen to. It had been settled that she was to go home that day for a Sunday to see her mother. She was glad to go, for she felt as if she could keep silence no longer, and might say something to George or to Horatia which she would afterwards regret. She felt that her mother's sympathy could help her to silence and toleration. She had but an hour more to be silent. Who can tell what an hour may do?

VII.

She had made her preparations and she was sitting that afternoon sewing in the window, until it should be time to go. Horatia was lying on the sofa, the sun was pouring in. It looked a peaceful little scene enough— flowers and young women, novels, needlework, silence, sunlight—when presently Horatia put down her novel, and began to talk; and as she talked, Berta began to sew very fiercely, and to blush up angrily.

'It is a shame,' Horatia was saying, 'that I may not choose my own company; that I am to be forced to receive a person so distasteful to me as Mr. Caton. His familiarity is really unbearable. Until your return, Roberta, I hope we shall see less of him. To-day he came up to me, and told me that I ought to take more care of

George. You and your brother cannot understand how distasteful this sort of thing is—what a real want this want of congenial society is to me.'

' You have George,' said Berta, stitching away.

' George is a dear, good George,' said Horatia, passing her hand wearily over her eyes; 'but he has not been brought up to many things that I have been accustomed to. I feel a little want of sympathy, a little lonely sometimes.'

A cleverer person than Roberta might have understood her better; but the girl was thoroughly provoked and offended. All her pent-up passion burst out; after all her days of silence she spoke, scarcely knowing what she said:

' Do you dare to complain—you, who have ·made George sad and lonely by coming to live with him—you, who don't appreciate him, who can't understand his goodness? He is the best, wisest, and dearest of men; his gentleness and forbearance are wonderful. You neglect ' him as no wife ever neglected her husband. You do nothing to help him. When he is worn out you complain to him about yourself—you are so used to think of yourself, Horatia. I must speak. I may never come into your house again; but it breaks my heart to see it all. And when he comes home sad and out of spirits, you don't look up—you scarcely heed him : you say, " George, shut the door," or " poke the fire," or whatever it may be. I always used to think George's wife would be the happiest, proudest woman in the whole world, until you came to undeceive me.'

Even Horatia could not bear this; she, too, got angry, and started up upon her sofa.

'You certainly shall never come here again, Roberta, unless I am away. You speak of things which are not your concern; and you should have been silent. I am quite able to appreciate my husband without anybody to point out his merits. But sometimes I think, Roberta, that either you or I had better go. Stay,' she said : 'I am not at all certain that it is I who should remain.' And she gathered up her papers and books, and drew herself up to her full height, and sailed out of the room.

And so poor tired George, coming home earlier than usual to see his sister before she left, found only Roberta crying and sobbing in the drawing-room. Horatia was upstairs with a nervous attack. A strong smell of burning and a black smoke came in whiffs out of the kitchen. The maids were in her room sympathising with the mistress; and the dinner was spoiling unheeded. The penitent Roberta tried in vain to stop crying.

'I am going away,' she said ; 'and oh, George, I don't

know when I may come back again. It is too disagreeable for Horatia to have me in the house. I have
behaved so dreadfully. I only wonder she did not turn
me out on the common. I am very sorry, dear George.
I will do anything. I will beg her pardon, if she will be
only kind enough to forgive what has passed, and let me
come and see you again. Because I do love you almost
more than anybody in the world. Please don't hate me
for behaving so badly.'

Then he had to go upstairs to Horatia. When he
came down he was looking very pale and biting his lips.
His wife had gasped out things about ' your relations ; '
about the way in which he preferred them and their
ways to hers ; about his being more happy before she
came ; about her loneliness ; about—— But there is no
use in recapitulating all her nervous griefs. ' Are you
packed up, Roberta ? ' said the doctor, with one more
sigh. ' I will drive you down to the station. I must
see you off. It is only four o'clock now ; if we catch
the five o'clock train it will still be light by the time
you get home. I think your sister will get over it
sooner if you are not here. Don't cry, dearest ; it will
be all right in a little. I can quite understand her
annoyance. Don't cry any more, Berta ; that won't mend
matters,' he said, cheerfully. Then he went into his

study, and shut the door, and fell down into his big chair, and let his head fall heavily on his breast. His pulses were throbbing with grief; it was all he could do to subdue his agitation. His wife's passionate indignation and reproaches had upset him; and that Berta, whom he looked upon almost as a daughter, should be estranged, and that he should be left quite alone—more lonely than he had ever been—was a cruel stab to this tender and sensitive heart. When it was time for Berta to go, he came out of his room, looking exactly as usual. He went to his wife's bedside, and said good-by, but she would not answer him; and then he came down again, and helped his sister into the little carriage, and took his place leisurely beside her, and they drove away.

The trees seemed to fly past them, the birds went wheeling over the fields, a blue-grey mist hung over the distant hedgerows and the haystacks, over the farmsteads and cottages nestling in the little hollows.

The landscape was painted in black and grey, with clouds and rain water. Now and then a rain-laden wind would come blowing freshly into Roberta's face.

As they were nearing the station, somebody came up alongside upon a tired horse. It was Mr. Caton.

' I was going to look for you,' said Dr. Rich, pulling up. ' Will you come in this evening, about nine o'clock ?

We can't wait now, we shall miss the train.' And
then he bent forward and said a few words in a low
voice. Berta wondered what it was all about, as she
nodded a grave good-by. Mr. Caton looked up with a
strange expression. She wondered whether it was because
she was going away ; and then she wondered whether she
should ever forgive herself, and thought what a comfort it
would be to tell her mother everything, and to be well
scolded as she deserved, and then kissed and forgiven like
a child. She gave such a tremendous sigh once, that her
brother began to laugh. 'You silly child!' he said ;
' forget all about it. I will undertake that Horatia shall
bear no malice. A little change will make all smooth
again, and you must come back directly.' Then he drove
on silently for a minute, and then he said, ' Berta, do you
think you could ever fancy Caton ?—he is a little rough,
but he is a thorough good fellow, and very fond of you.'

' I am very fond of him,' said Berta, smiling, ' but I
don't want to marry him. Perhaps, if you praise him very
much, George, in time—— Ah, here we are!' And
presently Berta had kissed him, and said good-by, and
watched him until the train had carried her away, and he
disappeared. By leaning out she just saw him for one
instant more, looking after her with his kind, smiling
face ; and then the train went suddenly on·through the

quiet country, carrying away Roberta, with her troubles
and puzzles. The doctor travels homeward, strangely
abstracted; and Horatia has risen from her bed, where she
had been lying, and is making desperate and angry resolutions.

'Was he indeed more happy before I came? He did
not deny it. When I gave up everything for him, I
thought, at least, that he would love me.' She smoothed
her tumbled hair, put on a shawl, and went downstairs and
out into the open air. ' It will do me good,' she thought,
as she opened the garden door, and walked along the
gravel walk towards the arbour. A book was lying on the
seat; George or Roberta must have left it. He sometimes smoked under the honeysuckles after dinner.
Roberta used to take her work there of a morning.
Horatia hated the place, and never went near it. The
faded summer green looked almost fresh again in the grey,
damp atmosphere; the birds flew over her head; and
across the common the dahlias were beginning to come
out.

It was chilly and dismal enough, and Horatia went
back presently into the house. She was shocked, and
hurt, and wounded. She was not angry exactly; she did
not like her husband less, but she was astonished to
find she had not made him happy. He had not denied it

when she accused him of unhappiness. She was telling herself, with some quiet scorn, that he wanted a house-keeper, like Roberta, and not a wife ; that if he had been really happier before she came to him, it would be perhaps as well that she should leave him now. She was in a hard and cruel frame of mind. She began to ask herself the old question, if it had not been better for them both if they had never married ? She began to wonder how she had ever been so infatuated as to give up everything for this commonplace man. She was sitting on the sofa, with her head against her hand, when he came in.

‘ You saw her off?’ said Horatia, by way of saying something.

‘ Yes, we just caught the train,’ her husband answered, ‘ or I should have had to bring her back.’

‘ I am glad you were in time,’ said Horatia, coldly, ‘ George, you must make Roberta understand that she is never to speak to me in such a way again.’

‘ She was over-excited : she is very sorry for what has happened; she told me to tell you so.’

‘ She may well be sorry,’ said the wife. ‘ I am very sorry that all this has happened; it has made me know—— made me understand——’ and she burst into tears.

Poor George sank back wearily into his chair. ‘ Go

on,' he said. 'Tell me all your troubles, you poor woman. What has it made you understand?'

' That we have failed to make one another happy,' said Horatia, in her wilfulness. 'I could have borne to be miserable myself, but I confess I cannot bear to hear that you—that you were happier before I came.'

' But it is not so. I have been more happy since you came, Horatia,' said the doctor, with kind and wonderful forbearance. 'I have been more happy and more unhappy. I have had you as well as myself to care for.'

' Ah, no!' cried the woman, foolishly and madly; 'it isn't so. I see it in your face, George; I have made up my mind. We shall be friends always, whatever happens, but I will go back to my aunt. Roberta, who is a drudge at heart, can come and keep your house, and satisfy you better than your wife could ever hope to do. Do you hear me?' she said, shrilly, for he did not answer. 'It is because I wish to be your friend, and not your housekeeper, that I am going; it is because people who do not agree are best apart.'

' I don't think so,' the doctor said, slowly, and looking at her in a strange, odd sort of way. 'Long habit brings folks together at last; forbearance is a wholesome discipline for one and for the other; a man and a woman who are both sincerely trying to do their duty can't fail one

·day to find their best happiness in it, and together.
Suppose we part—it may be for ever : the ways of Providence are inscrutable—what do we gain?—a life-long,
maybe an eternal, loneliness and estrangement and indifference ; or suppose we struggle on together for a little
time, Horatia, and learn at last to love one another, at
any rate to forgive, to sympathise, to endure ? Can you
hesitate one moment ? ' he said, in his sad voice.

' I should not hesitate,' said Horatia, sobbing still, ' if
it were not for Roberta. If she comes here, I cannot and
will not stay ; my duty does not extend to her. George,
we might love one another, even if we did not live together
—I might still be your best friend.'

The poor doctor, hurt, wounded beyond expression,
could listen no longer, and he got up with a great sigh,
and walked away out of the room. Horatia flung herself
down on the floor, and buried her face in her hands.
' He doesn't mean it,' she kept saying to herself. ' I know
he would be more happy without me. He is too good for
me. I own he is too good for me. I can't love him ; I
can't understand him ; I make him miserable. He looks
wretched, and ill, and unhappy, and it is all my doing ;
and it is his doing that I am wretched. Why did he
bring me here ? I must go ; it will be better for each of
us. Yes, I must—I will go.'

George was walking up and down outside in the garden. He once looked up through the uncurtained window, and saw her prostrate in her trouble. How could he make her more happy?—it was indeed a strange puzzle and bewilderment. He felt that she scarcely deserved kindnéss, and then he said to himself, kindness deserved was no kindness. 'What merit have ye?' he muttered, and something more about publicans and sinners, and so once more he went back into the warm little fire-lighted room. He went up to her, but she did not heed him; he stooped over her; he picked her up off the floor. 'Horatia,' he said, 'don't you care for me in the least; do you want to make me very lonely, very wretched? Go, if you like, but I tell you, you will be more miserable than you are now. Look at me, and tell me what you mean to do?'

How sad he looked, how kind, how enduring. Horatia could not help it. She was forced to give in. She still wanted to go, to turn back to her old easy life; but she had not the heart or the courage to say so. She was silent; and she left her hand in his. He accepted her silence.

'We will never talk about it again,' he said. 'And you must try and be more happy, my poor woman.'

Then he took a cigar, and went and lit it at the fire, and took up his hat, and said he would be in directly.

'I should like a cup of tea,' he said. 'I am only going to smoke my cigar in the garden. Call me when it is ready.'

Horatia watched him as he passed the window; and she then rang the bell and ordered some tea; and then once more sat down by the fire, staring at the embers. It was useless trying to get away. He would not let her go. By this fireside she must remain to the end. How inconceivably forbearing he was, how kind, how patient, how forgiving. Was it indeed impossible to love him? She heard his steps pacing the gravel outside. Why would he not let her go? What could make him wish that she should remain? What, indeed! Then, at last, she began suddenly to blame herself.

'I don't think I know how to appreciate his good- ness,' she said. 'Heigho! I wish he had married a model wife, who would have known how to make him happy, and at home.'

VIII.

BETSY brought in the tea and the candles. Horatia started from her low chair, where she had been sitting in a sort of dream of remorse, reproach, regret, indecision, and proceeded to make it; and then she poked the fire, and straightened her somewhat untidy locks, and then she went and tapped at the window for George to come in.

When she looked out at the end of five minutes, she was surprised to see that a shower of rain was falling. She opened the casement, and all the wet drops came plashing into her face. She said to herself that he must have come in at the garden-door, and gone up to his room. She went out into the passage, his hat was not there; she ran up the narrow staircase, and went and knocked at his door. Then she looked in. The room was dark and empty. No, he was not there; for she spoke his name, and no one answered. Horatia went down into the drawing-room to wait once more. The kettle was boiling over on the hearth, the candles were flaring, for she had forgotten to shut the window. As she went to close it, a great gust of wet-laden wind surged into the room, and one of the candles went out, and the door banged.

It was dismal and cheerless enough. She began to wish that George would come in. Had he gone across the common? No; she would have seen him pass. She went to the window once more; the trees were waving a little in the darkness. The rain was falling still when she went to the garden-door and called out, 'George! come to tea!' Do you not know the dreary sound of a voice calling in the darkness? She came back into the sitting-room, took up a book, and tried to read, glancing at the window every instant. Once she almost thought she saw her husband looking in, but it was only fancy. The book she had taken was the second volume of some novel. She looked on the table for the first, and then remembered that she had seen it lying, not on the table, but on the seat in the arbour at the end of the garden. And then suddenly she said to herself, 'That is where George has taken shelter from the rain; how foolish of him not to come home! I think I will go and fetch him.'

She went into the hall and tied on a waterproof; she pulled the hood over her head; she went to the garden-door a second time, hesitated a moment, and then passed out. It was darker and wetter than she had expected,

and she thought of turning back; but while she was
thinking of it she was going quickly along the gravel-
walk towards the arbour, brushing the wet gooseberry-
bushes and box borders, a little afraid of the blackness, a
little provoked with herself for her foolishness in coming.
She could just make out the arbour looking very black
in the night; as she came nearer, a sort of terror thrilled
over her, for she thought she saw something within the
darkness. 'George!' she said, in a sort of frightened
way, springing forward. 'Why are you there, George?'
she almost screamed as she came close up. She saw—
yes, surely she saw—his white face gleaming through the
blackness. She began to tremble with terror, for he did
not move or seem to notice her, though she came quite
close up, and stood before him, gasping. With a desperate fear, she put out her hand and touched the white
face. And still George did not move or speak.

A few minutes ago he had been a man with a tender
heart sorely tried, with a voice to speak, with eyes to
watch her reproachfully as she thrust him away, with a
kindly, forgiving hand always ready, and willingly outstretched. And now, what was he?—who was he? What
distance lay between them! Could he hear her feeble
wails and outcries across the awful gulf? 'George—
George!—Oh! George!' the poor woman screamed out,

hardly conscious. She did not faint; she did not quite realise the awful truth—she could not.

In a minute, with hurried voices and footsteps, the maids came up the garden, and with them the boy, who had brought a lantern. And suddenly flashing through the darkness, the light fell upon the dead man's face. It lit up the arbour, the dripping creepers, the wooden walls, the awful figure that was sitting there unmoved; and then Horatia fell with a sort of choking cry to the ground, prostrate in the wet, crushing the borders, the green plants that were drinking in the rain which still fell heavily.

The day had begun to dawn when Horatia came to herself, and opened her eyes in a dazed, wide, strange way. For a minute she hardly understood where she was, and then somehow she knew that she was lying on the sofa in the disordered drawing-room. A maid was kneeling beside her, the garden-door was open, the keen morning air was blowing in in gusts—so grey, so chill, so silent was it, that for a moment Horatia almost fancied that it was she who had died in the night; not George, surely not George. A man's low voice at her head, saying, 'She is coming to herself,' thrilled through her as she thought for a moment that it might be her husband.

What she seemed to remember was too horrible to be
thought of—too horrible to be true. It was not true.
The wild hope brought the blood into her cheeks. She
moved a little in an agony of suspense, and faltered his
name. Only as she spoke, somehow there was no response.
The half-uttered words died away, the hands that were
bathing her head ceased their toil. By the silence—by
the sudden quiet—she knew that she had spoken to the
empty air ; that though he might hear her, he would
never, never answer any more, never come, never heed
her call again ; and then, suddenly, with a swift pang of
despair, hopeless, desperate, she realised it all.

Caton, who had almost hated her, who had said to himself that he would be her judge—she had killed her
husband, she had wearied and embittered the last few
hours of his life, and he, Caton, would tell her the truth,
if there was no one else to speak it—Caton, who, in his
indignation, had thought all this, could not find it in his
heart now to utter one harsh word.   He came round, and
stood looking compassionately at her white wan face lying
back, with all the black rippling hair pushed away ; and
as he stood there, she put up her hands and covered her
eyes, and shivered.   How could he judge one so forlorn ?
Instead of the hard words he had meant to use, he only
said, ' He had feared it all along, Mrs. Rich.   He was not

afraid for himself, but for those he loved. It was a heart disease. It was hopeless from the first; he knew it, but he would not let me tell you. He was the best, the dearest——' the young man's voice broke as he spoke; he turned away, and went and stood at the window.

There was a long silence. At last, Horatia, speaking in her faint voice, said—

'I want you to send for Roberta. Can you send now, at once?'

'I telegraphed last night,' Caton answered, 'when I thought there might be hope. She will be here in the morning. I will meet her and bring her to you.'

Once more Horatia moved; she got up from the couch where she had been lying, and she tottered forward a few steps towards the door.

Caton sprang after her. 'Are you going upstairs to lie down? Where are you going?'

'Where, oh, where, indeed, am I going?' cried poor Horatia. 'Oh, my George, my George!' and with a sort of cry, she flung herself back into a great arm-chair which was near. 'Go—pray, go away,' she sobbed to them; 'only tell me when Roberta comes.' And so, scared, reluctant, they went away and left her.

Caton never forgot that terrible dawning. The black garden, the white mist creeping along the ground, the

chill light spreading, the widow's sobs and sorrowful outcries breaking the silence of the night.

It was Roberta who roused poor Horatia from a sort
of swoon of grief and remorse—Roberta, white, trembling,
silent, who led her into the next room, where all was so
peaceful that their sobs were hushed; so sacred, that it
seemed to them as if it was a profanity to even complain.
Only once more Horatia burst out. 'Forgive me, George!'
she suddenly cried, falling on her knees, and then she
wildly and imploringly looked up at Roberta's set white
face. The girl changed, melted, faintly smiled, and
stooped and kissed her sister.

'Oh, Horatia, what has he to do with trouble and
injury and sorrow now? Forgiveness belongs to this
world; only peace, only love to the next.'

Horatia was very ill for a long time after this.
Roberta was able to stay with George's wife, and to nurse
her very faithfully and tenderly in her sorrows. In time
Horatia got well, and prepared to live her old life again.
It was the old life, but the woman was not the same
woman. And George was carried away from his sister,
from his wife, from his home, from his daily work. He
was still alive somehow when Roberta thought of him.
She could see his face, hear his voice, love him more tenderly even than in his life.

One day Caton told Berta, as he had told Horatia, that. George had thought himself seriously ill for some short time, and though he did not consider the danger immi-; nent, he had taken pains to put his affairs in order, and to, leave enough behind for the provision of those he loved.

' When did he first know——'

Roberta hesitated, and her eyes filled with tears, and, Caton said that his first attack was one night when they, were sitting together in the study. Mrs. Rich had gone off to her grand relations. ' I remember she came back and talked about her partners,' he said.

' She did not know ? ' Berta said.

' Perhaps you never heard that he fainted away at that party at Mrs. Dumbleton's ? ' Caton went on, sighing. ' He went up to town next day to see a doctor. I am not. sure that he was right to keep it secret. He would not let me speak. I very nearly told you once, only you stopped me.'

And Berta remembered the day she had met Caton on, the road, and when she would not stop to speak to him. Things were changed now, for they had met in the lane by chance, and were walking on side by side towards the common. The common rippled westward, scattered with stones, and clumps of furze, and dells and hollows ; geese. cackled ; sunsets streamed across it ; roads branched here.

and there leading to other green lanes, or to distant villages, or to London, whose neighbouring noise and rush
seemed to make this quiet country suburb seem more
quiet. The river runs between these furze-grown commons and London. People coming from the city, as they
cross the bridge, seem to leave their cares and busy concerns behind them, and to breathe more freely as they
come out upon the fresh, wind-blown plains.

Caton and Roberta walked along one of these straight
roads, talking sadly enough; her eyes were full of tears.
Caton's voice was broken as he spoke of what was past; to
walk along with Roberta, even in this sorrowful companionship, was a sort of happiness : but even this was not
to last for long; she was going—Horatia was going; and
Caton was to succeed to the old place, with all its sad
memories, and he thought to himself that he had lost his
friend, and that Roberta would never care for him, and
that life was a dismal thing, and he almost wished it was
over. And he said almost as much. They had come to
the place where their two roads parted; Roberta said
good-by, and looked up shy and gentle, blushing under her
black hat. Caton put out his hand and said : ' This has
been our last walk. You will go that way by the gate,
and I shall walk straight on across the common, and we
may perhaps never even meet again.' His voice sounded

sad and reproachful, though he did not know it; and Berta's blushes suddenly faded, and she looked away and did not speak.

A number of birds flew over their heads as they stood there, parting. There was nobody near to heed them, only an old grey horse browsing the turf, a little flock of geese clustering round a pool hard by. Berta saw it all in a strange vivid way. She stood there, reluctant to wait, and yet still more reluctant to go. The roads gleamed farther and farther asunder; she hesitated, wondered, waited still; but she did not know all that she had tacitly decided until she looked up at last, and met Caton's honest bright eyes with her gentle glance. And so at last he was made happy, and the woman he had loved so well had learnt to care for him, touched by his faithful friendship for her brother, his faithful devotion to herself.

MAKING MERRY

MAKING MERRY.

'Such as the jocund flute or gamesome pipe.'

WE were all upon the terrace one morning, in front of
the old château. The *déjeûner* was just over, the sunshine had not reached us yet, and we were sitting under
the old grey towers, watching a river, and some wooded
slopes, all changing in the morning light. This September sunshine had turned the whole country to gold and
lovely red and russet. The rising grounds upon which
the old towers stand, the valley, the far-away hills, were
painted and chequered and shaded with bright crisp
autumnal colour. The trees were like the trees in
Aladdin's gardens, with gold pieces and jewels hanging
from the branches, or sparkling in the brown turf.

The morning seemed to come to us across fields and

villages, over the river which went shining and wending
away beyond the arches of the bridge at Meulan into that
dim and unknown country which seems to bound all that
is most beautiful. M. de V. had lighted his cigar, the
ladies were working, the gentlemen were making their
plans for the day, and the turkey-cocks came ambling
down the hill, to be fed by little Mary. ' *Tiens, voilà
ta St. Côme,*' said she, giving one of them a big piece of
bread, with which it instantly scrambled off in a fluster,
shaking all its red bags and tassels as it went. Winifred
asked what was a ' St. Côme.' Madame de V. smiled, and
said it was something that she must see. It was a *fête*
at Meulan, beyond the bridge on the little island in the
river, and they called the fairings ' St. Cômes' in that part
of the world. In the meantime the kind host was
making arrangements for every one of us to be driven
there and back in various open carriages, which were to
be in waiting at the very moment at which each of us
wished to go and to return. Some begged to go twice;
others, less enthusiastic, said once would content them.

St. Côme was a martyr : it is his memory which is
held sacred, and to which all these small altars are
erected, with their offerings of gingerbread, sugar-stick
toys and crockery, bobbins, cotton laces, and night-caps.
Popguns are fired off, a dentist with a drum comes all the

way from Paris, the celebrated two-headed child arrives in
its bottle of spirits-of-wine, pleasures succeed one another,
and all this cheerful clatter, all the little flags, all the
games and lotteries, which are going on, are to do the
saint honour. He was, while in the flesh, a wise Arabian
physician, who seems to have given his advice gratis, and
to have practised in partnership with his brother, St.
Damien. They were afterwards both martyred towards
the close of the thirteenth century; but the 27th of September ever since has been consecrated to the memory
of the good St. Côme, and the inhabitants of Meulan
and its surrounding villages have elected themselves his
especial votaries.

All the carts from all the neighbourhood seemed to be
jogging along the white dusty road which leads from V.,
with its white walls and vines and trellises, and glimpses
of the river, to Meulan. The country carts were heaped
up with delightful primitive-looking people, with kind,
smiling faces, and caps and satin bows, and bran-new
blouses. In one jolting conveyance I noticed seven happy-
looking girls, packed closely away, all in smart white caps,
with satin ribbons, and loops and ruffles quite crisp and
standing on end. They jogged on laughing, while the
young men of the party walked along the road by their
side. Other vehicles there were, with nice nutcracker old

women in the old-fashioned cap and red cotton dress of the last century.   They looked like the figures out of Noah's arks, like chimney ornaments, or water-colour sketches, or descriptions in books of travels.   They danced fat white doll-babies ; they held little girls upon their knees, tied up into pinafores, and with funny frill caps fitting close to their round little bullet-heads.   There were expectant little boys in pinafores too, and old fellows in snuff-brown coats and wonderful waistcoats, with patterns like maps and leopard-skins.   There were also donkeys, with tall wooden erections upon their backs, containing their mistresses, whose feet dangled into baskets.

All the people along the road came to their doors to see us go by, and presently we drove into the old-fashioned market-place, with the bridge spanning the river, and with the great town-hall, whose spire dominates the town, and strikes the hours.   It was an abbey once, and stands on the hill : the town clusters round it : the narrow streets climb the hillside, and wind corners and disappear.   The river flows down below between glittering banks.   Broad white roads lead to Vaux, to Poissy, and along them the carts come rolling through the dust.

We already begin to hear the distant booming of the fair, to the accompaniment of the screaming of a thousand pigs.   If the old men had put one in mind of

Mr. and Mrs. Noah and Shem and Ham (or Cham, as he
is called in France), it would seem as if all these animals
had been emptied out of a gigantic Noah's ark into the
market-place.   They are lying about, on their backs, on
their heads, on their fat sides, grunting, squalling, squeaking in the most distracting manner : whereas the little
donkeys are quiet and well-behaved, and stand in rows
under the cathedral walls, waiting to be bought.   There
is such a noise and chatter and confusion that one
scarcely knows at last which are pigs and which are old
women ; for they are all talking together, remonstrating
violently, and tumbling about over one another in the
straw.   The little children stand at safe distances absorbed in the bargains which are going on.   The poor
little pigs are poked and pinched, and caught up by the
leg and the ear, and flung anywhere and anyhow.   They
are small and lively, not horrible contemplative obesities
like those one sees in England.   Of all the interesting
animals I remarked on this occasion, I will only particu-
larise one little tortoise-shell pig with brown and red
spots, for I was struck by the wistful glances a pretty
peasant-woman was directing towards it.   'That is the
one I should have liked !' she said with a sigh to a sympathising friend ; and, indeed, who has not a little
tortoise-shell pig somewhere or other out of reach—

unattainable? If the pretty peasant-woman were to obtain her little pig, she would pop it into one of those great earthenware pots that are being sold by the bridge —they are something the shape of the Roman amphoræ, very gracefully designed and prettily ornamented— the pretty peasant-woman would then salt down the object of her desires, and eat it up by degrees during the winter.

But all this squeaking and moralising is only a flourish of trumpets at the opening of the entertainment. We hurry across the bridge to the little island where the fair is held: country blouses, babies, amiable papas in white linen with their families, elegant mammas in the last Meulan fashions. Here is one street of stalls for the sale of ginger-bread and gimcracks, with a cross-street for entertaining games and shows. The great time for the shows is at night; in the daytime we content our-selves with munching gingerbread and playing at *rouge et noir*. The fortunate may win seven dozen of maca-roons stuck at equal distances upon dubious sheets of white paper, with very little trouble, or exchange them for elegant chimney-ornaments, or water-colour sketches of dragoons, and ladies, and roses. It is a pretty sight— blue sky overhead, shining and twinkling through the branches of the avenue; people singing, talking, and staring at the gingerbread, of which perhaps the most delicious sort is called *semelle*, from its appetising like-- ness to the sole of a shoe. The grand ladies from the town are walking up and down between the stalls, grace- fully curtseying and dipping to each other. One élegante affects a blue Scotch cap, with a tuft of blue ostrich feathers ; all the ladies are neatly finished off with beau- tiful little frills, and many of them lean on the arms of gaitered husbands with broad-brimmed hats, evidently prepared to initiate their families into all the amusements of the show.

THE CELEBRATED TWO-HEADED CHILD invites us to enter and examine. He is represented alive and crowned with roses, and surrounded by an admiring throng. We are satisfied with the picture outside, for M. de V., who good-naturedly goes in to reconnoitre, assured us that the sight is not only revolting, but in a bottle. Next door, MADEMOISELLE RACHEL gives her interesting exhibition. Mademoiselle Rachel is a bright-eyed little bird, who hops out of a cage, and presents you with the card you selected at hazard from her master's well-worn pack. Her discrimination would be more extraordinary still if the cards in the pack were not *all* kings of spades ; but Mademoiselle Rachel is unconscious of the deception : she hops from her little perch with a clear conscience, neatly digs up the card with her bill, and takes a single grain of millet from her keeper's hand, as a reward, before she goes back into her prison. She has a rival; it is like Andersen's fairy-tale of the 'Princess and the Potsherd.' Mademoiselle Rachel is all very well in her way, but not to be compared to the wonderful singing-bird out of the snuff-box, who is to be seen next door for twenty centimes, together with the port of Niagara, the sultan of Turkey and his favourite sultana, and Robert Houdin at home *en famille.* Here at least is no deception. The singing-bird comes out of its snuff-box, and squeaks and wags its tail, and wrings its own neck in the most alarming fashion. The sultan of Turkey carefully rolls his eyes with a repugnant stare, which now rests upon his favourite sultana, now upon the alarmed spectators. All the ladies of the harem squat muslin-legged upon cushions round about him. The favourite fans herself spasmodically; while in the next compartment Robert Houdin, in majestic robes of black velvet and a sugar-cone hat, is playing thimblerig, surrounded by his numerous family. One spectatrix of about six years old, who is not afraid of turkey-cocks, is yet not quite certain that she derives pleasure from the entertainment; for, besides the glance of the sultan's eye, and the magic flow of Houdin's mystic robes, the terrific waves of green calico in the port of

Niagara have to be encountered. There are but three, but then they appear to be of enormous size and fury. A ship rests upon the crest of each one of them, and remains in that precarious position notwithstanding the stress of weather and the imminent dangers to which navigation must be exposed in that little-known part of the world.

The raging of the storm had not abated when we left the tent. As we escaped, we heard the exhibitor loudly calling upon the crowds outside to seize the auspicious moment, and not to forego their chance of admission. The mechanician has a rival opposite, who exhibits attractive sketches of all the celebrated crimes of the last fifty years. To judge from a hasty glance, murderers are invariably dressed in tights, top-boots, velvet caps, and elegantly floating feathers. This is a thing to be remembered, that such persons may be avoided in future. All this time the merry-go-rounds are twirling round and round, and we tear ourselves away from the dark exciting scenes of bloodshed to watch a little fat baby sitting quite happy and alone in its little flying carriage, a small ragged boy clinging to a horse, and some young amazons, who cast triumphant glances in our direction; the organ strikes up a military tune, and away they all go flying, men, women, children, one after another in the race.

There is something very cheering and inspiriting in all this. The people are lively, but not too loud; there is more vivacity, but more gentleness too, than there would be among our people at home. One's heart aches a little as one thinks of one's own fellow-countrymen, patient and dull, and strong and clumsy, and weary, not able to rest content with light passing interests, with half-happiness with small things, but hurrying up in wistful crowds with a violence of effort, an earnestness in their amusements even, that seems to carry them almost beyond bounds when they are once let free. One is always being told that nations are like individuals, and we all have to learn in our lives how to be happy with trifles, how to put away care in the passing sunshine of the moment, and to find pleasure even in the bright colours of a bubble.

If the sight was pretty in the daytime, it was prettier still at night. Madame de V. and her husband M. de V., Winifred and I, left the old castle about nine o'clock. It was all lighted up, turret windows and arched gateways; and from outside we could see the elders of the party sitting in the gallery in their quiet lampshine. It was pleasant to hurry down through the rustling woods and dark avenues, with the crisp leaves under foot, and the great stars blazing over the wide country. At the foot of the steep ascent and the avenue are great iron gates where the carriage was standing. All along the road we passed dusky forms hastening in one direction. The moon looked as if it was going to fall into the river and be extinguished with a great splutter; the wain travelled over the hills, the familiar triangles and figures blazed and hung in the sky. When we reached the island we found other illuminations: bright little arcades of fire were shining among the dark trees, and reflected in the water; and all the little gambling booths were lighted up in a simple fashion with candle-ends.

These games of skill are not very complicated. One energetic little man's whole stock-in-trade was an india-rubber tube, a halfpenny, and a soup-plate. The object of the game was to try and knock the tube and the sou together out of the soup-plate. He could do it, because he passed his life in practising his art; but none of the bystanders succeeded, and the professor always pocketed the halfpenny. Another exciting game was throwing a ball through a round hole lighted up by a candle.

The lady to whom the establishment belonged counted up the failures and payments with great rapidity: 'Un et deux et quatre font onze; et trois et

deux font vingt-deux, et six et trois, trente-cinq,' and
so on, with surprising àplomb and inaccuracy. Instead of
scolding her, M. de V. good-naturedly nodded his head
and said, 'Allez toujours, madame, ne vous gênez pas ; '
at which madame herself begins to scold, and gets very
red in the face, and vehement and angry. So we leave
her to her arithmetic, and go on past the little brawling
shops where customers are chaffering—(we saw one priest
buying quantities of gingerbread)—and people with white
caps and bright dark eyes keeping watch over their wares.
Crockery twinkles, little gilt ornaments shine and flicker
in abundance, lotteries whizz and whirl, some of the
prizes are of the most remarkable description, but the
trumpet calls and the rappel is sounded, and we all hasten
with the crowd to the central Place, where some one
is alternately discoursing and playing on the drum.

'Venez, venez, messieurs et dames, venez voir la
JEUNE SAUVAGE, qui mange de la viande TOUTE CRUE,'
roars the proprietor of· the booth. She is a native of
those distant countries where the inhabitants nourish
themselves upon the unfortunate crews of the vessels
which are wrecked upon their coast. This woman is in
noways related to the man you beheld last year. He was
dangerous, and was destroyed by order of the Govern-
ment. She can only speak her own language. Walk

in, walk in, 'et vouz serez-z r-r-récompensé de votre peine.'

So we walk in, much interested by the description, and behold the appalling spectacle of a being, whose name appears to be Juana, gambading behind the bars of a dark cage, grinning at us, and gnashing its teeth. Its face is painted of the approved cannibal brown; it occasionally shakes a great black woolly wig, which fills us with horror.

'Abawaba!' Juana bounds with delight, recognising the melodious language of her native isles; suddenly she stops, stares, with both hands eagerly outstretched. An extremley small and dirty-looking piece of meat is now produced out of the exhibitor's pocket. He carefully cuts off a minute portion with a pair of scissors. Juana glares at the delicious morsel, and then suddenly seizes it through the bars, and thrusts it into her mouth. 'Ah, see how savage she is,' says the man in the blouse. 'Nous allons maintenant lui préparer de la salade à la mode de son pays.' Some black stuff is then set fire to with a candle, which also goes into Juana's mouth. It seems that in her country the savages instantly expectorate their nourishment; and Juana accordingly deposits hers in a corner of the cage, dancing with rapture the whole time.

A *demoiselle de vingt-deux ans* now comes forward. The 'administration,' as the exhibitor calls himself, selects M. de V. and requests him to weigh the little dwarf, and to observe that she does not exceed two feet in stature nor ten pounds avoirdupois in weight. He then announces that the young lady will dance a little waltz *sans musique,* upon which she instantly twirls rapidly round two or three times. Her friend then begs to remark that she depends entirely upon the generosity of the public, '*n'étant nullement payée par l'administration !* '

Poor little dwarf! There was something affecting in the small, melancholy company. The administration looked very pale and hungry. Juana's life in the cage must have been somewhat monotonous. It seemed a weary way of gaining a livelihood. We hoped that their daily bread was not raw meat only, nor such very uninviting salad.

A great booth had been erected next door. All the simple country-folks had been gazing with delight at the glare and the tinsel on the coats of the pages and actors. We went up with the crowd. 'Quand on est marié on finit toujours par céder,' one man cried, appealing to us, when his wife insisted upon taking a place he had objected to. A melancholy, well-bred actor, in red silk,

with a quiet humourous manner, now came on before the
curtain, and said things which made the audience laugh,
but which it was impossible for our stranger ears to
follow. Everything he said was witty, M. de V. told
me ; and all he did was well done. He had a quiet non-
chalant way : he put one in mind of Mariclle, in George
Sand's charming *Théâtre de Nohant*, of Wilhelm Meister
among the players. The entertainment turned out to be
tableaux-vivants, behind a gauze curtain, on a revolving
stage. It put one in mind of the ' Pilgrim's Progress '
and the sights that Christian saw. There was the story
of Cain and Abel ; there was the history of Joan of Arc ;
and besides these there were things which seemed so
terrible to English eyes that I cannot write of them at
length. And yet it is not so long ago since miracle-plays
were performed. Every day we look unmoved upon
pictures and paintings of sacred subjects ; we listen to
descriptions and allusions which seem to approach with
far less effort, with far more familiarity, towards awful
mysteries. To me there did not even seem any great
want of reverence, though I was frightened and taken by
surprise. They had chosen two of Rubens' well-known
pictures for imitation ; there was not a sound in the
crowded booth when the curtain drew up for an instant,
and then fell again almost immediately. The figures in

this miracle-play were quite motionless. I have rarely seen nobler-looking people than the two chief performers. They enacted their parts with perfect gravity and harmony of sentiment. Both the man and the woman were tall, majestic, fair-haired, with a noble outline of form and feature, and a simpleness which was really grand and remarkable.

As Joan of Arc, this tall, straight, sorrowful-looking young woman, with all her fair hair falling about her shoulders, and her beautiful up-turned face, seemed the very personification of sweetness and valiance and misfortune.

It is only in Brittany that such noble types are found, our friends told us; but they also added, that though nothing could have been better and more decorous than the performance of these principal actors, yet before the curtain drew up, allusions were made which would have been far better avoided. Baroness Tautphœus has admirably described these miracle-plays in the Tyrol, which are looked upon in the light of religious ceremonies almost, and which must be less objectionable than these representations so near home. And yet, where no harm is intended, where none is understood, where, like children, the troops of simple country-folks come pouring in, quiet their laughter in a moment, say it is *la religion*, sit silent and hushed for a minute, until the curtain falls, and then pour out into the night, where the stars are shining, and the lamps flaring, and where, like children, they begin to laugh and talk again in the sudden glare and glitter—one cannot say how far all this is wrong or right. It does not strike one as it would in England, where feelings are more complex, faith less simple and unreasoning, and the natures of men more intricate and rough and dangerous to deal with.

The ball was a very pretty sight. There were quantities of lamps and festoons hanging round, a great boarded dancing-place, with an arched colonnade outside it for the spectators, who walked about upon the dried turf. Then came an inner row of benches for the chaperons, who sat round like real ones at a London ball, only they were little old peasant-women in their tight white caps, with their little shawls pinned across their shoulders, and they were holding other little shawls for their daughters when they should return to them. The middle part was crowded with dancers. The musicians were scraping away from a flowery bower. It was a pretty, pleasant, funny sight : glissades, galopades, gambades, like Juana's. Sometimes a good old couple would stand up and foot it with great intrepidity. One little wiry brown old woman with her husband in his high-shouldered coat, were hopping opposite to one another like a pair of lively old sparrows. As the night wears on, the excitement grows : the music plays faster and more gaily, the steps increase in rapidity, and they begin to skip and to bound, with immense sprightliness and variety. The ladies grin reprovingly at their partners, but at their smiles the gentlemen's spirits only seem to leap like fire when a little water is thrown upon it.   There is one delightful little man with an immense tall partner, and a very tall hat with a curly rim ; either of them would have seemed quite sufficient to weigh him down, but he is equal to the occasion. His evolutions and revolutions, his inflections and ascensions, and flights and inspirations, are something quite wonderful. Retreats, advances, salutations, clapping of hands—one does not know which to admire most. His lady joins in with great spirit. Their *vis-à-vis* try in vain to surpass them. The gay refrain of the waltz echoes, and the dancers seem to sway with the tune : the chaperons nod their heads, and look on with smiling approbation.   At last the dance comes to an end, the young ladies return to their mammas, but carefully lift up their dresses before they sit down.

We see the little man with the tall hat walking off with his partner to treat her to gingerbread outside ; they seem conscious of a triumph, and some of the lookers-on shake their heads, laughing as they march past.   One or

two ladies who have the gift of the dance jerk with peculiar adeptness; but these are far less interesting and more
sophisticated than the simple peasant-women delightedly
jumping, and bobbing, and flouncing, or rolling like the
friendly teetotums of one's youth. There is scarcely a
pretty face in the whole room. They are 'gentilles,' that
is the most that can be said for them. Their hair is
smartly dressed, parted, and twisted up tight and spruce.
Most of them have their petticoats neatly looped up over
tidy brodequins—quite different from the splay, web-
shaped chaussure of the inhabitants of our native isles.

. The lamps were beginning to go out and to splutter
when we came away, only the stars seemed brighter than
ever in the dark sky, and almost starting from their places.
The moon had not set, and we climbed the hill and came
out from the avenue of lime-trees and nut-trees into a
great calm sea of moonshine rippling over the old towers
and pointed roofs. It was late, and everyone was gone
to bed. Only one red lamp was left burning for us when
we returned. But until the early morning I heard the
carts rolling homeward with their weary, happy burdens,
and the distant voices chaunting cheerily through the
silence of the night. They rolled through the darkness to
their peaceful villages all round in the valleys and among
the hills; and this distant, odd, pleasant music only ceased
with the dawn.

SOLA.

SOLA.

'Where are the great whom thou would'st wish to praise thee?
Where are the pure whom thou would'st choose to love thee?
Where are the brave to stand supreme above thee,
Whose high commands would cheer, whose chiding raise thee?
Seek, seeker, in thyself, submit to find
In the stones bread, and life in the blank mind.'

I.

ONCE two hundred years ago, or more, in an old Italian city where the workers still knead their clay in the sun and set it drying along the walls of the deserted streets, some workman designed an open dish. It may have been meant as a gif for a betrothed maiden; it may have been ordered by a fanciful customer. There was a rough garland of citrons and green leaves all round about the edge, and then came a circlet of oranges, and then, in the centre of the platter, two clasped right hands and a scroll upon which 'Sola' was written. The dish was old and chipped, the varnish was covered with a fine network of hair-like cracks; but neither time, nor cracks, nor infidelity could unclasp the two hands in the centre, firmly grasping each other through the long ages. Strangers speaking a different tongue still guessed that 'Sola' meant the only one—a life's fidelity: for there is a silent language belonging to no particular time, or age, or place, which all sorts of people can understand.

I do not know how the plate had come to be one of the ornaments of the china cupboard in the morning-room at Harpington Hall. There it stood on the faded old shelf in the old grey room, looking eastward; with the spindle-legged chairs standing against the panels, the faded Turkey rug before the fireplace, the two deep window-sills where Felicia used to sit a blooming little girl in the midst of these ancient appurtenances. One almost wondered where the child found her youth, her bright colours, her gay spirits; she was like a little Phœnix rising out of the ashes at Harpington. The old Hall was haunted by ashes and dust and rats; by all sorts of ghosts, and sad memories of the past. The poor old owner's dead children's pictures hung in the mother's dressing-room; Mr. Marlow's gun was slung up in the dining-room; the stables were empty; the state-rooms were closed. Sometimes if people asked her to show them over the house, Mrs. Marlow would take them quickly round from one great wooden room to another, and perhaps stop for an instant at the china cupboard, and point out the plate as a quaint old piece of Italian ware, and then shut the glass doors quickly. She had a nervous, hasty manner, and never seemed to be quite in the same mind as other people, but in a world of her own and her husband's. And Mr. Marlow did not certainly care either for cracked china or sentiment; it was only Felicia, the grand-daughter, who had sometimes wondered what it all meant as she looked at the lemon wreath and the grasping fingers. 'Sola,' clasped hands—it all seemed very meaningless to her until one day, when her eyes were opened, and she understood once for all.

When Felicia was fifteen she was told by her grand-parents that she was engaged to her cousin, James Marlow, a gentle, good-humoured little fellow, who was to be master after the old Squire's death. The old Squire made some broad jokes on the occasion; Mrs. Marlow treated the business in a very dry, off-hand way. James took it as a matter of course, and went back to college, and Felicia remained at the Hall.

The way of life in the old house was a close and narrow way, not leading to salvation, though year by year Mr.

Marlow added more and more to his store, and counted up with satisfaction various items of moth and dust.

These were largely eked out by his own and his household's discomfort; Felicia's little shoes were rubbed out at the toes. Mrs. Marlow's Sunday dress was shining with age, but the five guineas a new one might cost were safe in the bank. Loneliness, stinginess, self-denial, and denials of every sort, had added to a moderate fortune until it was now a large one. That trembling, bandy-legged old fellow, with his gaiters and his felt hat, did not look much like a speculator, but such he had been, in fact. He was sly, he was dull, he had been lucky. His wife had sympathised in his ventures, and the narrow economies of the household had been begun by her years ago. Now Mr. Marlow was old and timid, and afraid of loss. He speculated no more, but still, from habit, the two ground down life to its narrowest compass. Such people would like to prevent the sun from rising so early for fear of wasting its heat; they would only have leaves on the alternate branches of the trees, or keep the autumnal sprays over for another year. But they could not prevent nature from being bountiful, and lovely, and wasteful, and from flooding Felicia's life with youth and wild girlish spirits, with sunshine, with full fresh country winds and sweet rural sights, to all of which she turned more readily than to the house-stinting and keeping her grandmother tried to teach her. All the summer-time she was happy, wandering about the deserted gardens, where the straggling flower-beds travelled over the ill-kept lawns; and the great trees gave shade upon the grasses and the laurels. The little chestnut trees in the wood, where the birds hid their nests, rustled and trembled; now and then dividing their close branches to give a sight of the tranquil furrows in the spreading fields beyond, where the great elms were sailing like ships at sea. . . .

The house, with its high sloping roof, stood on a hill, and might be seen for miles. From the front blistered door, with its broken steps, an avenue ran down to the road. There was an old gateway, of which the iron doors stood always open. The ivy had crept up in slender sprays, covering the hinges, and hiding the brickwork, and wreathing over the stone balls at either side of the entrance. One day, Felicia, picking periwinkles in the avenue, tried to imagine a vision of herself at some future day, as a bride, passing through the gate, on her way to the little church close by. Somehow, in this fancy of Felicia's, she was the bride, scarcely changed, except that her stuff gown was altered to shining satin; but poor James was strangely transformed and metamorphosed. He was a great deal older, taller; he had broad shoulders, and

P

a set straight figure in this representation; he had a fiery, quick, scornful sort of way, quite unlike his usual gentle manner. The fiery manner softened in the vision when the bridegroom turned to his bride. He was holding her hand close in his. What was it he whispered? something out of the marriage service: 'To thee only,' 'Sola!' Was it James's voice? It was certainly James's voice that Felicia heard in the avenue calling her, 'Felicia! Felicia!'

Felicia was seventeen by this time. She had been engaged two years. She started and blushed. She knew she ought not to wish James to be different from what he was. She jumped up hastily from the pile of stones and periwinkles upon which she had been kneeling, dreaming her little love-dream, with her head bent over the flowers. She heard voices. A great dog came running down the avenue, and jumped upon her faded gown; and James, no taller, no more mysterious or romantic-looking than usual, followed with his grandmother, looking for her down the avenue, to say good-by. 'Felicia,' said the young fellow, 'why did you run away? It is time for me to be off. Good-by, dear; take care of yourself.'

'Good-by, dear James,' said Felicia, kissing his cheek. 'It is you who must take care of yourself; and mind you wear the comforter I knitted you.'

' James,'—this was the old grandfather on the house-step,—' you will miss the train.'

' Here I am,' cried James, kissing both his grand-mother and Felicia, and hurrying off. Only he stopped at the foot of the steps to look a good-by and to take breath. ' London—10th—don't forget,' he cried.

Some people said that James, who was of a delicate stock, was ailing for want of care and of necessary comforts beyond the bare allowance his grandfather made him. He never complained, and I am sure it never occurred to Felicia to complain for him. She believed her grandmother, who assured her that the doctor was mistaken in ordering another climate—what air was so good as Harpington ? Felicia had thriven upon it, and James could come home from college whenever he felt inclined. He was making but a poor thing of his career there. The old lady spoke a little bitterly. Felicia was sorry. She herself sometimes felt angry with her cousin for the way in which he submitted to the tyrannical rule of the old people. Felicia had been so little away from home that she had no standard by which to measure its ways. She did not care about a brilliant career in the world. She scarcely knew what it meant ; but she could not but feel a secret vexation when she saw how poor Jim was a cypher in the determined old hands that ruled both their destinies. Felicia, who was wayward and impetuous, sometimes revolted against the discipline in which she was kept; the young fellow never did. It did not much matter whether the children revolted or not, for the grim old couple were not to be stirred from their strange fixed ways by all Felicia's reproaches and girlish demands. The old lady was not even angry; she had taken her as a child, and brought her up with a vigorous rule, and it was not a quick passionate creature like Felicia who could move that rugged rock.

In summer Felicia laid up her store of youth and brightness; but the winters were long and dreary. Poor Felicia! How the cold blasts used to pinch and bite her. Her somewhat languid circulation seemed stopped and frozen by the wooden echoes of those long bare passages at Harpington. There was a window looking into a court past which she used to run, giving a wistful glance at the warm-lighted kitchen-window, looking out upon moonlight in winter. The kitchen was the only really comfortable corner in the house,—long wooden passages, stone stairs, up which winds blew shrilly. Some old people do not feel the cold, and Mrs. Marlow was one of them. 'Shivering again, Fay?' It was absurd that Felicia should shiver when there was a fire in the dining-room.

This old house seemed, like its owners, in some fashion

dreary, yet capable of better things—of warmth, and comfort, and brightness too ; a stately old place, with all that was wanting for a generous life, and yet, through some curious whim of chance, all shabby, and closed, and narrow. Jim and Felicia in some measure belonged to the sad past, and were expected to keep up its traditions. He was a son's son, and she a younger daughter's daughter. The pictures of the dead children were hanging carefully guarded in an inner closet ; no new interests were admitted. The doors opened not to the living joys or interests of others, but to calculations of interest, and money-getting, and money-saving, and to the remembrances of a few dead people. It was for this reason Felicia was to marry Jim ; for this, and also because old Marlow hated strangers, and liked his own way. One of the young people was indifferent on the subject. This was Felicia, who told James what her grandmother had told her. James, who had seen more of the world, looked at her earnestly and curiously for a minute.

'You must think of it, dear,' he said.

II.

FELICIA, being now solemnly engaged to be married, had settled that it was time that they should give up keeping rabbits. It seemed a pursuit scarcely consistent with the dignity of a young betrothed couple; and yet from day to day she put off the execution of this stern decree. It was not to be any very tragical transaction, for rabbit-pie, which the Squire affectioned, was a horror and an abomination in Felicia's eyes. Jim had made a private arrangement with a little gardener's boy, who consented, after some bargaining, to accept the unconscious creatures upon payment of twopence apiece from James. The gardener's boy did not make an unfair bargain: it is the usual charge for giving away rabbits. But besides the twopences, there was also the pang of separation. It must be confessed that Felicia was the most to be pitied on this occasion. The rabbits went on nibbling their salad-leaves to the last moment, nibbling and relishing up to the very edge of the stalk.

'Why don't you keep them?' said James, seeing the girl's eyes full of tears.

'No, I don't want them any more,' says Felicia. 'Good-by, Puck; good-by, Cobweb; good-by, Mustard;'

and she stroked the stupid sleek ears, and laid her soft cheek upon them, and kissed them with an affection which was scarcely requited.

It was some joke of her grandfather's which had determined Felicia to part from her favourites. She had a morbid horror of being laughed at. I think she was deficient in humour, and people who are wanting in fun, as a rule, are those who can least bear being laughed at. James's was a different nature. He used to smile at life. It had been a hard one for him on the whole. Weak health, small powers of application, failure, a generous and tender heart, and a narrow meed of love in return. All this did not go to make his fate a very bright one. Little Jim Marlow was a fatalist in his way: he resigned himself to his narrow destiny. As for Felicia, that was a hope too bright for him to reckon on ; he never expected to win his cousin's affections, though he did not say no when Felicia came to him that day, saying, 'Jim, is it true we are to be engaged ?' He loved her so truly that he would have almost consented to give her up if he had felt convinced it would be for her welfare. His nature was so gentle and peaceful, that no thought of himself or of his rights ever seemed to trouble him. Some people worry over their own interests, but he let them alone. Perhaps he had a secret presentiment that there were not

many more for him. Reproofs which would have been an
indignity almost if they had carried any bitterness with
them, he scarcely noticed. He went his own way : he
dreamt over his books : Felicia was the one person he
loved best in the world, and in her service he would wake
up from his dream of peace to face the troubled realities
of life ; or perhaps I should say from his realities of
peace to face the troubled dreams of life ; but that is the
problem.

'I don't know what you will do without your rabbits,
Felicia,' said Jim, feeling that this moment had now
come for a little good advice. 'You will have to take to
reading, or music.'

' Jim,' said Felicia, suddenly turning round, and opening her grey penetrating eyes, ' do you know any other
young ladies besides me ? '

Her cousin blushed up. 'I know one or two,' he said.

' What are they like ? ' says Felicia, looking quickly
at him, and then again stroking her rabbit. ' I suppose
they all talk French and play the piano ? '

'Some of them do,' said Jim. 'Felicia, I wish you
knew something of music.'

' I am very glad I don't,' says Felicia, changing
colour. ' It's too much trouble.'

' I know a Miss Flower who plays all sorts of charming

old tunes,' said James. 'I should like you to know her; she does not live very far from this: though, after all, perhaps you would not like her.'

'I hate young ladies,' said Felicia; 'they are all so silly.'

'Only now and then,' said James, smiling.

'Is Miss˙ Flower silly?' says Felicia. 'I think you are very unkind;' and her grey eyes circled deeper, and she drew herself up slight, white, against the old stable-door.

'Miss Flower may be silly for all I know,' said James. 'I hope not, for I think some day she will marry a friend of mine—Baxter—you know. She is his cousin, she lives with his aunt and his little girl, and he seems very——'

'Shut the door,' says Felicia, still very cross. 'I hear grandpapa's voice; he will be laughing at my rabbits again.'

So James shut the door as he was bid, and the two stood waiting silent in the stable darkness, with the great lines of brightness shining through the joints of the planking, and red lights where the knots were in the rough boards against the windows, while the rabbits went on nibbling and crunching. The empty stalls gloomed dark and mysterious. The two stood silent, waiting for the voices to pass.

'There, you can see the boundary from here,' old Marlow was saying, outside. 'You can think my offer over, Captain, and let me hear from you in a day or two. It will make a pretty addition to the farm, whoever buys it.'

'I have almost determined upon buying the farm,' said the other.'

'It's Baxter,' whispered James.

'Hush!' said Felicia.

The voice went on. 'This is rather a fancy price for the field, Mr. Marlow, and I am afraid I must give up thinking of it. I will speak to my lawyer, and——'

'Why did you come to me if you didn't know your own mind?' growled old Marlow. 'I thought you wanted the field as a favour. Who told you I wanted to sell it?'

'I was told you were thinking of selling it,' said Baxter; 'and I asked your grandson if you would give a neighbour the refusal.'

'I thought so,' says the old man, more and more angry. 'James is a meddlesome blockhead, and it is all along of such chattering fools as him people think my land is going about begging, d—— him; I believe he does it on purpose.'

James turned away, as this growl reached the two

young folks in the stable. There was a sort of low angry
sound from Felicia, then a silence, then—'Why, why
don't you go and contradict him ?' cried the girl, giving
her cousin a push. ' Go.'

James hung back. ' What is the good?' he said with
a sigh. ' He is an old man. I hate a scene.'

But if James hated a scene, it was not so with
Felicia. There was something new stirring in her nature
that seemed to cry out for a vent for action, for spectators.
Baxter should not hear James insulted. 'I am not
afraid,' said Miss Marlow, magnificently ; and before
James could stop her she had sprung to the great stable-
door, flung it wide open, and was standing outside in a
blaze of sunshine, confronting the two—the old grandfather and Captain Baxter, whose dark face didn't show
much of the surprise he felt. For that the old stable-
door should fly open before them, and an avenging
goddess should appear, sudden, overwhelming, breathing
vengeance and retribution, was certainly the last thing
the angry old schemer, or the disappointed neighbour,
had in their minds. Felicia's eyes were radiating, her
lips pouting, her cheeks brilliantly flushed. She had
never looked more beautiful—certainly never so angry.
' How dare you say such things of poor Jim, grandpapa ?
It is cruel of you and unjust; yes, and you know it. I
told Captain Baxter about the field.'

'Oh, listening!' says grandpapa, quite unmoved; 'and James too. Come out of your hiding, James, and you' (to Felicia) 'go back to your grandmamma.'

'You know it is not James who chatters,' persists Felicia, stamping; but her courage begins to fail a little at the two steady shaggy old eyes fixed upon her. As for the stranger, she indefinitely feels that there is protection in that straight, dark-looking figure now greeting her cousin. But she scarcely realises this. Some sudden storm had been stirred; some sudden flame had burnt up fiercely, only to go out as such flames do after a minute's flashing and flaring.

'Do you hear me, Fay?' says Mr. Marlow; 'go up to your grandmother. I'm busy with the Captain, and don't want you here.'

'But you have been unjust,' cries Felicia, worked up, more and more passionately. 'I will not have James spoken of as you have done.'

'Do you hear me or not?' roars old Marlow; and then James came forward and pulled Felicia's arm through his, and led her off without a look or a word at the angry old man. Baxter looked after the two as they walked away. At first Felicia clung to her cousin, trembling and sobbing; then in a moment she pushed him violently away, then she set off running; and when she ran poor James could not follow her, for his breath failed, his heart beat so that he could not hear or see ; he sat down upon the steps of the house, and there Baxter found him a few minutes after, almost fainting and utterly exhausted by the morning's work.

III.

FELICIA, having pulled her arm away from her cousin, ran back to the house in a troubled, furious, tearful mood. She was indignant with her grandfather, angry with herself; for James she was feeling something almost like scornful pity. Why had he been so silent?—why did he allow that intemperate old man to speak of him in such a way? She had seen Captain Baxter give one glance at James and then at her grandfather. Why did not Jim do something instead of putting down a basket of lettuces, and offering her his arm? He was more like a rabbit himself than a man. Oh, why was she not a man herself? as she stamped in a fury.

'Where is James?' said her grandmother, meeting the girl in the hall.

'I don't know; how should I?' said Felicia, and

she passed on, flitting from room to room, till she found herself at the end of the house in a certain play-room which she considered her own. Here she began to cry afresh; then she dried her tears; then Felicia, defiant, ran to an old piano, and began strumming noisily on the keys. 'Miss Flower, Miss Flower,' she sang, banging with all her might, and thumping.

And meanwhile, outside in the hot garden, poor Jim was still struggling and panting for breath. When he heard a quick foot upon the gravel, the sound turned him faint and sick with apprehension. He thought it was his grandfather, and, in his present state, everything seemed to him terrible. But it was only Baxter, who, black as his face was, and fierce of aspect, sympathised with anything that was in want of help, or that was weak or in pain. He stopped short, sat down on the stone step beside his friend, and asked him if he was ill?

'Ill!' gasped Jim, 'no—that is—I—I'm used to it. Is Felicia——'

'Felicia!—is your cousin coming back?' said Baxter, guessing more than poor Jim meant to reveal.

'If she would come—she would know—' said the young man, panting still.

'I will fetch someone,' said Baxter, really frightened;

and he hurried up the steps and along the stone terraces, and hearing a sound of noisy music coming through an open window, he stooped under the creepers that were hanging over it and went in. He only came into an empty little passage room; but from a door he heard loudly now the jangle of some old cracked piano, and he knocked impatiently, and entered without waiting for an answer.

Felicia was still playing; for, notwithstanding her protest, she could play a little, and she was strumming at some old-fashioned jig, I think she called it, which had grown out of the noise. She was standing, and playing, and bending over the music. The room was not a sitting-room, but some sort of lumber-place, such as people who live in big old houses can afford to spare to old boxes and scraps and odds and ends of furniture, and the discarded piano had been put away there among the lumber. The room was dark: great green wreaths were hanging before the windows. There were no other blinds, and none others were wanted. There was nothing to shade except old boxes and fishing-rods, some broken chairs; a great cracked looking-glass, leaning against the wall, reflected the chequered light and the whole slim length of the musician. She stood in her green faded dress among the rakes and geranium-pots, where feeble sprigs were sprouting; and close by was an old chest, upon which stood a ship full sail, and three bald-headed goggling dolls. Any other time Aurelius might have paid some martial compliment, and admired the pretty girl making merry among the rubbish; but he scarcely noticed her. It was only after he got home, in reply to the questions they asked him, that he seemed to see it all again, and remembered how she had looked, and where he had found her. Tum-tum-te-tumty! clattered Felicia, stopping short as the door opened. She was somewhat taken aback when the dark lean figure came marching up to her straight and grim-looking.

'Will you come to your cousin?' said the Captain, without any preamble. Her feelings did not require much tender handling in his estimation. 'He seems to me very ill. Perhaps you may know what to do for him.'

'Ill!' exclaimed Felicia, starting away from the piano with a slight crash among the geranium-pots. 'Have you seen grandmamma? she always nurses him when he is ill.' And she stooped to pick up the flower-pots, and to stick back the sprigs and cuttings that had fallen out of them. Felicia did not appear to think much of James's illness.

Baxter was more and more indignant.

'Poor fellow,' said Aurelius; 'he does not seem to get much nursing from anybody.' The Captain was downright angry, and did not care whom he offended. At home, if his little finger ached, aunt and cousin and attendant maids were in tears almost; his little daughter would turn pale. It was foolish, and Aurelius made fun of their solicitude, but how infinitely better than this cold-bloodedness.

'He must have some wine,' cried Felicia, carelessly. She did not choose to let Baxter see she had noticed his taunt, and she went on before him leading the way with a little careless dancing step. 'Oh dear me, who has got the keys? Scruby, Scruby,' sang the girl, and at her call a dilapidated-looking man put his bald head out of the dining-room door. 'Scruby, Master James isn't well; have you got any wine out?'

The three o'clock dinner-table was set, and a bottle with a little wine in it was put ready by the old Squire's seat.

'Not that,' said Scruby, feebly proceeding to explore various drawers and cupboards. But Baxter impatiently seized the bottle and poured its contents into a tumbler.

'That's grandpapa's wine,' said Felicia, a little awe-stricken, and Scruby made a toothless exclamation.

Q

Baxter did not say a word in reply, but walked off quickly. As he hurried along, Felicia followed him. 'I thought you cared for your cousin,' said the Captain to the girl as she came up a little timidly to the place where poor James was lying. He was better; the colour had come back into his cheeks, and he was drinking the wine which Baxter had brought him. He looked up, smiled, and held out his hand to Felicia, and she, without speaking, held it between her own two soft palms as she knelt leaning against the stone banister of the terrace.

So the Captain left them. He met Mrs. Marlow coming out of the house with a reproof on her lips.

'He should not excite himself over trifles,' said the old lady, briskly. 'I have never had a day's illness in my life.' Mrs. Marlow seemed to think that it was her own good sense which had kept her well all these years. She did not mean to be unkind, but she never pretended to anything she did not feel. It was her way; she had no morbid terrors, no hidden pains and shrinking nerves, wherewith to sympathise with others. All this had died out in her; now-a-days no impressions reached her, though the old ones of fifty years before sometimes came to life again. She loved her husband, and she loved Felicia. She tolerated James. When

her children had died, in her despair she had almost
blamed them for their weakness—she had mourned
them after her own fashion. The whole generation of
sons and daughters and sons and daughters in law had
passed away, but the tough old folks lived on, tending
the two little orphan grandchildren.

Here is one of them dragging himself up the steps
with the help of. the other. Felicia at least bears no
sign of illness or premature decay. How blooming she
looks as she drags Jim up with her arms. Mrs. Marlow
thinks in her heart there never was a sweeter, brighter
face, and ·half pities the girl linked to poor little Jim
for life.

As Aurelius rode off he thanked Heaven that all women
were not like those two. He had found it very sweet to
have to come back after years of hard work and loneliness
to the tender solicitude of a gentle old aunt, and Lucy his
little daughter. They were of a different type and order
to those two women he had just left. Good and tender
and unselfish, and living for others instead of existing
scarce alive in that strange silence and exhausted atmosphere which oppressed him and. everyone else at
Harpington.

Baxter had often heard James Marlow speak of
Felicia; this was only the second time he had ever seen

her. His first impression was of something that he never forgot—a wild, bright, sudden gleam. In later days he sometimes thought of the beautiful angry face that had flashed out upon them from the darkness. When he thought of this he melted and softened, and by some contradiction he told himself that it was a pity that such a bright brilliant flame of youth and unreserve should be dimmed and chilled down by rough cold blasts, and by time, and by indifference. But that is the story of many and many a beautiful flame. Just now, however, it was Felicia's indifference and not her beauty that was paramount in Baxter's mind: her indifference shocked him. He thought of her more than once that day.

'Is she pretty?' asked his aunt, and Aurelius paused for a minute before he answered.

'I forget—yes, she is wonderfully pretty. Those may admire her who like.' Poor James had got a bad bargain for all her brilliant loveliness. Sometimes the Captain relented a little, and then he thought of Felicia as a thoughtless child; but again he would tell himself that she was at best but a hard-hearted little siren playing jigs in her beautiful golden hair, while her victims drowned round about her. That hateful tune he had heard her play kept nagging in his ears; he found himself humming it at night as he paced the quiet lane in front of the house, smoking his midnight pipe before going to bed, long after the other members of the peaceful little household retired.

IV.

THE poor siren was also sitting up in the dark in her little room at that minute. The great hall clock had struck one, but the child had not gone to bed ; and yet midnight was a much more terrible affair at Harpington than in the cottage where Captain Baxter was staying, and where you could hear the cat purring in the kitchen all over the house. At Harpington far-off rats raced down the long passages. Far-off creaks and starts sounded in the ears of startled watchers. Felicia was frightened, but she was used to being frightened. If anything terrible came out of the barred door which led to the empty rooms, she could run down the passage screaming, and her grandmother, who rarely slept, would hear her. Room after room, dark and gloomy and ghostlike, dim passages, staircases winding into blackness—all this was round about. Jim was under the roof at the other end of the wing, and the old people were sleeping in state in the great front rooms. Felicia had opened her window. She had heard a dog bay somewhere across the dark fields, and seen a star or two shine out through the dim veil of clouds overhead. She could not see, though she peered out ever so far with her two bright grey eyes, where the line of the fields met the heavens. It was all dark, and sweet, and dim, and fresh with that indescribable calm of sleeping night. The air was touched by the scent of the fresh green blades, and of the pinks in the kitchen-garden. Some young owls began to hoot and whistle, but only for a little. Then everything was silent again. And when everything was quite silent, Felicia once more sat listening to a voice that began telling her the events of the day over and over again. These voices are apt to speak in the silence of the night, and to keep people awake.

'I thought *you* might have cared a little more,' the voice said to Felicia.

' He thought me hard, cold, cruel,' said Felicia to herself; and she began to remember how Baxter had looked at her—just as he had looked at her grandfather—with a curious hard, indifferent look, such as no one had ever given her before. Then she went over it all again, and saw James lying straight out on the stone step, and the broad shoulders of Aurelius bending over him. She saw the orange-trees on the terrace, and her grandfather crossing by the side-walk to avoid them, and her grandmother coming out of the house. There was the little scene bright painted on the darkness before her. She was sick of it, but there it was.

'Poor fellow, he does not seem to get much nursing from anyone,' said the voice again; and then again, 'I thought *you* might have cared for your cousin.'

This time the voice sounded more forgiving; but no, there was the vision of the tall unrelenting figure walking away without another word. Why was she not angry? Oh, he was right—he was right; that was why. She should have been more gentle with her cousin. She should not have pushed him from her. How kind he had been : yes; he was right to take her away when her grandfather stormed. He (Jim) had no strength for scenes and fights, and she had no strength. She only stormed and failed. She had never loved Jim so well as at that moment. Even though she had been so angry with him, she never before understood his goodness and gentleness as she did now. And then no one had ever told her before what was right : what she ought to feel and to do. Oh, if she had but one friend in the world whom she could trust, who would help her a little ; then she would know how to be good, and how to take care of Jim, and how to make him happy. Captain Baxter should see that she did care —that she was not utterly heartless. . . . So Felicia, sitting there, dreamt her waking dreams through the night.

Poor little Jim, tossing on his bed in the garret under the roof, did not know of Felicia's remorse and love, as she sat wakeful at the foot of her little iron couch, and yet—this is a theory which people may scout if they will —the unconscious magnetism of her good-will reached him in some mysterious fashion, and by degrees the fever left him, and he was soothed and quieted and fell asleep. Felicia longed for the morning to come that she might go to him, comfort him, make him forgive her. Jim was peacefully dreaming: he thought he was eating his dinner off the old china plate in the morning-room, and that Felicia came in and tossed it up in the air.

He came down late, and breakfast was over. The old couple were already on their rounds; but Felicia, who was sitting on the window-sill waiting, jumped up and ran to meet him. As she came up, Jim, looking into her face, saw a sweet, troubled, tender look that he had never seen before; grey eyes half tearful, a trembling colour, a quivering mouth.

'Dearest Jim,' she said, with both hands put out to meet his; 'forgive me, I was so cruel yesterday; I have been so unhappy about it;' and she held up her sweet face to be kissed. Never in all his life before had he seen her look like this. It was almost more than he could bear.

' Forgive, dearest Fay ! Don't talk of forgive,' he said, putting his arm round about her, and leaning his head for a moment on her shoulder.

' You are still quite tired and weak ; here is your tea and your egg,' she said, jumping away. And all breakfast-time Felicia waited on him, bringing him at last a bunch of ripe grapes she had stolen (though she did not tell him so), by breaking a pane of the grape-house.

' If Captain Baxter could see us now,' thought Felicia, ' he would see I am sorry to have been heartless.'

Poor Jim ! How delicious the grapes tasted, how happy it made him to be a little comforted and loved ! He could hardly realise his own happiness, or believe that this was in truth his own Felicia.

When Aurelius rode over that afternoon to see his friend he found him quite restored, reading in the window of the old lumber-room. Felicia, in her green dress, was still strumming on the piano, *La ci darem* : she was playing, with a great many false notes, out of an old music-book she had discovered in a corner. She shut up the piano with a bang, however, when Aurelius came into the room, and soon after disappeared, leaving the two young men together.

Baxter sat on for some time talking to Jim. He tried to give him good advice, and tell him to hold his own. James, as usual, shrugged his shoulders, and smiled and sighed: so long as he had Felicia he did not care what others said or did or thought of him, and so he said. Baxter did not answer, but soon after got up and went away.

He was very sorry for his friend. It did not seem to him, for all James told him, that Felicia cared for him in the least. Once more he told himself that she was a hard-hearted, ill-tempered little creature; and so thinking he walked away, and down the old stone steps along the periwinkle walk leading to the road. And then he looked up, and saw that there was a figure at the gate sitting waiting on the grass-grown step. The figure jumped up quickly, and came to meet him. A wild, nymph-like little figure, in her quaint green dress, with her hair flying. It was Felicia, who had taken a great resolution.

'I was waiting for you,' she said, opening her grey eyes wider and wider. 'I have something to say to you: I want you to listen.' And she stood before him so that he could not pass. 'You think me heartless,' she said. 'You think I do not care for James. You think I am not good enough for him. Oh, Captain Baxter, you are right; that is what I wanted to say to you; but—indeed, indeed—I know how good he is, and I do love him, and do try to take care of him; and I can't bear that you should think me quite wicked and heartless.' And the tears stood in her eyes.

'Wicked! heartless!' said Aurelius, feeling in his turn ashamed. 'It is I who am wicked and heartless, ever to think anything of the sort, and I thank you for making me know you as you are.' And he held out his hand, and went away touched and melted by the girl's confidence.

James, who had seen the two from his window, came down the walk a minute later, and found Felicia standing quite still in the middle of the path where Aurelius had left her.

'What have you two been talking about?' Jim said.

'Never mind,' said Felicia. 'Do you want to know? He told me I was heartless that day you were so ill, and I wanted to say to him that I do love my friends, and am not quite without a heart.' She said it so prettily, so shyly, so quickly, that Jim's vague jealousy melted away, and he looked down admiringly at the sweet, bright face beside him.

This was only a very little while before Jim went back to college for his last term. Baxter came once or twice to see him, and then, when he was gone, the Captain's visits ceased. Mrs. Marlow gave him very plainly to understand she did not care for him to come, and there was nothing

at the Hall that Baxter cared to come for; not even
Felicia, although he often thought of her in her slim
green dress.

Once or twice he met her in the lanes; once, the very
day he left for town, in a buttercup field with a great golden
ball of flowers in her hand. That day little Lucy was with
him, and Felicia gave the child the flowers. Little Lucy,
who had read of princesses in fairy tales, firmly believed
Felicia to be one of them, and talked of her all the way
home. Felicia was a very silent princess, and never
spoke, but always ran away.

V.

My story, as I am telling it, seems to be a sad one, of
which the actors themselves scarcely know the meaning.
What does it take to make a tragedy? Youths, summer
days, beauty, kind hearts, a garden to stroll in; on one
side an impulsive word, perhaps a look, in which an unconscious truth shines out of steadfast eyes, perhaps a pang
of jealousy; and then a pause or two, a word, a rose off a
tree—that is material enough for Tragedy. She lays her
cold hand upon the best, the fairest, and sweetest, and
most innocent. For my own part, Tragedy seems less

terrible, with her dark veil and cold, stern face, than Comedy in her tinsel and mask. Tragedy is terrible; and as she passes tears flow and cries of pain are uttered; but along with these are heroic endurance, faithfulness, self-denial, and tender, unflinching love, that her dark veil cannot hide nor her terrors dismay, and she passes by, leaving a benediction behind her. Flowers spring up along the road, her arid wastes are re-peopled, the plough travels over the battlefields, and the living stand faithful by the sacred memories of the past.

But Comedy seems to scorn her victims. How can they rise again from her jibes and jeers? For Comedy take middle age, take false sentiment, and weakness, and infidelity; take small passions, unworthy objects, affectations, rouge-pots, calculations, the blunting influence of time. It makes one's heart ache to think of the cruel, cruel comedies of life, into which good people are drawn, and gentle natures, only to be cast out again, sullied and mortified, and broken-spirited and defiled. When the crisis comes, Comedy grinds her mad teeth and tears her false hair, and cries and writhes, and the spectators laugh and shrug their shoulders; but they love and pity Tragedy, as she passes along despairing, but simple and beautiful even in her woe. We pass through all these phases, youth and tragedy and the comedy of middle life, and then, I suppose, if we are sensible and honest-minded people, comes the peace of age, and, at all events, the silence that follows all youth and life and age ; when at last Comedy shrinks away abashed and powerless.

This silence was hanging over the old house at Harpington : its unconscious inmates came and went as usual, sitting out in the lovely summer sunshine, living the same still life.   For the last time—it was all for the last time—and yet it seemed like any of the other summers that had flooded through the old place, across the fields, into the remotest nooks and corners of the neglected gardens, shining on the high tiled roofs and the ancient elms and rooks.   Even old Marlow would come out and bask in the lovely summer weather, conning his account-books and making his calculations under the trees to the singing of the birds.   One day two butterflies came flitting and bobbing about his head.   Felicia burst out laughing at the sight.

Jim had gone off, telling them to remember the 10th. He was to come back from Oxford in the beginning of July, and it had long been settled that Felicia and her grandmother were to accept an invitation they had received, and meet him in London, and spend ten days there, and buy Felicia's wedding-clothes.   Mrs. Marlow was to see her doctor and lawyer at the same time ; old

Marlow had desired this arrangement—I don't know in what fit of generosity—it was a whim; a sort of remembrance of the week he had spent in London, before his marriage. The clothes were unnecessary, but he would not have to pay for them; so he chose to do the thing handsomely for once; and all this being accomplished, there would be no further reason for delay. Jim and Fay should come back and be married out of hand. It was also a sort of intended encouragement to Felicia, who certainly showed no eagerness to enter into matrimonial bonds; but, if going to London depended upon being married, here was Felicia as eager as anyone to be married, for London was her dream, her heaven upon earth, her soul's aspiration. Why she should have sighed and longed after all these millions of brown half-baked bricks, piled one on the top of the other, I cannot tell. Jim had sometimes told her stories of London streets and parks, and promised that he would take her to see the sights. They were to stay with an opportune old sister of Mr. Marlow's, from whom a letter had come one morning, to everybody's surprise:

'Queen Square, June 27.

'My dear Brother,' wrote the old lady—'When I think how many years we have both lived, and how many have passed since we last met, and how very few more we can expect to be together in the world, it occurs to me to write to you and ask you if it is not time to let past things be past. This is our mother's birthday, and I have been thinking over old times, and I feel that I should much like to see you once more. Are you coming to town? and if so, will you give me the great pleasure of receiving you, and come to me with your wife and your grand-daughter? I hear Felicia's marriage is to take place before very long; and she must be doubtless thinking about her trousseau. I should like to contribute a hundred pounds towards it, in token of the goodwill of an old maiden aunt who has not quite forgotten her earlier days. She can expend it to the best advantage during her stay with me.

'I am thinking of going abroad, so that I would only beg that I may soon have the pleasure of welcoming you in my house. With love to your wife,

'Your affectionate sister,

'MARY ANNE MARLOW.'

'Well,' said Mrs. Marlow, as she finished, 'Mary Anne seems to be flourishing—going abroad.'

'I shall answer that letter,' said the Squire, in a determined voice. 'You had better go, and take Fay with you.'

'*Me!*' cried Mrs. Marlow. . 'I am not going to leave home, Robert. I am just making my jam.'

'Jam!' said the Squire, 'who wants jam? But I tell you what, Mary Anne seems disposed to be liberal, and I don't see why we shouldn't get the benefit of our own as well as anybody else. That house in Queen Square ought to have been mine at this minute.'

'Nothing will induce me to set foot in it,' cried Mrs. Marlow, 'after all that has passed. You can take Felicia yourself, Robert, if you choose to go.'

'Go! It is out of the question,' said old Marlow. 'I must look after my crops. What should I do in London?' said the Squire.

As usual, the old fellow had his way in the end. He frowned and insisted, being determined not to lose that chance 100*l.*

'Harpington, June 29.

'MY DEAR SISTER,—I thank you for your letter, inviting us to your house, and alluding to old times. Although I am unfortunately prevented from accepting your invitation, my wife and grand-daughter will avail themselves of your kindness, and Felicia will be glad to do her shopping under your auspices.

R

'It is many years, as you say, since we met, and we are both, doubtless, very much changed.   Believe me

'Your affectionate brother,

'R. MARLOW.'

Felicia felt as if they were really going when she went into her grandmother's room one morning to find doors and cupboards wide open, and strange garments and relics piled on the floor, and on the bed, and on the window-sill, and Hannah Morton, the housekeeper, dragging in a great hair-trunk and a rope.   The old lady was selecting from a curious store of wimples, and pockets, and mittens, and furbelows, and out of numbers of faded reticules and bags, the articles which she thought necessary for her journey. Felicia's experience was small; but she asked her grandmother if she thought so many things would be wanted for a ten days' excursion.

'Who is this, grandmamma?' cried the girl, holding up a black plaster silhouette.

'Put it down, child,' said Mrs. Marlow.

She could not bear her treasures to be inspected.   Few old ladies like it.   They store their keepsakes and mementoes away in drawers and dark cupboards—cupboards fifty years old, drawers a lifetime deep.

And so even these slow, still, wall-enclosed days at

Harpington came to an end at last. They ended as the
old trap, with its leather straps and chains, drove up to
the door with George, the gardener, on the box, and the
drag swinging. The carriage was at the door; the sand-
wiches were cut; the old hair-box was corded. Felicia,
who even now, within ten minutes of her going, expected
that an earthquake would come to engulph London before
she should see it, that her grandfather would change his
mind, or, at least, that the white horse would take to his
heels and run away down hill, began at last to believe in
their going.

The thought of it all had been so delightful that the
delight was almost an agony, as very vivid feelings must
be. Felicia had been wide-awake all night, starting and
jumping in her little bed, and watching the dawn spread
dull beyond the trees (as it was spreading behind the
chimney-pots in the dream-city to which she was going).
Now she stood, with her little brown hat tied over her
hair, watching the proceedings with incredulous eyes.
The old gig, with its bony horse, was no miraculous
apparition; but miracles take homely shapes at times, and
we don't always recognise them when we see them. The
grey hair-trunk was hoisted up by Hannah and George,
the bags were brought down, and then Mrs. Marlow,
walking brisk and decided, equipped for the journey, with

strange loopings and pinnings, with a bag and a country
bonnet, appeared arm in arm with her husband. The
grandfather had sometimes driven off for a day or two,
but the grandmother's departure was a much more seldom
and special occurrence. So Felicia felt, as well as Mrs.
Marlow, as she stood on the threshold, with her arm still
in the old Squire's. It is affecting to see some leave-
takings: outstretched hands that have lost strength in
each other's service; eyes meeting that have seen each
other's brightness fade. I don't know if the end of love
is a triumph or a requiem: the young man and woman
are gone, but their two souls are there still in their
changed garments; the throb of the full flooding current
is over, but it has carried them on so far on their
way. Here were two whose aims had not been very
great, nor could you · see in their faces the trace of
past aspirations and high endeavour. Two mean worn
faces looking at each other for the last time with
faithful eyes.*

' Good-by, Robert,' said Mrs. Marlow, wistfully.

---

* 'Tous les hommes sont menteurs, inconstants, faux, bavards,
hypocrites, orgueilleux ou lâches, méprisables et sensuels; toutes les
femmes sont perfides, artificieuses, vaniteuses; le monde n'est qu'un égout
sans fond où les phoques les plus informes rampent et se tordent sur des
montagnes de fange: mais il y a au monde une chose sainte et sublime;
c'est l'union de deux de ces êtres si imparfaits et si affreux. . . .'

'Take care of yourself. You will find the cellar-key on the hook in my cupboard.'

'Good-by, my dear. Give my love to Mary Anne,' says the Squire, signing to the man to help his mistress up. When the old lady was safe hoisted on the seat of the little carriage, once more she put out her thin hand, and he took it in his. 'There,' said he, 'be off; don't stay beyond your time.'

'You will have to come for me,' said Mrs. Marlow, smiling; and then Felicia jumped up, and they drove away. Then the Squire tramped back into the house again. How dull and lonely it seemed, all of a sudden. Empty rooms; silence. Why did he let them go? Confound Mary Anne and her money! It was all his own doing, and he loved his own way, but it was dismal all the same. What was this? his wife come back for something. For an instant he had fancied her in the room. Marlow pulled down the blind noisily, making his study still darker than it was before; then he pulled on his wide-awake, and trudged out through the stable-yard into the fields, where he stayed till dinner-time, finding fault with the men for company's sake. Mrs. Marlow had not yet left home in spirit, though she was driving away through the lanes: she was roaming through the house, and pondering on this plan and that

for the Squire's comfort; and Felicia was flying ahead
of gigs and railways, through a sort of dream landscape,
all living and indistinct, like one of Turner's pictures.
That was London—that dim, harmonious city; and
Jim was there; and Captain Baxter, would he come
and see them, she wondered? Perhaps they might meet
one day suddenly; and then her London heart, as she
called it, began to throb.

VI.

THE old house in Queen Square stood hospitably
waiting for the travellers. An old butler came to the
door; an old lady, looking something like the Squire
in a bonnet, beamed down to meet them. Two old
four-post beds were prepared for Felicia and her grandmother. There was some indescribable family likeness
to Harpington in the quiet old house, with its potpourri
pots, and Chinese junks, and faded carpets, and narrow
slit windows. But the welcome was warmer; for Miss
Marlow nodded, and brightened, and twinkled more
often in five minutes than the Squire in his whole lifetime.

'How do you do? Welcome, my dear. Well!'—

taking both her hands—'are you very much in love?
Pretty thing, isn't she? Eliza, I wish you had brought
my brother with you. Come up, come up. There, this
is the drawing-room, and this is the balcony, with a
nice little iron table for lovers to sit at. Now come
upstairs. There is someone to dinner. Matthew, send
my maid. We must make the bride look prettier still
for dinner; mustn't we, Jim?'

Miss Marlow enjoyed nothing so much as a romance,
for she had been in love many, many times herself.

'And so you say Robert is not a bit changed since he
was last here? why, that is a century ago at least. We
are a good wearing family; and as for Felicia, I hope
she will look just as she does now for twenty years to
come.'

They all had some tea very sociably together. Miss
Marlow poured it out, with her bonnet very much on one
side. Mrs. Marlow imagined it to be London fashion,
and mentally railed at new-fangled London ways; as for
Felicia—breathless, excited, with radiating grey eyes—
she took in all that was round about her—the aunt,
the old servants, the potpourri, the fusty cushions and
gilt tables, the winding Westminster streets outside,
the Park, the distant roar of the town, the tops of
statues and turrets, the Horse Guards—and ah! the

Prince of Wales actually in person, riding down Birdcage
Walk.   She went upstairs to dress for dinner, and presently Mrs. Marlow came in with some ancient amethyst
ornaments.

'Here, Felicia, I shall not wear them myself; you
may have them,' she said.

Felicia, who had been looking disconsolately in the
glass at a pretty face and shining hair, was charmed, and
instantly· fastened the bygone elegance round her slim
white neck, and felt herself beautiful.

'Oh, *thank* you, grandmamma.   Shall you wear your
jaspers?' Felicia asked.

But Mrs. Marlow answered abruptly, she was tired,
and she should not come down at all.   She looked black
and rigid, and it was in vain Felicia implored her to
relent in her determination.

'Your great-grandfather's will was iniquitous,' said
Mrs. Marlow, absently.   'Mary Anne has no possible
right to this house.   Yes, I shall remain in my room.
You may stay with me, Felicia, if you feel as I do on
the subject.'

'Oh, grandmamma!' gasped poor Fay.   'It happened such a *very* long time ago.   I think I will go
down.'

'You can do as you like in the matter, and judge

for yourself,' said Mrs. Marlow, coldly. 'Send me that volume I gave you to read on the way.'

And so Felicia left her grandmother reading a volume of Porteous's sermons, and escaped much relieved, and went and knocked at her aunt's door to tell her of the change. Miss Marlow popped her head, still in her bonnet, out of her bedroom.

'Not coming! Dear me, what a pity. Ready?— that is right, my dear : make yourself pretty, for Captain Baxter is come.'

. . . .

A kind fate sometimes gives people what they wish for long, long before they have ventured even to expect it. Felicia had hoped to see Baxter once, perhaps, or twice—meeting in a street just before she left—and now, the very first evening of her arrival she was told he was come—downstairs, actually in the house! Make herself pretty! Her cheeks brightened up of their own accord, her lips began to smile, and such sweet, gay, childish happiness beamed from her grey eyes, that Miss Marlow was obliged to come out of her room and embrace her on the spot then and there.

Felicia lingered a little as she went, and as she lingered it was with an odd feeling that she recognised the twins of some of the old home things—some chairs like those at Harpington, and some old Italian china, and a plate not unlike the Sola plate at home, with arabesques and ornaments; but no clasped hands were there. Felicia came to the drawing-room door at last, hesitated, and went in very slowly. James had not come down. Felicia, in her amethysts, turned pale, as Baxter, who was standing alone in the room, came up to greet the young lady.

At a first glance Aurelius thought Felicia very much changed. She looked older, graver; perhaps the dusty damask, and gorgeous picture-frames, and gilt tables made a less becoming background than the ivy walls and periwinkles at Harpington.

'I am so glad to see you again,' he said. 'It was very kind of Miss Marlow to let me come and meet you.'

As Aurelius finished this little speech he looked at her again. What had he been dreaming of? she was prettier—far, far prettier than he remembered her even. A sort of curious bright look, half conscious, half doubting, was in her eyes; she blushed and smiled.

'I am so glad you have come. I was afraid I should only see you by chance,' said she.

'We have not had a talk since that last time we parted,' said Aurelius, stupidly; 'but little Lucy treasured up her flowers.'

' And you believed me ? ' Felicia cried, earnestly, flushing as she spoke.

' I never doubted you,' said Aurelius; and he believed he was speaking the truth. Beauty is the most positive of all convictions.

The others presently came into the room, Miss Marlow resplendent, and ushered in by gongs.

' James, take your bride in to dinner,' she cried, with a nod and an intelligent look at Baxter, who glanced at the two, and then stiffly offered his arm to the old lady. The Captain was a favourite with Miss Marlow, who liked good looks, and had not yet got over an early penchant for the army. She had asked him first at James's suggestion, and now counted on him as an agreeable escort on the many occasions she had already devised for taking herself and Felicia to see sights, theatres, parties, toilettes. There was no end to the things Miss Marlow wanted to take Felicia to see.

Mrs. Marlow let her sister-in-law go her own way. She could not forgive her, and would not join many of the schemes and expeditions. She was envious, lonely, and home-sick : after that first day she would come down and sit dismally in a corner; but, in her way, she was touched by Felicia's delight, and perhaps she wondered if she had always done enough for the happiness of the two children she had reared. Felicia and her betrothed behaved exactly as usual. Jim tried to find a proof of Fay's affection for him in the long hours she spent among the ribbons and gauzes of her trousseau. The girl brightened, chattered, ruled her kind and patient little lover with an iron rod, and then rewarded him by one word of happiness. If she was happy, it was all he asked. Poor Jim! his was but a small share of all this excitement and pleasure. Fay wounded him one day by saying before Baxter, 'You don't look at all like a husband, Jim; you are much more like an uncle.' This was the first time she had ever talked about their approaching marriage. In vain Jim spoke of coming times, and tried to find out what was in her mind. She shifted, parried, doubled, and finally would run away altogether; she was too happy in the present to face the future, and all Felicia's present, like a dissolving view, had opened and revealed delights more endless even than any she had imagined for herself.

Many people, seeing her sitting in the Park one morning between Jim and Captain Baxter, looked a second time, and smiled at the dazzling young creature. There was a great flower-bed of red·rhododendrons just behind her chair. She had put on one of her pretty new trousseau dresses; she was gay, glad, happy, beyond any happiness she had ever conceived before. As for her approaching marriage, I do not honestly believe she had ever given it a single thought; all she knew was that she was sitting there with Jim to take care of her, and to wait as long as ever she liked, with Baxter—who was kind now, and who no longer thought her heartless—with a sight so glittering and cheerful that that alone would have been enough for her. The horses went by with their beautiful shining necks and smooth clean-cut limbs; the amazons rode along, laughing and talking as they passed; the young men, magnificent and self-conscious, were squaring their elbows and swooping by on their big horses; the grand dresses and ladies went rustling along the footpath; the pleasant green park spread and gleamed; a sort of song of talk, and footsteps, and sunshine was in the air. High overhead the little pinkish-grey London clouds were sailing across the blue sky, and the long distant lines of white houses were twinkling with light. And yet nothing is quite perfect; why did Aurelius ask her just then when the marriage was to take place?

'Marriage!' said Felicia, 'what marriage? Ours do you mean? Oh, any time.'

'My grandfather talks of August,' said James, gravely.

'August! when is August?' said Felicia, looking a little strangely. For the first time a swift quick pang of certainty seemed to come over her. It was like nothing that she had ever felt before. But she was brave, young, and confident; she wanted to be happy, and so in a moment her dancing grey eyes were raised to Baxter's.

'You must never talk about our wedding again,' she said; 'we don't like it. We mean to be happy while we can, without troubling ourselves about the future; don't we, Jim?'

'I hope we shall be happy any way, dear,' said Jim, gravely.

Aurelius looked from one to the other, and thought this was the strangest love-making he had ever witnessed. The next time he came he brought a little parcel in his hand, which he asked her, in an ashamed sort of voice, to accept as a token of sympathy on an occasion he was not permitted to name. Felicia had heard of wedding presents, but had not thought they would come to her. She screamed with delight, seeing a beautiful little gold glittering ring for her arm, from which a crystal locket was hanging.

'Oh, how pretty!' she cried. 'Is it for me—really for me? Oh, thank you. Look, Jim; look, grand-mamma.'

Mrs. Marlow looked, and dryly said it must have cost a good deal of money. As for Felicia, she was radiant. The loan of her grandmother's amethysts had charmed her; how much more this lovely thing, glittering, twinkling—her very own. It was a link, poor little soul, in her future destiny.

.   .   .   .

Days went on, and the time was drawing near for their return. Felicia's pretty gowns were bought, and Miss Marlow's hundred pounds expended. The old Squire wrote to his wife, bidding her come home, and bring the girl. Our poor little Proserpine, whose creed it was to live in the present, and to pick the flowers, and not to trouble herself with what she did not see, woke one day to find that the present was nearly over, and the past was beginning again. The past!—was she to go back to it, to leave life and light for that tomb in which she had been bred; to see Aurelius no more, London no more, living men and women no more; live with only sheep, only silence, only shadows, and the drone of insects, to fill up the rest of her life; only Jim, Jim, whose every thought and word and look she knew by heart? 'Oh! it was horrible; it was a shame. It shouldn't be. She couldn't go,' said Felicia to herself. 'She would stay on with her aunt. She would ask her. She would not go.' She began walking up and down her little bedroom, like a young tigress pacing a narrow cage. Her grandmother looked in, hearing a hasty rush of footsteps, and Felicia stopped short in her walk.

'Is anything the matter?' said Mrs. Marlow.

'Nothing, grandmamma,' said Felicia. And then when the door was shut again, once more she began her fierce gymnastics. A few minutes before, James had said, 'We must come again when we are married, Felicia, and see all the sights we leave unseen now.'

'There is plenty of time,' says Felicia.

'Three days,' says James.

'Three days!' cries the girl; 'but I don't mean to go—I don't want to go; I shall stay, James; do you hear? Aunt Mary Anne will ask me. How unkind you are.'

'I am afraid Aunt Mary Anne is packing up to go too,' said poor stupid James. 'Dear, some day when I have the right to bring you, you shall come for as long as you like.'

'Some day! I want it now,' cries Felicia. 'I haven't seen the waxworks or the lions. I—I *will* stay,' she flashed at him in a passion. And then, as usual, she ran away, realising that she was talking

nonsense, that she was powerless, that she was only
a girl, and that here was happiness, delight, interest—
a world where every hour meant its own special delight,
sympathy, friendship ; and friendship was more than love,
thought Felicia, a thousand times, and she might not
taste it. To be her own self, that was what Felicia
longed for. Here, in London, life seemed made for her ;
there, at Harpington, it seemed to her, looking back,
that she was like one of the periwinkles growing round
the garden-gate.

VII.

BAXTER was, as I have said, a widower ; he looked back
to his early married days now from the heights of thirty-
five. Life was not to him the wonderful strange new
thing it seemed to Felicia, coming from her periwinkle
haunts, from the still lichen-grown walls of brick, which
so effectually keep out many spiritual things, and within
which all her existence had been enclosed. When
Baxter found himself gratefully accepting Miss ·Marlow's
invitations to dinner, coming day after day to the old
dark house, patiently waiting among the needlework,
chairs, and cushions in the gorgeous drawing-room ;

s

planning one scheme and another to give pleasure to
little Felicia, who was so happy, and in such delight
at his coming—when he found himself thinking of her
constantly, and living perpetually in her company, he
said to himself—for he was a loyal gentleman—that this
must not be. It was a pity, but it must not be. He
had respected his wife, but she had never charmed him.
People generally destined him for her cousin, Miss
Flower; but now he began to tell himself that this also
was impossible. There had been one real story in his life,
of which people knew nothing, which was told now, and
to which (for it was there written and finished) there
were no new chapters to add, for the dictating spirit was
gone for ever. As for Emily Flower, she and Aurelius
understood each other very well : they were sincere
friends, nothing more, and they let people talk as
they perhaps talked of others in turn, without caring
or knowing very much of concerns that were not their
own.

If Felicia had not been going back so soon, and her
fate decided, and if James himself had not asked him
again and again to come home, to join them in one
excursion and another, Baxter might have kept to his
good resolves, and avoided the bright, sweet young
sylph who had beguiled him. But it was for such a

little while, surely there was no harm in it, he told himself. She would not guess his secret, poor little thing—sacrificed to the old people's convenience and cupidity. Suddenly, thinking of it all, of Felicia's unconsciousness, a sort of indignation seized the young man at the thought of this marriage. Someone should save her ; someone should hold her back—say a warning word before it was too late. He would interfere ; he would go to Mrs. Marlow and protest. But then came a thought of Jim, generous, gentle, unselfish, full of heart and affection—worth a dozen Felicias, thought Baxter, who was not blind to her faults—only he loved her all the same— and Jim also loved her, and Felicia was indifferent ; that was the cruel part of the bargain.

Who are we, to judge for others ? In after days, Baxter remembered his indignation—remembered it in shame and in remorse. It was too late then to change the past, but not too late to regret it.

Felicia cried herself to sleep that night, and again Mrs. Marlow came into the child's room, and stood by the great four-post bed, where the little creature was writhing and starting.

' Fay, my dear,' said the old lady, ' you forget yourself. Wake up. What is it ? '

Felicia woke up, with her great sleepy eyes full of

tears, stared about her vaguely, and then fell asleep again, as girls do.

I think, if she had spoken then, the old lady would have helped her; but she slept quietly, and Mrs. Marlow, who had been frightened, left her. Felicia was so little used to talk to her grandmother that she did not know how to do it. She would as soon have thought of telling the marble washstand that she was unhappy.

But, nevertheless, Jim had spoken, and Felicia's looks had implored, and Mrs. Marlow, with heroic self-sacrifice, had written to ask for leave to stay another week. Felicia, hearing the great news, never for an instant doubted that all was right, and once more she embarked in her golden seas of contentment.

There was a little expedition she looked forward to with some excitement. It should be the last, Baxter had mentally decided. There was to be a river, a row, a tea-making in the woods. Little Lucy and her cousin, Miss Flower, were to come to it, and James, and Fay, and Miss Marlow, who was always ready to enjoy herself. Mrs. Marlow, according to her wont, said she should not be able to go.

Felicia came down early that morning to breakfast, and flung open a window to let in a fresh gust of early London soot. Some distant cries reached her ears. A morning sight of busy park and passing people spread before her. Some far-away bells were ringing. All was wide, bright, and misty. She tried to realise her own happiness for a minute, but couldn't. A whole day's pleasuring—a whole week's respite. Her grandmother had written, and all was well. Another week! Another week was another lifetime; and she need not trouble herself about what would come after.

'Oh, Jim, I am so happy,' she said, going up to him as he came into the room.

And then came post, tea-urns, old ladies, and funny old mahogany tea-caddies; and then came, once more, swift, and sharp, and overwhelming, a pang of disappointment more cruel than any that had gone before.

'I have heard from your grandfather,' said Mrs. Marlow, quite cheerfully (as if it did not seem a matter of life and death to poor Fay), 'and he says, my dear, that we have been away quite long enough, and that we must start to-morrow, as we first arranged.'

'To-morrow?' gasped the girl, in a strange numb horror.

'I suppose you have got your finery, and I hope James has bought the gold ring' (reading). 'There is nothing to wait for now, and the wedding may as well take place on your return. The banns shall be put up next Sunday, and there need be no more talk about the matter. As for Parsons, the way he has behaved about that horse was only what might have been expected. I shall have him up at the next assizes, and let the county see that I am not the man to be put upon. Remember me to Mary Anne. . . .' So read the old lady.

Felicia heard no more: she listened, turning white and red over her teacup. She looked up once imploringly at James, and met a shy adoring glance that made her hate him. Mrs. Marlow nodded relief. Miss Marlow was beaming and kissing her hand; the old butler, who had come in with some boiling water, seemed to guess what was passing, and he too smiled. And Felicia was cold, pale, furious, in a strange, desperate state of mind— desperate, and yet determined, and sure even in her despair of some secret help somewhere—she did not tell herself whence it was to come. She could bear it no longer, and jumping up, white as a ghost, she ran out of the room.

Felicia never forgot that day, in its strange jumble of happiness and misery. Baxter was right when he called her cold-hearted. She no more cared for Jim, no more thought of his possible pain, than she thought of the feelings of the footman who opened the door, or the stoker who drove the engine.

The sun shone, the engine was whistling; Aurelius, holding little Lucy by the hand, and accompanied by a smiling young lady in a hat and long blue veil, met them at the station. Jim, still unconscious of his companion's silence and pre-occupation, pulled her arm through his, and carried her along the long line of carriages, leaving his aunt to Aurelius' care. All the way Jim had talked and asked questions in his unusual elation; every word he said worried and jarred upon the girl. Now, in his happiness, he went on talking and chirping; but Felicia was in a cloud, and did not listen: sometimes waking up, she thought of appealing to him then and there, in the carriage, with all the others to take her part, and of imploring him to help her—to what? to escape from him. Sometimes she felt that her one chance would be to run away, and never be heard of again; sometimes, with a start, she asked herself what was this new terrible thing hanging over her—this close-at-hand horrible fate, made for her—such as no one before had ever experienced. Then for some minutes, as was her nature, she put it all away, and began to play cat's-cradle with little Lucy Baxter, who was sitting beside her.

They reached Henley at last, scudding through broad sunny meadows, with a sight of blue summer woods, and of the hills overhanging the flooding river; they lunched at the old red brick house, with the great lilac westerias hanging and flowering, and then they took a boat and rowed against the stream to Wargrave —sliding, gliding along against the rush of the clear water, past the swirls of the wavelets, and the rat-holes, and the pools; among the red reeds and white flowers, along damp, sweet banks of tangle and grass. It soothed and quieted poor Felicia's fever. By degrees a feeling came to her of a whole world passing away in remorseless motion, and of a fate against which it was vain to struggle. This was life and fate, to be travelling along between green banks, with summer sights, and flying birds, and woods, and wreathing green things all about; while the stream of life and feeling flowed away quick in a contrary direction, with a rapid rush, carrying the sticks, and leaves, and mementoes, and passing lights along with it. And so at last she was soothed and calmed a little as the boat swung on. Perhaps there is happiness even in travelling against one's fate, thought poor Felicia, despairing. The happiest person in that boat-load was little Lucy, who had not yet reached her life, and next to her the old lady, who was well nigh over it, who sat talking and chirping to Miss Flower. James was silent, for he had at last discovered Felicia's

abstraction, and he had seen that she did not hear him
when he spoke to her. But when Aurelius once made
a little joke, Felicia brightened up again, and suddenly
seemed to throw off the cloud which oppressed her.

As the boats touched the shore, they saw a fire
burning in the little wood; the smoke was rising blue
and curling, and the flames sparkling among the sticks.
All the summer-green slopes of the wood were bright
with leaves, twigs, buds, fragrant points; faint showers
of light, and blossom, and perfume seemed falling upon
the branches : it may have been the effect of the sun-
beams shining on the woods lighting the waters. The
lodge-keeper's wife had lighted the fire, which smoked
and sparkled ; and Emily Flower made tea. Aurelius
laughed and shook his head when she offered him some
—tea was not much in his line, he said; nor was Felicia
yet of an age much given to tea-drinking : that is a
consolation which is reserved for her elders, who are
more in need of such mild stimulation; but she stirred
her cup, and set it down upon the grass, and waved
away the flies with the stem of a wild rose that James
had picked for her.

Every now and then Felicia stole a glance at Miss
Flower. She could not understand that demure young
lady, who looked so little, spoke so rarely. She seemed

so unlike any of Felicia's experiences (experiences, by the way, which were chiefly confined to herself, for she had never had a companion), that Felicia could not understand her. Emily Flower, however, understood Felicia very well, and the two did not somehow seem to amalgamate. Felicia wished that she could be sure Miss Flower and Aurelius were nothing to each other. She looked from one to the other more than once.

'Are you still happy, Felicia?' said Jim, sadly, coming up to her as she stood there waving her rose-branch.

'Happy?' said Felicia. 'No; I am miserable.'

'What makes you miserable?' James asked.

For a moment she had a mind to tell him; then her courage failed.

'I can't go back,' she cried, evading the truth, with a sudden impetuous burst of emotion. 'Oh, Jim, if you loved me, you would help me; but you don't, and I hate you!' Then a minute after she was suddenly sorry for him, for the first time that day; and, as he stood silent and hurt, she put her hand on his arm. 'You know I don't hate you, Jim,' she said, piteously. 'How silly you are to mind.' And she dashed the rose-branch across her face,·to wipe away her tears.

Nobody noticed this little scene except perhaps Aurelius, who had been standing near, and who walked away with little Lucy, and began pulling down ivy-wreaths for the child.

I don't know how he knew, but at that minute Jim, in his turn, looking from one to the other, seemed to understand it all. He left Felicia for a minute, and then came back, wistfully.

' Can't you trust me, Felicia? ' he said, in odd, doubtful voice.

But poor Fay had not even trust to give him as yet. She did not understand, and stared with beautiful list-less grey eyes. Then she went and flung herself down by the fire, and watched the flame crackling and drifting among the glowing twigs, and listened to her aunt talking on and on to Miss Flower, and to the sound of the river running by the bank, and washing against the leaves and the grasses. . . .

VIII.

THE tea-party was over—they were floating with the stream again, and travelling back at a rapid pace past the trim green rustic lawns at Wargrave towards Henley —past a desolate-looking island, where a barge was floating ; past banks of wild roses, flowering and hanging in fanciful garlands : golden flags were springing, and lilies opening their chalices ; and stars, white and violet, were studding the banks of this lovely summer-world. Then they left it all, and passed into a dark cavernous dungeon of waters, shut in by great wooden doors. Felicia was not yet used to locks, and she and little Lucy grasped each other's hands as the boat began sinking into the depths, sinking to the roar of the weir and the mill into slimy green profundities, hollowed and destroyed by the discoloured tides. The little rose-cottage where the keeper lived went right up into the air—so did his little children, who had rushed out to help to open the sluices.

Down went the boat to the very depths : the great green dripping walls were covered with slime and weeds ; up above, roses were flowering on the surface of the earth ; down here, the sunlight scarcely touched the gloom, and dank dripping mould and creeping vegetation. Little waterfalls burst through the rotten gates, and fell roaring and rushing into the dark waters.

' Oh, what a terrible place,' said Felicia.

Miss Marlow gave a little shriek as the boat bumped suddenly against the side of the lock.

' Are you frightened ? ' said Baxter to Felicia.

'Yes,' said Felicia ; and then she looked up and smiled. 'I mean no,' she said, 'not if you——' Then, seeing that James was looking at her, she stopped short.

Jim, who was standing up with the boat-hook in his hand, turned away ; and, stooping over the edge of the boat, looked at something deep down in the river. Per-. haps a minute may have passed—it seemed a very long while to him. When he looked up again, Felicia was blushing still ; the great gates were opening, the water was pouring through, and a glimpse of the sweet flowing river shone once more between the great portals : it all looked more lovely if possible for the gloom in which they had been waiting.

Then Jim and Baxter pushed with their long boat-hooks, and the boat began to slide out from the dark jaws in which it had been enclosed. The gates creaked as they opened wide : the boat was almost between them—when something happened. I cannot exactly tell how, a great barge that was waiting outside began to move, and struck against the gate. The lock-man had been called away, one of the boys turning the pulley tripped and fell, the other boy's hand slipped ; the windlass began to untwist rapidly, and the great gates to close fast upon the little boat.

'Pull! pull!' shouted Baxter, who was at the bow, to James, who had instinctively begun to back.

Their two contrary efforts delayed them for an instant; James, seeing the danger, with a great effort caught at the gate with his boat-hook, and, with an impetus from his whole body, urged the boat through. It was just in time; the boat was safe, the barge was stopped; but the boat-hook stuck in the wood, and before anyone could help him, Jim was over and splashing in the water.

It was no very great matter: a punt close at hand came to his help, and the little boat's crew landed, and waited in the garden while the lock-keeper dried Jim's clothes. The man lent him some of his own while the others were drying; and Jim, coming out of the little rose-cottage in a fustian jacket, top-boots, and a fur cap, found Miss Flower sitting on a little green wooden bench under a rose-tree. He saw old Miss Marlow's broad back as she stood, placid, gazing at the river, and Aurelius and Felicia and little Lucy were wandering along the banks under the little row of willow-trees in the meadow, where the cows were crunching the buttercups. There was a bird singing somewhere, and a dog leaping in the grass, and a sweet flood of peaceful light.

Miss Marlow turned round from her contemplation

of the river, hearing Jim's voice. She came up and took his arm, and leaning heavily, proposed that they should follow the others.

'Come, Miss Flower, you are not doing your duty,' said the old lady, 'allowing your cousin to flirt as he does with engaged young ladies.'

But Emily said gravely, 'No, thank you. I am tired, and I will wait for you here.'

Felicia and Lucy had found great bunches of forget-me-nots growing down by the river. They were trying to tempt the cows to come and eat them.

It was about eight o'clock when they reached the station. Little Lucy was to go home immediately, and to bed. She and Emily Flower had come up for a two-days' visit to a friend. Miss Marlow, like an old goose, instead of saying good-by, cordially invited Captain Baxter to come back to supper with them. Wouldn't Miss Flower come too, if they dropped little Lucy on their way? But again Miss Flower refused very decidedly.

'I think Lady Mary expected you, Aurelius,' she said.

'Then I will go with you,' said Aurelius.

'Oh, Miss Flower, our last night!' cried Miss Marlow, reproachfully.

And then poor Emily, who could not bear to seem grasping and unreasonable, said, blushing, that she could easily explain to Lady Mary, and she begged Aurelius to call a hansom for her and Lucy, and the two drove off to the house in Chesham Place, where they were staying. They were to go home the next morning.

Felicia and her aunt went off together in a brougham which had been waiting, and reached Queen Square some little time before the two gentlemen arrived. Felicia's first question was for her grandmother. The old butler said that Mrs. Marlow was in her room. She had been out that afternoon, and came home about four o'clock, complaining of faintness. Felicia thought her looking ill, when she ran in in the glad way that girls burst in after a pleasant day.

'Are you ill, dear grandmamma? We have had such a day,' said the girl. 'Oh dear me, why is it over? I wish you had been with us. Oh, how I wish we were not going to-morrow. What has been the matter?'

'I don't know,' said Mrs. Marlow, a little strangely. 'I have been ill and out of spirits. I could not have stayed away longer from home, Felicia. I have suffered too much for your pleasure as it is.'

Felicia flushed up, hurt. 'My pleasure, dear grandmamma! I don't have so very much.'

'You never think of anything else,' said Mrs. Marlow. 'Girls are always thinking of their pleasure : they don't mind what pain they give others,' the old lady went on, still in this strange excited way. 'There is your grandfather alone; here am I, quite ill and overdone. I shall be thankful when this marriage is over.'

'You need not tell me that,' cried the girl, indignant. 'I know it.'

'When a thing is settled and determined, the sooner it is done with the better,' said Mrs. Marlow.

Fay's heart began to beat.

'Determined and settled, grandmamma!' she cried. 'I think it is cruel the way in which you and grandpapa talk : you have settled everything for us, and it is cruel, yes, cruel! I can do nothing, and no one will help me; and you care for nothing, so long as grandpapa has his own selfish way,' said the girl.

'Hush!' said Mrs. Marlow, white and angry. 'This is not the way for you to speak of your grandfather. I am frightened by your impertinence.'

The poor lady was ill, nervous, thoroughly unstrung, almost for the first time since Felicia had known her. She had never before taken any of the girl's outbursts seriously. Fay, too, was excited, unreasonable. The idea of breaking off had never occurred to her till that day;

T

she was in an agitated state of mind, impressionable, easily upset.

It all happened in a moment. Miss Marlow had barely time to pant upstairs to find the two in high controversy—Felicia in tears, Mrs. Marlow flushed and agitated.

'What is the matter? My dear Eliza, I am so sorry to hear of your indisposition. Fay, go and get ready for dinner,' cried Miss Marlow.

It would have been better, far better for Felicia, if they had ended their little quarrel; fought it out, and made it up with tears. As it was, Miss Marlow separated them, and when the gong sounded, Felicia, still indignant, came into her grandmother's room.

'I am going down, grandmamma; are you ready?'

The old lady was busy packing in the hair-box.

'You had better go, Felicia,' said Mrs. Marlow, without looking up. 'I will follow. Pray remember never again speak to me of your grandfather as you did just now. It is what I cannot listen to.'

She spoke so coldly, that once more Felicia felt a thrill of injured indignation; and she swept downstairs with a heart aching sorely, notwithstanding all the pleasures of the day.

IX.

It was in the evening. They had all finished dinner. Mrs. Marlow had gone up again to see to her packing; Miss Marlow had got up from table and come away into the after-dinner drawing-room, holding Felicia's hand in hers. Baxter—(Miss Marlow, as I have said, had insisted on his coming. I cannot imagine how a woman of her sentimental experience can have been so silly. Is it possible that a thought of thwarting her brother may have added a little malice to her hospitality?)—Baxter, who had come back at the old lady's request to say good-by, was sitting with James in the dining-room. The great windows were wide open upon the balcony, and the dusky park gloomed without, at once hot and cool and mysterious. Felicia, who had scarcely spoken all dinner-time, who was angry still, was summoning up her courage to speak now—to say what was in her heart —to implore Miss Marlow to help her. She loved Jim dearly, dearly. Some day, years and years hence, she would marry him if he wished it; but now, ah, no! it was impossible. She fell down upon her two knees by her aunt's low chair, then for a minute was silent, looking out across the grey evening, watching the distant lights, the bright stars shining clear in the faint summer sky. She thought of the river flowing on—of Jim and his faithful kindness, with more affection and remorse, I think, at this minute, than in all her life before; and then suddenly she burst out, in her childish, plaintive voice, seizing Miss Marlow's hand tight in her two eager little palms—'Oh, tell me what is to happen—what is to happen! Oh, aunt Mary Anne, what shall I do?'

Aunt Mary Anne was a coward at heart. She turned round and stared at the imploring face upturned to her; she had not realised the edged tools with which she had been playing when she brought two impulsive young people together. There had been, as I have said, a little quiet spite in her doings; a little selfishness, for she liked the Captain's company; a little common-sense and good-will, and a feeling that Felicia should see some other man in all the world beside Jim, before she retired with him for ever to the solitudes of Harpington. But Miss Marlow had judged by her own vague and manifold sentimental experiences. Felicia's strange looks that afternoon, her sudden cry of pain, frightened the elder lady.

Miss Marlow felt for a moment afraid of poor eager Felicia, and started up all flustered. 'Do just what you like, my dear,' said the old lady very nervously. 'Nobody can force you to do anything you don't like. I—I must go and see how your grandmother is getting on.' And so saying, the old maid trotted out of the room.

She was gone in a minute, and poor Fay was left, frightened and disappointed — bitterly, bitterly disappointed. 'What was the good of being old, of having lived all those years, if she had no help, no kind word to spare for a poor little thing in trouble?' thought Felicia. There was a something wild and self-reliant in the girl's nature that would not be daunted. She set her teeth. 'I will *make* her hear me,' she said to herself: she would speak again when this evening was over, when Aurelius was gone, and the last happy hour of her life ended for ever. Presently, sitting there still, she found that Baxter had come in and was talking to her; she had hardly noticed him at first, so busy was she thinking about him. She jumped up confused, and then they both with the same impulse went out upon the terrace. 'James is gone off for a smoke,' the Captain was saying, as he followed her. 'There he is under the trees.' Felicia looked and saw that it was not James, but she did not speak.

A sort of sleepy apathy had come over Felicia after her day's excitement. She did not care what happened just at that minute. It was like one of her many visions to be sitting there with Baxter—to hear him speak, to listen to his voice in the dusk. What was he saying? He had been praising Jim for the last five minutes. He felt as if by praising the poor boy he made amends somehow for the unowned treachery in his heart against him.

It was some such feeling which irritated Felicia; she was not going to sham and pretend what she did not feel. In all her life this faculty had been hers, of speaking the truth boldly. Some people have loved her for it; others have hated her. All this day the poor child had been driven to the very utmost end of her powers by inward assaults, and doubts, and terrors, born of the very excitements and happiness of the last few weeks. When Baxter spoke, she said quickly that 'it was not Jim's goodness she cared about, and yet he was a hundred times too good for her.'

'Too good for you!' Baxter said, speaking his thought inadvertently. 'Ask him. He does not think so : why, it would break his heart to part from you.'

'Do you think so?' cried Felicia, desperate. 'Do you think people mind very much when others break their hearts—when these sort of things are broken off? Don't you see how unhappy I am?' she went on.

Was she false to Jim, poor child, in being true? She trusted Baxter so utterly; she was so young, she

felt so convinced that she might trust him; she had
begun the talk just now with her aunt—it was but going
on with it now, leaning forward with her piteous little
face upturned, and waiting for an answer. But no answer
came; no one would help her. Baxter was too loyal to
want her confidence.

'Come and let us talk to Miss Marlow,' he said, very
gravely; 'she will want you to come in.'

'No one—no one will help!' cried Felicia, desper-
ately. 'She won't help me. You won't listen to me,
you won't help me,' she said, as he turned to go; it was
all over—there was no hope anywhere.

'Poor child!' he said.

'Are you sorry for me?' said Felicia, simply. 'Then
I don't mind so much.'

'Sorry!' cried poor Baxter, at an end of his courage.
'Don't you see how it is, Felicia—that I am trying to
be an honest man?'

'Oh, what am I to do? Tell me what I ought to
do!' said Felicia, breaking into tears.

Poor little thing! Her heart beat, her tears flowed.
She trembled so she could not stand, and she put out
her hands wildly to grasp some support. She had no
strong sense of duty. When had she ever seen duty
practised in that dreary self-seeking household? She

did not love Jim as she loved Aurelius. She could not understand that, loving and trusting him, she should not appeal to him.

'Oh, help me!' she said once more, wringing her hands. 'Oh, I cannot, cannot go back.'

You blame him, and so do I, that he was weak; that he did not turn away and leave her; that he caught her two poor little outstretched hands.

'Oh, Felicia,' he said again, 'do you think it is you only who are unhappy? Don't you see that I—— that some debts are almost more than we can pay?'

And then he stopped short. What was he saying? What could he say or do that was not a treachery to his friend? And yet these two loved each other; and was it fair that their whole love and life should be marred so that one person should be made half happy, half content? Only, somehow, Aurelius could not reason thus.

'James trusts us; and he is right,' said he, in an altered voice.

Poor Aurelius! If Felicia had been older, different, more able to decide; but, as it was, he felt that it was for him to take a part. Felicia, heaven bless her! was ready to give up her faith, her word, if he had desired it. He had dropped her two hands. She stood crying still, and leaning against a chair.

'I will do what you think I ought,' she said.

It was at that minute that a light from the room fell upon the two, and that someone came and stood in the window,—some one with a pale face, who did not speak for a minute; then Miss Marlow, following quick and bustling out—

'Why, James, where have you been?' she said. 'I have been looking -for you. There is a telegram for you. Dear me, it is getting quite chilly, and they have not brought the tea. Would you ring, Captain Baxter?'

'I am afraid I must be going,' said Baxter, in a steady voice. No one would have guessed from his voice that anything unusual had happened, though his face might have told the story, had the light been upon it. He nodded to James, shook hands with Miss Marlow. Felicia never moved or looked up, nor did he look at her again. Aurelius went down the stairs and passed out by the narrow iron wicket into the Park, and then all his strength left him. He went and leant against the railings, resting his arm upon the iron, and covering his eyes with his hand. Shut eyes or open, he saw that trembling, wildly-appealing face. It was no use,—it was in vain he had known Felicia. He would do his duty, heaven help them both. His part was clear for the present; he must go, and see Felicia no more.

When Aurelius had said good-night to James, the young man had scarcely responded. Baxter did not know how long he had been standing in the window or how much he had heard of what had passed. Aurelius, sorry as he was, vexed, troubled, unhappy, could not but feel that he had acted as an honest man as far as James was concerned. Towards poor little Felicia his conduct had been less praiseworthy. Leaving her, he felt like a traitor, poor fellow; and yet what could he do but leave her? Where it was all to end, Aurelius could not tell. He was a man not greatly given to self-dissection and examination. His life had been too active for more than a sort of *jour le jour* conscience. He knew that on the whole he hoped to do his duty as a gentleman and a soldier: to wrong no man or woman, to speak the truth, to take a fair advantage of the enemy when he saw a chance. For all his thirty-five years there was a certain boyish rigidity about him; and having said that black was blue, or discovered that he intended to leap a five-barred gate, or be in such a place by such a day, black was blue in his eyes, he leaped the gate, he went through any inconvenience to keep his word. I do not know that there is any particular advantage in playing this sort of game of skill with fate and inclination. But it is a way some people have, and they are honest people for the most part.

Aurelius, contrary to his wont, had allowed himself to drift a little along the stream in the pleasant company he had been keeping of late. Now he stopped short, and as he stood for a minute by the iron railing, he made up his mind. No; he would not go any more to the house. He would not say good-by to Felicia. He would not meddle in the business. He could not help it if the girl was to be sacrificed. She was not the first or the last woman to make a mistaken marriage, and it was no affair of his. So Baxter walked away angry through the twilight of the summer's night, quick, straight, rigid, disappearing rapidly into the gloom. As he went along he saw Felicia's sad eyes appealing everywhere, through the glimmering twigs on the trees, shining from the stars, and once in the gas-lit windows of a shop-front. He did not care, he hardened himself and walked on quicker. Poor Aurelius! he thought it was a shame to leave her. He told himself again that it was a crime that two people should be sacrificed for so little cause. He knew James well enough—that scrupulous soul—to be sure that a word would set his conscience swaying and whirling, and secure Felicia's liberty. He knew all this, he knew it would be right. He felt that he was acting wrongly and cruelly, and inflicting unnecessary pain; and yet, somehow, right as it might be to interfere, he (Baxter) was determined that the deed should not be of his doing. He should not be the one to hand his friend the weapon with which to destroy his happiness, nor to suggest to Felicia the possibility of inflicting upon her lover a deadly wound. And so he walked away with brisk steps farther and farther from the dim balcony where the passionate cry had so nearly touched him, where the poor, pale, trembling little creature was still crouching in the dark.

Poor little Felicia! Baxter was gone, and the child, shrinking out of sight, sat down upon one of the low window-steps. James went to find his telegram. The tea-tray was brought up, then Miss Marlow came and called her, and went away. Fay gave no answer. She only wanted to be alone—to be left to hide herself there in the grey darkness and melancholy of the night. There was a black corner behind a little laurel-tree in a box. Felicia—poor little Daphne that she was—longed to creep into the narrow dark hole and stay there. Never come out again, never hear her own voice speak again, never ask people for help and be refused any more. No one helped —no one cared for her. She covered her face with her hands at the thought—abandoned and despised. Ah! if she could only be nowhere; but wherever she was she cumbered the earth, thought poor little Fay in her despair. Would there be vast groves of laurel, I sometimes wonder, if men and women possessed the power of changing themselves at will into inanimate trees in moments of shame and bewilderment? What a terrible boon it would be to humanity! One can imagine the fatal wish granted—leaves springing from the slender finger-ends, the wreath of laurel creeping round their heads, the narrow choking bark enclosing them in its rapid growth. And then the faint aromatic breath of the prussic acid, and then the wind shivering among human leaves. Poor Fay would have wildly grasped at the power if it had been hers at that minute; but now-a-days, little girls in trouble can only cry and sit with their faces hidden in their hands, instead of becoming stars and streams and plants. She had spoken in an impulse, and now that the impulse was over, what would she not give to have been silent—her life, her right hand, anything, everything. So the night wore on, the black leaves rustled close to her shining head, London was rolling itself asleep and quiet by degrees.

Felicia at last hearing some clock strike eleven across the house-tops, pulled herself wearily up, and came out of her hiding. Very pale she looked, with a black smudge upon her white muslin dress, and wild, sad eyes, with great pupils. She could not see, coming into the dazzle of the drawing-room lamps, but she heard voices calling her, 'Felicia, Felicia!' They seemed to be everywhere; and then James, who had come into the room, rushed up to her. 'Oh, Felicia,' he said, ' I have been looking for you. Go—go to grandmother—there is terrible news from home. . . .

While Felicia had been absorbed in her own griefs and pre-occupations the great laws of life and death and fate had not been suspended, and the news had come that the Squire was dead.

He had been seized with some fatal attack in a field, and carried to a cottage close by, where he died. He had been found by some labourers.

X.

JAMES and Felicia never forgot that terrible night. When the morning came, her despair of a few hours before seemed like a remembrance of some old tune played out and come to an end abruptly in the midst of its most passionate cadence. The tunes of life stop short just in the middle, and that is the most curious part of our history. Another music sounds, mighty, sudden, and un-expected, and we leave off our song to listen to it, and when it is over some of us have forgotten the song we were singing. Perhaps in another world it may come to us again.

This death-music was now sounding through the old house in Queen Square. The poor grandmother lay crushed and stunned by its awful thunder; the old aunt, to whom it was familiar enough, came and went with a troubled and yet accustomed face.

' You had better not go to your grandmother, child,' she said, looking into the room; ' she is best alone.'

Fay appealed to Jim, who looked distressed and took her hand in his, and to comfort her he said they would go together, when aunt Mary Anne was below.

And so about midnight there was an opportunity, and the two went upstairs together. The unshuttered windows let in the gleam of a starry sky, for the vapours had drifted away. They came along the passage to the door of the dim front bedroom, where Felicia had left her angry grandmother a little while before, and where she was now lying stricken, cold, and motionless, and stretched at full length upon the great bed. There was a dim night-light in the room, and they seemed to feel the hard, stony grief as they came in; to meet it,—a presence with a vague intangible form. Felicia, with a beating heart, stood by the bedside. Mrs. Marlow never moved nor spoke. At last the girl knelt down, and softly and imploringly kissed the old brown hand. It was moved away. 'Grandmamma, dear grandmamma!' sobbed Felicia; but her grandmother, in an odd, harsh, hissing voice, said, 'Is James there?' and when he came said, still in this quick strange way, 'I want to be alone, James. Take her away.'

Poor Fay! she was trembling like a little aspen, and as she got up from her knees she held to the chair by the bedside. She was hurt and wounded almost beyond bearing. She put her hand to her heart: 'Oh, grandmamma,' she faltered, 'I who love you so——'

But Mrs. Marlow never moved, or looked, or answered, and James putting his arm round Felicia, brought her away gently and closed the door. Once outside in the passage, Felicia cried and cried as if her heart would break. Miss Marlow came upstairs, and finding Fay there tried to scold her.

'You should not have gone to her when I told you not. She is not quite in her right mind,' said the old lady; 'and people in her state often turn against those they love best. You must be good and patient, and James shall come and fetch you. I think—Jim, don't you think—Fay had better stay here and pack up after we are gone, and then you can come back for her to-morrow?'

And poor Fay meekly assented, crying still, and

utterly crushed and worn out. But she would not go to bed : nobody went to bed that night. There was an early morning train at six o'clock, by which the travellers were to go. A conveyance had to be found, preparations had to be made, packing done, and notes written. Felicia fluttered about, trying to help, utterly weary. Then at last she lay down, about two in the morning, on the golden sofa in the drawing-room, aud slept till a cab driving up through the silence awoke her. She knew it was the cab which had come to take the others away, and she jumped up from the sofa and went out on the stairs : she was afraid to go to Mrs. Marlow's room.

Felicia stood with a wistful face waiting to see them off, but her grandmother passed her without a word or a look. The women came down together, followed by James, with bundles and cloaks upon his arm. Miss Marlow stopped to kiss Fay and bid her go to bed and try to sleep. Jim said with his kind face that he would come back ; and then they were gone, haggard mourners, in the light of the clear early dawn. The cab-wheels rolled and echoed through the silent streets. Fay stood where they had left her, listening to the sound, but presently a kind housemaid came and begged her to come to bed, and helped Felicia to undress, and brought her a cup of tea and sat by her bedside till she had fallen asleep.

When Felicia awoke it was ten o'clock, and a misty morning sun was streaming into the room. The housemaid had been opening and shutting the door and peeping in many times, and she now appeared to ask Miss Marlow if she would come down to breakfast, or if the butler should clear away.

Felicia said she would come down, and dressed in a hurry and ran downstairs, with an indefinite impression of a scolding from someone. But there was no scolding: only the teapot, *The Times* all to herself, a little dish of cold buttered toast, a new pot of strawberry jam sent up by the sympathising housekeeper. Felicia liked the jam, but she had no great appetite, and presently she forgot to eat, and sat looking at her own reflection in the teapot, and conjuring up one last scene at home after another, and picturing the sad home-coming.

There was her grandfather standing before her, as she had seen him that last time, stooping to button the leather apron of the gig. She seemed to see him riding off on the white horse, with his grey wideawake pulled tight over his grey head; or coming home and walking into the morning-room where she and her grandmother were sitting: then she saw him under the tree that sunshiny day busy over his accounts. Poor grandfather! he had mended her wheel-barrow for her when she was a little girl ; and one delightful day she remembered he had taken her in the gig to a farm-house, and given her a cup of milk with his own hands. A crowd of thoughts and remembrances came, and were driven away by a crowd of fancies of what was now, of Harpington all gloomy and shut up. Felicia was so frightened at last that she rang the bell for old Matthew to clear away (Matthew was a portly and prosperous old butler, very different from the poor drudge at Harpington). Matthew stopped a long time, but at last Felicia saw him carry off the last plate and knife, and then she found herself alone once more with the bare dining-room table before her : the mahogany sideboard, the mahogany wine-cases, and the print of Queen Adelaide over the chimney. She tried the drawing-room for a change. When animate things are away, inanimate things attain to a strange life and importance of their own. All the gold tables and couches seemed to spread themselves out to receive her. Felicia sank down in a corner of the sofa and took the first book that came to her hand; but somehow she could only see the legs of the chairs and the tables, the stuffed birds, and the bust of Miss Marlow in her youth nodding. When she had tried to read for ten minutes, she thought she had been sitting there for hours and hours, with Roger's *Italy* open before her, and the prints of the mountains, and the reflection of

the little boat sailing in the finely-etched lake. Was that
horrible little boat never going to reach the shore?
Felicia shut up the book and threw it down on the cushion
beside her. She was accustomed to being alone; but
alone was different at home, where she knew every corner
of the house, with the garden, and the farm, and the village children to play with. This was hateful. How could
Miss Marlow bear such a life, so strange and still, and
crowded with chairs and tables? Felicia did not feel
that she might run from the top of the house to the
bottom, dive into outhouses and cupboards,—as she did at
home: here to gaze through glass-doors at the shells and
Japanese gods, and through glass-windows at the silent
old houses opposite in Queen.Square was all that she dared
to do. Felicia had taken a horror of the balcony. She
went into the passage, and looked for a long while at the
old brown house opposite, with the dim slit windows; at
the statue of Queen Anne standing calm in all her ruffles
and frills. It must be very dull to be a statue, Felicia
thought. She wandered up to her own room, but the.
grandmother's door was open,and through that open door
passed a troop of sad hobgoblins : all the grandmother's
stern looks, all the miseries of the night before, coming
with a rush, and surrounding her.

Felicia fled into the passage again. She looked at

the pasteboard effigy, painted and glazed, of a little page in the corner. In one of the glass cupboards on the stairs was a plate which put her in mind of the old dish at Harpington. There was a garland and some scroll-work. But it was not the same, for the clasped hands were missing, nor was Sola written on the scroll. What a horrid thing it was to be alone. Sola—Sola meant alone as well as the only one. Fay made up a little story of some Portia asking her knights to choose off which of the two plates they would dine; and one knight said,—' I will dine alone, lady, for I have a good appetite, and don't care to share my meal.' And the other knight said he would never touch food again unless one only lady would consent to break bread with him. And then Felicia began to wonder what the lady would say, suppose she liked the greedy knight best. That was a difficult question to answer, and as she was debating it she heard a ring at the bell, and she leant over the banisters to see who it could be.

One of her two knights was at that minute standing outside the door, and she knew his voice when he asked if Miss Marlow was at home, and if Mrs. Marlow was gone back to Harpington.

Then Matthew began a long, long story, and when finally he made way for Captain Baxter to come into the

hall, it seemed to Felicia that it was like the stream of
life rushing into the hushed house again, and that the door
of the lock had opened, and that her boat was rising upon
the rising waters; but she started away as usual, and ran
and hid herself in the little dressing-room out of Miss
Marlow's bedroom, where, after a long search, the housemaid found her.

XI.

MEANWHILE poor Baxter was waiting in the dining-
room and looking forward with some perturbation to his
interview. He had had two lines from James that
morning begging him to call in Queen Square, and
telling him what had happened. 'If I cannot get back
to-morrow, I am going to ask you to bring Felicia
to us,' James wrote. Aurelius confounded James's
stupidity. Why was Felicia left behind? Why was
he, of all people in the world, chosen to escort her to
Harpington?

Baxter could not pretend to any great personal regret

for the old Squire, but for the poor widow he felt a great compassion, and as for Felicia, well, it would delay her marriage, poor little thing, and so far at least she was the gainer. It was not in human nature not to be glad of the excuse to see her again, although all the way Aurelius railed at his friend, and said to himself he deserved his fate for his dulness and want of comprehension.

Was Jim so dull? He knew Baxter better than Baxter knew himself, and by the light of his own honest heart he judged his friend. Baxter need not have been afraid of the meeting. The long sad night had come like a year between Fay and the indignant tears she had shed for herself the night before. They were wiped out. Baxter's first word brought other tears into her eyes, tears of regret and of feeling for others. Felicia was a whole year older in experience than she had been when he last saw her. As she came into the room with half flashing eyes, Baxter felt ashamed of his alarms, and met her quite humbly, saying something about the shock that they had had and his note from James. 'I came to see if I could do anything for you?' he said.

Felicia shook her head and sat down listlessly in the big chair by the empty fireplace.

'I am alone here,' she answered, looking away. 'There is nothing wanted. Poor grandmamma went away

before six o'clock this morning. She could not bear
to have me with her, and so they left me here to wait.
I want nothing, thank you.'

'Poor child!' Aurelius said. He was more sorry for
Felicia, left alone for a day with these gloomy fancies,
than for the whole life-agony of the widowed woman.
He was, poor fellow, in a state of indescribable pity,
vexation, that he could do nothing to help this poor
little stricken creature. This time it was not Felicia
who appealed to him; it was Baxter appealing to
Felicia. 'I wish you would let me do anything for
you,' he said. Something in his sympathising looks
roused the girl's indignation. It was too late; she
did not want his kindness now. For Felicia was used
to be adored, and to command poor Jim, and to
speak her mind plainly enough. Her almost childish
admiration and confidence in Baxter had received a
shock. She had discovered that their friendship meant
very little after all; that to count upon people outside
is of little use in home affairs. To think of her own
feelings seemed a sort of sacrilege now at this time.
Last night, when she asked him to help her, he left her;
to-day, when she did not want him, he came with offers
of help that meant nothing at all. There was a certain
combativeness, a certain determination in Felicia's cha—

racter—a horror of ridicule, a want of breadth and ,
patience of nature, all of which feelings kindling
suddenly brought a bright flush of angry colour into her
pale cheeks. 'Jim will be here before long,' she said.
'He will take care of me. *Now* I want nothing from anyone else.'

'Good-by,' said Aurelius. 'Please remember, however, that if you want me ever at any time anywhere I
will come.' He spoke so humbly that it was impossible
to be angry. Felicia looked at him steadily with her
curious grey eyes; her mouth quivered, the colour died
out of her cheeks.

Felicia's heart began to sink as soon as Baxter had left
the room. She sat quite still, and the minutes became
hours again, and time appeared interminable, and release
so far, far off, that it seemed to this impatient little creature as if in that one instant she had waited for an eternity
—an eternity with James at the end of it! Felicia had
said good-by, the door was closed, the parting was over,
time had passed, and now, with a very simple impulse, she
sprang up and ran out into the hall. Aurelius was still
there, turning at the many complicated locks and chain-
works that Miss Marlow considered necessary for her
security and old Matthew's. They had done Felicia good
service on this occasion.

.   Baxter turned, hearing his name called, and saw Fay in the doorway. 'Will you do me a kindness now directly?' she said impetuously. 'Will you take me home? I want to go. I can't bear to stay here any longer.'

'Had not you better wait till you hear from Jim?' said Baxter, coming back, and not much surprised. 'I am ready at any time, but he may be on his way.'

'I have been thinking of it. He will not come till to-morrow,' said Felicia, sharply. 'Will you do this for me or not? Please do,' said the girl. 'I do so want to get away. They must want me; they can't be so cruel as not to want me. Don't you think so?'

'They only want to spare you,' said Baxter, but when she begged again he could not resist her any longer. 'Will you like to go by the five o'clock train?' he asked.

'Yes,' said Felicia, eagerly. 'Is that the soonest? Please come and fetch me.' And Baxter said he would come, and then went to put off half-a-dozen engagements. He thought the girl would be better off in a home, no matter how sad, than vexing and chafing in the solitudes of Queen Square.

And so it happened that Felicia came back to Harpington all of a sudden. She and Baxter scarcely spoke to each other during the three hours they were on the road. He had come to take care of her, and not to make himself agreeable ; and he conscientiously read the paper in a corner of the railway carriage. Fay looked at him once or twice, surprised at first by this silence, and then she watched the fields flit by the telegraph-posts, the cows, the cottages with their smoking chimneys and all their inhabitants; and so they sped along from one county to another ; here and there came a shining hamlet, now a gig passing a bridge, now a woman carrying a bundle. Felicia tried to follow some of the people with her mind, but another cow, another gig, another tree-stump, would come and drive out the remembrance of the last. Fay, as I have said, had almost put away the remembrance of the night before. She had thought she should never be able to look at Baxter again to speak to him, but now she felt that they might be friends once more. He was changed, but Felicia was too full of her own thoughts. to perceive this. What a strange progression of new feelings and realisations had hold of her—visions of home—visions of London delights—visions of the sorrowful, terrible present, and of the happy past, and of the future of marriage, of loneliness, of doubtful hope.

And so, if Baxter was changed and silent, Felicia, too, was changed and silenced. There were some other people in the carriage who did not find out the two were travelling

together. One old gentleman, interested by the pair of
innocent, penetrating grey eyes that he caught scanning
him, asked the young lady if she was travelling alone, and
if there was anything he could do for her.   Then for the
first time Baxter looked up from his paper, and said in his
blackest and stiffest manner that the lady was under his
care.

It was nearly eight o'clock when they got to the
station. Baxter had telegraphed from London, and he
expected to find Jim upon the platform; but there was no
Jim, no sign, and the only thing to do was to walk to the
inn and order a fly. They waited under the rose-grown
porch in the twilight. Everything seemed sweet, and
still, and peaceful. A gardener belonging to the inn was
pumping water for the pretty old garden flowers—lillies,
and lupins, and marigolds, and white honey-suckles; the
sky was sweet with sunset, and the air with perfume. A
couple of dusky figures stood in the middle of the street
talking quietly; an old woman came to the door of her
cottage. This purple dusk was making everything beautiful, and how fragrant the air was after the vapid London
breath they had been living in !

They had a long, sweet, silent drive across the fields,
and between dim horizons and wooded fringes. The evening star came and shone over the twilight silver and purple

world before they got to their journey's end. Baxter was silently happy and so was Felicia, who, for a mile or two, had almost forgotten the sorrow to which she was travelling, in the peace and sweetness of the journey. But when the house appeared above the hedge at the turn of the road, her heart began to beat and everything came back to her.

'The gates are closed,' said the girl, startled, as they passed the front of the house.

The gates were closed for the first time since Felicia could remember, and the ivy and wild creepers had been crushed and torn in the process.

This one little incident, perhaps, brought all that happened more vividly to Felicia's mind than anything else that had gone before. They stopped at the back door, the front gate being locked, and Aurelius desired the fly-man to wait, and came with Felicia to see her safe into the house before he drove away. They crossed the stable-yard and the end of the garden, and so reached the terrace along which were the windows, barred and fast, except one looking more black than the rest. And suddenly came a cruel minute for Felicia, in which all the pain of parting, all the sadness into which she was going, all the gloom of that great shut house and of her hopeless future, seemed realised and concentrated.

Baxter, too, looked up at the gloomy walls behind which little Fay was about to disappear; there stood the hall, closed and black, and he thought of the poor raving widowed heart aching within, and with a pang he thought of the little white victim standing beside him.

'Good-by,' he said, putting out his hand quickly.

'Oh, I am frightened,' said Felicia, not taking it, not looking, and trembling and standing irresolute. 'Oh, what shall I do?'

'There is nothing to be afraid of,' said Baxter, kindly. 'I have seen a great many people die. It is a much more peaceful process than living. I don't think you need be afraid.' Felicia sighed, but did not answer.

'Look, is not that study window open?' Baxter asked.

'Yes, but—but I could not go in there alone,' said the girl, as with a shaking hand she tried to unfasten the door. 'Don't go yet, please don't go,' she said.

'I will wait here as long as you like,' said Baxter. 'Perhaps James will see me for a minute. You can send me word.'

'Yes,' said Felicia. She had got the door open at last. Once more she said—'Please wait, please don't leave me yet. I will come back to you.' She spoke in a shrill, nervous voice, and the words travelling through the silence, woke up James, who had fallen asleep on the study sofa, utterly worn out and tired after his journey, his sleepless day and night of agitation and excitement. Had he dreamt them? had he heard them? He did not know—he started from his sleep, from a vague dream of Baxter and Felicia in the garden outside. He sat up and listened,—'Don't leave me yet! I will come back to you!' He heard her voice plainly ringing in his ears,was— it to him she was speaking? Was it Felicia come to make him well and happy by her presence? or was it Felicia speaking to someone else? Felicia false, Felicia lost to him for ever!

XII.

Poor Jim! It was when they were going down into the lock the day before that he had made up his mind to it, and told himself that cost what it might he must give up his darling. Felicia was not for such as him. She was too bright and brilliant a creature to mate with any but her own kind.

Little Jim was a hero in his way. His whole life had been a forlorn hope. He had made up his mind, but in this feverish dream from which he was waking, he had forgotten his calmer self-decision and courage—only the natural pain was there, the jealousy, the humiliation, the heart-burning. Aurelius' telegram had come, and he had meant to go and meet them, but as he was waiting, turning over papers in the study, till the time should come to start, he had fallen asleep. Miss Marlow was upstairs with her sister-in-law; the whole house was silent, and no one had come near the study, and Jim for the last hour or two had been lying in a fever, dreaming uneasy dreams and moaning in the deserted room. And now when he started wide awake from his sleep, he was wide awake, but dreaming still in a sort of way, forgetting all his resolutions, remembering only the fancies that had haunted his sleep. Felicia outside with Baxter! Ah false! ah faithless! As the door opened, and she came in, Jim had groped his way to the table, and struck a light.

'I knew you were there,' he said, turning his haggard face to greet her. 'Oh, Felicia, I was dreaming. Are you going to leave me, quick, tell me? How could I bear it? How can I bear it? It will kill me. I have little enough life; you will take it all if you go.'

He looked so strange and so excited that his cousin was frightened.

' Going, Jim ? What do you mean ? '

' I heard you say so to someone outside,' he went on, in his strange agitation.

' Dear Jim,' said Felicia, trembling still, ' be quiet. Hush ! pray hush ! See, lie down here. I—I won't leave you,' she said ; and a faint glow came into her pale cheeks. ' Lie still. Don't be afraid. You have had some nightmare,' faltered the girl, knowing full well that it had been no nightmare, but her own words, which he had overheard.

' I thought I heard you say you were going,' Jim said, still half distraught. ' It was a dream then—I had fallen asleep. Oh, thank heaven ! Oh, my Felicia ! '

She soothed him, she quieted him with a hundred kind words and looks, and all the while her heart smote her. She was ashamed to meet his honest upturned loving glance.

' Poor boy,' said Felicia, passing her cool hand across his forehead. ' Lie still, dear,' she said. ' I am going for one minute. I shall come back to you.'

He sprang up with a frightened sort of cry.

' Ah ! now I know it was true,' he said. ' Felicia, Felicia ! You are going. I shall wait and wait, and you will never come back.'

x

'I swear I will come back,' said Felicia, earnestly, fixing her great grey eyes upon her cousin.

A minute after, as Baxter stood waiting, listening for the voices, Felicia appeared for one moment in the darkness of the doorway. 'Good-night, good-by, and thank you,' she said. 'I am not afraid any more, and I am thankful I came,' and she gave him her hand and was gone.

'Did Baxter come back with you?' James asked, as Felicia came back to him. He seemed like himself again, calm and different, and with his own natural expression. 'Have you sent him away? It was a pity,' he said. 'A pity, a pity,' he repeated, thinking, poor fellow, of himself as he spoke. 'Dear,' he said. 'I think I was half asleep just now. I don't know what nonsense I talked. Forgive me.'

'You are quite tired and worn out,' said Felicia. 'You must go to bed, Jim, directly. May I go to grandmamma?' But James begged her to wait, and he went and found Miss Marlow, and then he went to bed as he was bid.

Miss Marlow was surprised to see the girl, but welcomed her kindly. 'So Captain Baxter brought you? Well, I am glad you are come,' and then she told Felicia a long long history of their coming home.

The old lady was very gentle, and cried a little, and

she came with the girl to her own little room, past the door of the state apartment where the poor old grandfather was lying. And Fay followed her about meekly, seeing all with her startled grey eyes. Aurelius was gone, but she did not mind. When everybody else was so unhappy, Felicia accepted her own share with more resignation. Her grandmother would not see her—that was the thing which most troubled her. Jim was very ill— that was evident—she must do what she could to help him. And then, utterly wearied out, Felicia fell fast asleep, with all the trouble and doubt round about her, and the darkness and gloom of the night, and dreamt the hours peacefully away till the morning light came to awaken her.

XIII.

Two days more, and the closed gates were opened to let the old Squire's funeral pass through, travelling down the periwinkle walk, and followed by the steps of a few old neighbours. Baxter came to the churchyard, but did not come back to the house; and then the blinds were drawn up, and the business of life began once more; only Mrs. Marlow remained still in her room, and scarcely ever left it. The lawyers came to read the will. It was dated many years back. The house and the chief part of the estate had been left to Jim's father, and now consequently fell to the share of the young man himself. There was a jointure settled upon Mrs. Marlow which (under a stringent clause) she was to forfeit if she married again. Felicia (whose mother had married an offending cousin) was only to have a hundred a year. Another later will had been prepared, but never signed; it was much to the same effect as the first, only that the jointure was increased and more in proportion to the bulk of the old man's property. He had left nearly 6,000*l.* a year behind him, and Jim, who had never until now possessed a spare sovereign to do as he liked with, had money in stocks and land, and cheque-books, and credit without stint. . . .

James was closeted all day with different people, lawyers, and agents, and tenants; and one day a doctor came over from the neighbouring town, and Jim declared next day that he had business in London. Little Lucy, who happened to meet Felicia that day, told her her papa had gone to town with Mr. Marlow.

James came back, and Felicia tried to think that he

was the same, but she felt a difference. He was busy arranging, docketing, putting away. People came and went; Felicia scarcely spoke to him. She dined with him (Felicia was surprised to see that Jim could carve), but immediately after dinner James would go away into the study.

As for Aunt Mary Anne, being naturally of a cheerful and gregarious disposition, she found it all very dull, and packed up at the end of a week and went off to Cheltenham for a change.

The day Miss Marlow left Felicia begged her grandmother timidly to let her be with her a little more.

'No, no,' said Mrs. Marlow, with a little shiver. ' Pray don't ask it ; go—you agitate me.'

So Felicia went away, pained and forlorn, flitting about with a feeling of disgrace, and the strange uneasy sense of being some tamed animal that had lost its master and was suddenly set free.

One day—it was a little thing, but she took it foolishly to heart—her crystal bracelet, that she liked to wear, came unclasped and fell off her arm. She went roaming about a whole morning looking for it in the empty rabbit-house, in the kitchen-garden, on the terrace walk.

James, coming out of the study for a little turn on

the terrace, was struck by Felicia's scared, wobegone
face.

She had been sitting on the step for half-an-hour in
the sun.

'Fay, what is the matter?' said Marlow, in his old
familiar voice, as he came up to her.

'Nothing,' said Felicia, looking up.

Nothing! That was just the answer to his question.
Nothing to hope, to fear, to love, to try for. She did
not think that James loved her now: she knew her grandmother had taken a strange hatred and aversion to her
presence.

'Nothing?' said James, looking gravely at her
troubled face.

'I have lost my pretty bracelet,' said Felicia; 'but
that is nothing, of course. And everything is horrid, but
it does not matter.'

'But is everything horrid?' said James, sighing.
'You have lost a bracelet,' he continued, absently, feeling
in his pockets. 'I picked one up this morning on the
landing.' And he pulled out Felicia's beloved gold and
crystal ring.

She seized it with a little cry of delight. 'Oh, how
glad I am!' she said. 'Thank you, James; how clever
of you to find it.' And she began fastening it on her
slim wrist again.

'How clever of you to let it fall upon the landing,' he said, smiling. 'And now I want to talk to you, Fay,' James went on, sitting down beside her on the step. Then he was silent for a little, then he began very nervously : 'I have been thinking about a good many things these last few days,' he said, 'and happiness has been one of the things. Don't you think, dear, we must not care about it too much?'

'Not care!' his cousin said. 'How can we not care when we do?'

James looked more and more nervous.

' "We bow to heaven that ruled it so," ' he said, hesitating, quoting from a lay preacher. 'I saw Dr. —— when I was in London, and he told me that matters were more serious with me than I had imagined. I don't know how much more, or what may be in store for us ; but, Fay, you and I—our two lives, I mean—belong to something greater than our own happiness, at least one hopes so ; for one's own happiness seems a stupid thing to live for altogether, doesn't it, dear?'

Felicia's circling eyes were fixed upon him. She was twisting her gold bracelet round and round. Jim looked paler and paler as he spoke.

'I think,' he said, 'our duty in life, Felicia—yours and mine—is not to think whether we are very happy or not, or satisfied '—and the poor fellow's voice ached a little as he spoke—'and, perhaps, the mistake we have both made has been that we have thought a little too much of our selves and our own feelings, and not enough of something beyond them . . . .'

' Dear, dear James!' said Felicia, and her eyes filled up with tears.

James went on steadily, holding her hand in his,—

' And I have been thinking that we have both other things to do just now than marrying and giving in marriage. I must go away and try and get well, to live to do a few of these things; and you must—darling Fay, don't cry—take care of grandmother, and be patient with her, and wait here, and love me a little. And then,' resolved to finish what he had to say, he went on hastily, ' There is poor Baxter, who wants to come with me ; and some day, if he comes back to you, Fay, I think you would be doing wisely to try and make him happy. Perhaps, you may not like to think of it just now, but in a little time ——' Jim's voice faltered—' One cannot foretell the future——'

' Oh, Jim, what a hateful, hateful creature I am !' burst out Felicia, covering her face with her hands. I have not deserved anything, and you want me to have everything ; but I will never—never——'

'Hush, hush!' said Jim, gravely; 'take care of grand-mother, and don't make any vows, and—and—trust me a little, Felicia,' he added, smiling a little sadly himself as he got up to go away.

And so Jim cut the knot that bound him—cut it, and all the difficulties that had beset him of late were van-quished. No one had guessed at the depth of his secret grief, and the pain of the parting—not Aurelius, not Felicia, looking up into his calm face, not Jim himself, who thought himself a foolish stupid fellow, but no hero; only it was all over now.

It was the last of the late summer days. As he stood he heard the distant thrill of the birds, the drone of buzzing insects : the warm touch of the sun came fall-ing upon them both. A feeling came to Jim as if he was looking at Fay, with her sweet upturned face, for the last time ; and it was in truth their real parting, though he did not sail for some days later. And yet, of the two at that minute, it was not Jim who was most unhappy. The light of his true heart was shining in his eyes. Felicia never forgot his look : a man of gentle will, stand-ing there, that summer's day, with a gift in his hand, priceless, a life's gift, a true heart's love. And Jim, as he left her, felt that he loved her as she ought to be loved. Loved her enough to leave her with a benediction. He

was a sick, and dull, and stupid fellow; but he had.
played his part like an honest man. Felicia was the only
woman he ever loved, hers the only hand he ever cared to
grasp; but while he held it, he had held it by force, and
when he loosened his hold, the fair hand fell away. And
he was content that it should be so, and he wisely accepted.
the very pain as part of his love.

There is something in life which seems to tell us that.
no failures, no mistakes, no helplessnesses make failure; no.
successes, no triumphs make success. And so James
walked away victorious, leaving the poor vanquished
victress alone upon the sunny steps. Was it Felicia's
wish to be the only one? It was granted, and she did not
care for it. She was alone now, but free. She stood
watching the young fellow as he walked away. Jim's
heart was sad enough, but at rest. Felicia's was beating
with passionate gratitude, with anger against herself, with
a dim new hope for the future, and, at the same time,
with a great new love and regret for the past, for the
tie that was now broken for ever. It was a pang that.
lasted her for all her life.

Later that day, as she was passing through the morning-room, she happened to catch sight of the old Sola
plate through the glass of the china cupboard, and with
one of her quick impulses, Felicia opened the glass doors,.

took it quickly off the shelf, and flung it to the ground, where it lay broken in many pieces at her feet. . . . . Is this the end of the story? Does any story finish while the flame of light is alight, burning up, and reviving and changing from day to day. Fay's story was a blank for a time after Jim left her in charge at Harpington; a blank from all those things which had seemed to her so all-important. In after life her love-story may have begun again. But that was when she was alone in the world; when those who loved her best were gone; and Baxter, coming back after years of absence, met her as of old—lonely, sad, glad, eager, and unchanged, flitting between the grey walls of the old Harpington House.

MORETTI'S CAMPANULA

MORETTI'S CAMPANULA.[1]

I.

'That very time I saw, (but thou could'st not,)
Flying between the cold moon and the earth,
Cupid all arm'd : a certain aim he took
At a fair vestal, throned by the west ;
And loos'd his love-shaft smartly from his bow,
As it should pierce a hundred thousand hearts :
But I might see young Cupid's fiery shaft
Quench'd in the chaste beams of the wat'ry moon ;
And the imperial vot'ress passed on,
In maiden meditation, fancy-free.
Yet mark'd I where the bolt of Cupid fell :
It fell upon a little western flower,—
Before, milk-white ; now purple with love's wound,—
And maidens call it, love-in-idleness.
Fetch me that flower. . . ."

A Midsummer-Night's Dream.

IF you could see Dorchester House, age-worn, sun-burnt, and wind-beaten, with many wooden shutters flapping in the sun, with strange sweet southern tufts of weed springing along its cornices, and from one and another marble window-ledge, house-leeks with soft pink heads, delicate

[1] Moretti's Campanula is a flower that grows among the Alps on precipitous rocks.

feathery grasses; here and there a trailing nasturtium hanging like a fringe and swinging against the wall, and in the courtyard an orange-tree and a cactus or two, and a mountain-ash with its burning flame of scarlet berries—you would see the palace of the family of Pavis, one of the oldest in South Tyrol. It stands in a little sun-baked town, half-way between Italy and Germany, among the Venetian Alps, and its many shutters open out upon a green and deserted-looking piazza, where a donkey feeds and women spread their linen strips to bleach. . . . There is an hotel upon the piazza and a coppersmith's shop, from whence comes a monotonous sound from the blows of the great hammer; and then on the opposite side of the green stands a church, vast, and empty, and tawdry, as many of these North of Italy churches are, of which the silent dusty gloom and emptiness suggest a curious contrast to the fervour of North Tyrol. Here the vast wide open doors show fading deceptions of pasteboard and tinsel ornament, and admit a dazzle of dust-flickered light into the gloom. Worshippers are scarce now, but in the time of the father of the present Count de Pavis they were more numerous. The Countess and her daughters were often to be seen in their places.   In these churches brazen plates are affixed to the benches with names engraved thereupon; those of Claudia, Irminia, Valeria de Pavis, are still to be deciphered upon the worn brass plate that marks the seat of the Pavis family, though Claudia, the mother, is long since dead, and Irminia and Valeria have married and left their old home in the mountain city. Another name, that of Saverio de Pavis, is also inscribed upon the family plate. He is the owner of the palazzo, but it is said that he does not keep up his mother's pious practices.

One day I wandered into the church: the only worshippers were two girls kneeling near a small open side-door. The light fell upon their youthful heads, upon an altar ornamented with cotton laces and paste-board vases: outside the door was a bright white wall, a creeping pumpkin with great starry golden flower and pantomime-like fruit, and the lizards darting from stone to stone. The girls came away presently, passing out by this white wall to the piazza again, where they had tied up their donkey at the copperman's shop.

The ooppersmith, with whom I had had some dealing, was a kind old fellow. He seemed to love his great saucepans, over which he might now see the two pretty girls' faces, and the donkey's head, and the Palazzo Pavis, and the mountain beyond; and he nodded a friendly greeting as we all passed together.

How delicately lovely the mountains looked, in fair ridges round about the little town: strange peaks of dolomite, crushed, shivered, splintered sharp, with a

Y

network of lines and modellings, of light and passing
shadows; now a cleft, now a pinnacle standing out sharp;
now a shadowy black veil hanging from some topmost
point; and then see it melt away, and the shining crys-
tallised peaks flash quivering and clear. . . . It was a
wonderful fairy country through which we had been
wandering for ten days past—among alps and rocky passes:
—wild fairies they surely are who inhabit them : mossy
trunks hang over precipices; thousands of flowers shine,.
sweet autumn cyclamen, starry parnassus; above and
below, the waters dash, filtering through rocky cups, and
foaming crystal among the fringing leaves and mosses.
Green alps, too, flow from rock to rock along the
mountain-side, where the grey cows are feeding; tranquil
little villages perch along the wandering track, whence
dark eyes watch you as you pass on your way to the
smiling valley below. Strangers are strangers still, and
not yet tourists on the road. The host greets you with
friendly gladness; the fresh straw beds are covered with
the winter-spun linen. The fare is scant sometimes, but
quaint and good. For the chamois-hunters are out upon
their raids, the valleys are spread with waving fields of
Indian corn; there are trout in the lakes and streams.
Along the road the pumpkins are swelling in the sun, and
the flax grows with its fringed plumes, or hangs drying in
yellow bundles from the eaves of the cottages.

All this smiling land lies along the frontier between Austria and Italy. We had crossed the line a dozen times on our way to the little sun-baked town, which seemed to us dreary, and tattered, and saddening, after the prosperous villages. We were going on again that day to the neighbourhood of Marmolata, the noblest mountain of the Rhætian range, and thence home by Bötzen, where civilisation begins.

I, for one, do not wish to cry out against it. The jolts and difficulties in the world of civilised life are mental, instead of physical. The problems are human. There are byways and bold ascents, precipices to skirt, deep and distracting as any of these. Opinions grow instead of crops of Indian corn ; sympathies and aspirations dazzle us and thrill us, in the loneliness of our souls, as do still mountain ranges or wide-spreading horizons. The music of civilised life is not in the song of birds, or the flow of streams, or the tinkling of flocks. Alas ! it is a music sadder and more boisterous and more incomplete ; but it may be there is a deeper tone in it than the calm self-satisfaction of pastoral completeness. Because the cries are loud, the instruments unequal to the tunes they should play, shall people decry it ? Is Nature divine ? Perhaps in the darkest London slum, where dirt and sorrow and filth are massed together, there may be a deeper divinity than in the widest, sweetest valley where sheep are browsing, evening lights shining on the hills, hamlets sprinkling in still nooks, crops ripening in their season, and wayside crosses casting their shade across the precipitous road.

II.

UNDER the dark entrance-porch of the hotel our luggage was piled, and H. and my nephew Tom were looking out for me. The carriage had not come, and all my Italian, such as it was, was wanted to urge the stout old padrona with the garnet necklace to wake up from a sort of trance, and send for it. 'When we pleased; when we pleased. Ah, we were going on to C——. The Count had ordered the carriage. It should come back for us. There was no hurry—no hurry.' But here a tall, pale-faced young man, with spectacles, with a straw-hat, and a green case for plants slung across his shoulders, came striding hastily into the hotel. He nearly tripped up over the strap of my nephew's knapsack: he flushed up impatiently, and kicked it away. 'I have come to say I shall not want the carriage,' he cried, in a harsh, quick voice. 'Supper? No. I shall not sup here to-night.'

'Then Beppo can conduct these gentry by the equipage,' cried the old padrona, brightening up for a single moment to a gleam of intelligence. 'Your servant, Signor Conte.'

The young Count, still impatient, shrugged his shoulders; then, recollecting himself, raised his straw-hat to us, as if to make up for the shrug, and began striding off as quick as he could go, flying along with an odd, swinging walk.

'He is an original,' said the hostess, speaking in her sleep. 'He only thinks of herbs—always herbs—he studies them from one season's end to another. Ah, his father was not of that sort.'

In a few minutes more a little old trembling convey-ance, with swinging handles, bits of string and broken straps, and a youthful but incompetent driver, shivered and.ambled up to the door. Our way led through a melancholy defile, where the white road wound in long zigzags, overhanging the depths below; while the peaks seemed to crowd higher and closer with a wild melan-choly monotony, to which the moan of the torrent flowing in its white stony bed, and straggling between arid flats, seemed to respond. In the distance, far, far a-head of us, down in a dip of the valley, we could see a donkey and someone following, and at a turn of the road we met a little calf, driven along the pass by a peasant-woman. It looked at us and at the horse with lively and suspicious interest; but the calf and the poor old horse were respectively urged on by their drivers, who nodded as they passed. The calf-woman was worn-faced, brown, and kind-eyed. She wore a bead necklace and took off her hat. I don't know why it all seemed so dreary to me, like a presentiment of impending ill. It was but a fancy, for no harm came beyond a variety of bumps, and jerks, and lurches over into the abyss by which we were travelling, so numerous and alarming, that H. exclaimed in horror, and Tom, indignant, jumped down at last and led the horse down the steeper places; while the vivacious young driver amused himself by winding and unwinding the drag at the wrong minute, with immense energy and many exclamations.

Our advance was not very quick, but by degrees we gained upon the donkey, and as we got nearer we saw that there was a young soldier with the two girls, whom I recognised as those I had seen in the church. One girl was sitting on the donkey's back, the other walking a-head, with a free, striding peasant step. Both had their great fair plaits pinned round with many long pins like little arrows. The pedestrian wore a conical hat on the top of her plaits; she had white sleeves, a black bodice and a skirt, and a coral necklace, and her dress was a little above that of the peasants. As she walked she looked up and around in a free yet dreaming way. Her companion on the donkey had discarded the white country sleeves altogether. She was small and delicate-looking, with beautiful red hair and brown eyes; her dress was only black alpaca: she, too, wore a coral necklace. The young soldier spoke to her now and then, but she scarcely answered him: they were evidently brother and sister, from their likeness and peculiar red locks. The donkey tripped along lively and careful; every now and then the young people called it by name: 'Hu, Bruno! Ehu, Bruno!' Bruno seemed to be an independent little fellow, with a very decided will of his own. At one place, in the descent, we all came together to a stream that flows across the road into the torrent below. Bruno and the soldier seemed to have some difference as to the place where it should be forded. The girl jumped off in a fright; the soldier tugged; Bruno pulled, and set his forepaws. Some one cried out from above; the soldier looked round; Bruno seized the moment, jerked the reins out of his leader's hand, and was over before his master could come near him. 'Look, Mary,' said my sister-in-law, 'there is that young man from the hotel.' He was coming scrambling down the side of the pass, leaping with wonderful agility from one splintered rock to another. Every movement looked wild and clumsy and unpremeditated, and yet his progress was secure and unfailing. It seemed a horrible-looking place and impossible to get over; but there he was in a minute, safe on the road, and hurrying after the little party, with his swinging green canteen behind him.

'Well,' said Tom, my nephew, 'I couldn't have done that better myself.' (Tom was a sailor for some years, but he came into a fortune, and is a country gentleman now, and only exerts himself once in a hundred years or so, when my sister-in-law drags him abroad.)

The athlete joined the little party, and after walking with them a short way, suddenly left them, flying off at a sharp ridge of rock and disappearing by degrees. We had got to take an interest in them all by this time. Bruno completely won our hearts by a last sudden dash he made at a haystack that was coming walking along on two blue worsted legs and brown kneebreeches: he overpowered his conductor and got a good bite of sweet dry hay before anyone could prevent him. The hay was going to a little stony lodge on the wayside, from whence a raven and flamingo maiden stepped out to see us pass. Then we began to ascend, and left our fellow-travellers and Bruno behind us, conversing with the apparition; and the dismal gorge came to an end at last in fields of Indian corn, in a tattered village with falling balconies and blackened gables, and fences, and children with wistful faces swarming out to see us pass.

We all breathed more freely as the road climbed up again by the mountain-side into a wider fresher world, while a lovely green valley opened, and high cliffs came rising from still green alps, with evening clouds like bubbles trembling along their ridges; and then, still passing on, we presently reach a terrible valley, where a hundred years ago the crest of a mountain thundered from its height, crushing houses and people and flocks in its fall—crashing up the river, and creating a calm blue lake. Great masses lie scattered as they fell, for who can raise prostrate mountains? But they are wreathed and pine-crowned, and their fierce edges are softened by the sweet-spreading green veil which hangs over all this Alpine country: a veil which only seems rent here and there by the sharp rocky points that burst through it.

III.

'Presently a maid
   Enters with the liquor,
(Half a pint of ale
   Frothing in a beaker).
Gads! I didn't know
   What my beating heart meant;
Hebe's self I thought
   Entered the apartment.
As she came she smiled,
   And the smile bewitching,
On my word and honour,
   Lighted all the kitchen!'

WE were only going a short day's journey to C——, at the other end of the blue lake, and it was still light when we reached the village. There was a cheerful sound of music as we came down into the street, and an echo of one of the Alpine chants that the young men catch up and troll out with great skill, spirit, and good tune, and presently we met a row of five young fellows walking arm-in-arm towards the town, with plumes and flowers in their Tyrolese hats, short sleeves, and long flowered waistcoats, loudly chanting their evening song. It was a feast day, our driver told us, a feast day as far as the bridge (where, by the way, he sent us over, fortunately, in a place where the earth was heaped up to support the planks, so that the horse was able to pull us safe back

again). All the white shirts had turned out in honour of
St. Bartholomew, the little children had their best clean
faces on, the mothers sat in their door-ways resting from
their heavy burdens, the fathers smoked their silver-
topped pipes, the young men walked about arm-in-arm,
as I have said, and a grand game of *pallone* was going on
in the village street.   Our arrival distracted some triflers,
but not so the real players of the game.   The marker stood
under an old arch with his two strange little wooden implements. The balls flew high over the house-tops, rolling
down and dropping from the wide-eaved roofs, sometimes
flying in at a window and violently thrown out again—
the young men leapt after them, and the people shouted
in excitement.

These Tyrolese houses are stables to enter by, with
horses and carriages and cows stowed away ; but as you
mount the stairs each floor improves.   The first floor is
the kitchen and the public room, where you catch a glimpse
of peaked hats, of gaiters, of bottles of wine and shirt-
sleeves.   The hostess comes out of her kitchen to greet
you, and takes you up to the second floor, which is quieter,
fresher, and with flowers in the balcony at the end of the
passage, where you dine.   At Signora Sarti's 'Black
Eagle,' the flowers were brighter, the bedrooms lighter and
more comfortable than any we had yet seen.   The rooms

were clean, great pots of carnation stood promiscuously
on the stove, and in the corner and in the window of the
sitting-room; we saw wooden benches against the wall,
wooden floors, some odds and ends of poles, and then in
the bedrooms huge beds, so high that you had to leap from
ledge to ledge to reach them. A back-door from our bed-
rooms opened upon the outer wooden balcony running
along the back of the house. The balcony looked out upon
what they call the piazzetina—a little grimy back-yard
sort of place, with six dozen arched doors and windows at
all possible angles, looking over and under one another.
Here, too, were more carnation-pots and dried wisps of
flax under the roof hanging out to dry.

Before and behind us were casements with wide open
wooden shutters through which we could see into the lives
of the people. Strange little framed pictures of unknown
existences. How much can four feet by three of one's
daily habits disclose? Not much, perhaps, in a world
where everything is changing and flitting; but here,
where day by day the sun shines upon the same peaceful
sights and customs, it may be enough to give a hint of
them. There was the old tailor sitting on his bed on the
second floor—there was a daily dinner laid at a certain
window at twelve o'clock—there were the three washer-
women living on the first floor. They looked out of

window, stretching their long brown necks with the bead necklaces, their wisps of hair were pinned up like the plaits we had admired on the road, with aureoles of silver pins. (As their brown necks were constantly stretching through the window, the aureoles beamed down not un-frequently upon the passers-by in the street below.) Now comes music again. An air out of the 'Trovatore,' an air out of the 'Dame Blanche.' The musicians are two soldiers in the Austrian uniform : they are singing as they sit at a little table, and we see their glasses filling among the red and yellow cloves that are falling from the window-sill.

Clatter—clatter! 'Here is the donkey,' says Tom, look-ing out of window, and we heard a sound of little hoofs, exclamations, embraces, cheerful girls' voices, and presently the padrona comes in with flushed happy cheeks to ask us what we would have for our meal.

'I should have come sooner, but my son is just arrived,' she said. 'My daughter Fortunata, and Joanna my servant, went into Agordo to meet him.'

'Is he a soldier?' said H., smiling. 'Was there a donkey?'

'Yes, yes,' said the beaming signora. 'The gentry must have passed them. It is two years since I had seen him; now he comes home because I——on business. And here her face fell. 'A mother's heart is in many places,' says the padrona, with a sort of little chronic sigh.

Tom, who was very hungry, and not so much interested as we were in these family details, now asked somewhat inconsequently if there was any fish to be had for dinner.

'Fish? No. The fisherman had to be told the day before, and then he went out at sunrise and caught it; but' (hesitating) 'a friend had sent some wild partridges, and if we liked she would roast a couple. Would we choose white wine or black?'

With the white wine came our dinner :—

1st. A rice soup with little sausages floating in it.

2nd. Slices of a sort of fried plum-pudding.

3rd. Biftek. This is a mince with a sweet garlicky batter, and polenta to eat with it.

4th. The partridges, with prunes.

5th. A sort of white cream-cheese eaten with cinnamon.

Tom complained that it was all puddings, but he ate them with good appetite; and then we went and drank our coffee in the window, watching the lights gleam away on the mountain-tops above the roofs. I could see some one down below also supping off wild partridges at a sort of little terrace where his table was set. From the number before him, and the way he cut them up, I guessed that he was the sportsman who had brought them down. It seemed to me that I knew the green box lying on the table, and I also recognised in the sportsman our wandering Count.

IV.

WE had, strange to say, an acquaintance living at C——, an old lady whom we had met a year before drinking the waters at a watering-place in the Alps, where H. had been sent by a German doctor. She was only a humble sort of companion, she told us, to another old lady, who owned the country-house in which they spent their summer months. She seemed to be loved and trusted by her employer; and able to do as she liked, and she had begged us to come and see her if we passed her way. She assured us that their garden was well worth a visit. We had taken a liking to the gentle, intelligent, somewhat melancholy woman, with her simple Italian ways and ready sympathies. Signora Elizabetta della Santa was tall, with many bones and wrinkles, and a few black and grey hairs. She spoke slowly in a deep guttural voice; she was dressed like an old wall-flower, in dingy yellows and greens for the most part. This evening, strolling out along the street, it occurred to me to look her up, and when I came back to the hotel I thought I would ask for news of my old acquaintance. I went upstairs in the twilight of the landing beneath ours; it led to the terrace, where Fortunata and Joanna were both standing talking to the Count. He seemed to be emptying his vasculum of all sorts of plants, ferns, roots, and flowers, and I did not like to disturb them. Tonina, the padrona's eldest daughter, was very busy in the general room, coming and going from one table to another, with her leathern bag of office strapped to her waist. I looked into the kitchen to see if the mother was there. Yes, the padrona was standing in the last sunlit window with her son. I noticed that Mario, as they called him, was looking odd and flushed, and that his honest face was as red as his hair, but I put it all down to the evening glow, and asked my question without any thought of trouble.

'What does the Signora ask?' said the padrona, hastily. 'Signora della Santa and the Marchesa are here; they live close by. Mario will—no, Fortunata will—you turn to the right by the bridge; you——' but here suddenly her voice failed, and the poor thing burst out crying. 'It's nothing, nothing,' she went on, volubly. 'Don't ask; don't ask; and oh! do not tell the girls that

I am troubled ; they at least shall never know what a cruel——' Mario, who was hissing and spluttering between his teeth, stopped her with a kind impatience.— ' He is here,' said the poor thing, recovering herself, and wiping her eyes. ' He will take care of us, and all will be well now.' And she laid her hand on her son's arm and looked at me, and then at his carrot-face, with wistful tender eyes.

I went away sorry to have come in, and left them in their window. There was a roar of laughter from the tap-room as I passed. The Count seemed to have done with his botanizing, and to be beginning a course of astronomy from the little terrace. Upstairs I found Tom with a pipe, and H., who was much interested when I told her of the padrona's unknown trouble. ' I am afraid money matters must be wrong,' said H. But there was no sign of any want of prosperity in the little household. Fresh piles of linen were carried in from the bleaching-field, cows came dragging stores of hay for the stable, bare-legged assistants brought fruit and corn and wine, like people in the Bible. The padrona was walking about with a carpenter early next morning devising alterations, and I found Fortunata displaying a perfect store of ribbons and laces she had bought for Tonina in Agordo the day before. Tonina, the eldest daughter, wore a gold brooch and earrings, and two horns of black hair; she was engaged to be married, and was shortly to depart, earrings and all, for the town where her intended was employed. Tonina was a big handsome young woman, with a perfect passion for dress. I never heard her speak with interest on any other subject. She would waylay us, feel our gowns, settle our bonnet-strings; she was for ever straggling into our rooms and trying on our clothes.

I did not care for Antonina at all, but little Fortunata, with her sweet, quick, gentle ways, was irresistible. She was spoiled by them all, and she seemed to me like a little brownie at work, sparing her mother, helping Joanna, and stirring about us with a kind energy. She could sing all sorts of songs, mountain catches, and opera tunes too. She had brown startled eyes and red hair, plaits upon plaits that Joanna used to put up with the silver pins in a sort of true-lover's knot every morning. She used to be up quite late, till midnight and even later, and again at six in the morning this young woman was about—often at four if any early traveller was starting. 'Tonina would never get up,' Joanna said, shrugging her shoulders.

But the person who most interested me in the household was the padrona, with her dark sweet anxious face and her tender care for her children. The woman was a born lady, whatever her station in life might be. I liked

to see her receiving her guests, with a gracious courtesy
that was shyly returned by funny red-faced, blear-eyed
men with kneebreeches and conical hats, coming to drink
vino nero; and slouching young conscripts, half-shy, half-
proud, with their flowers and numbers stuck into their
caps. If there was any disturbance the padrona would
walk boldly in and quell it with instant measures.
The gentle decision with which, on one occasion, Beppo
was summoned to assist one of these young fellows out of
the house amused me. It was a handsome fair-haired
boy, dressed in green, with a great bunch of pink roses,
and neat white knitted hose. With a sudden yell, he
tore off his gay hat and flung it on the ground, trolling
out something between a hymn and a drinking-song in a
hoarse tipsy voice. The padrona laid her hand on his
shoulder. Her grave look seemed to steady him. 'Angelo
Soya,' she said, 'enough of this; go home, my boy.' And
Angelo actually got up and disappeared without a
word.

Italians, if they trust you, will speak of themselves and
their feelings with an openness that is touching to people
of a more reserved habit. Very soon the signora spoke to
me of impending anxiety, of Fortunata, and her eyes
would fill with tears of love and care. Something was
amiss in the little household; good and affectionate as they

all were, and tenderly devoted as was the mother, she had not been able, even in that lonely mountain-enclosed village, to keep her young ones safe and away from harm and evil speaking. Joanna's indignant fealty, Mario's manly protection, what is of avail against spying eyes and spiteful tongues, and three long brown necks stretched out? I could have wrung them with pleasure when I knew the harm they had done. The rest of the household consisted of a wild undermaid called Jacoma, of Beppo the old man, and numberless assistants, with bare legs and short petticoats, appearing and disappearing, carrying tubs, gourds, great baskets of Indian corn, inflated pigskins, and what not. Labour is cheap in these parts, and garments are dear. This was hard upon Tonina. In houses where everything is made at home,—soap, bread, wine, linen, cheese, &c., there is, of course, an infinity to see to. They had a farm from whence provisions came; they had granaries, fruit-stores. I could see sacks heaped and heaped in the store-rooms on the ground-floor, and often there, too, was Joanna at work among them with an assistant. barelegs.

V.

JOANNA seemed to have a temper of her own. I was passing the open door of one of those ground store-rooms next morning on my way to join H. on the hillside, when I heard Joanna rating her unlucky assistant at the pitch of her voice. Barelegs answered, tossing her head. Joanna, with a sort of shrill, contemptuous, whistling noise, orders barelegs off; and finally the poor creature slinks away with a basket full of polenta meal on her head, leaving Joanna triumphant.

'What was it?' said Mario, who had been standing in the door with his usual long weedy cigar in his mouth. 'Joanna, don't scold poor Jacoma.'

'Ah! you pity La Jacoma,' said Joanna, sharply. 'Now Mario has come back he is to set everything right. Go and console her, and ask her if she does not deserve my indignation.'

'What the devil is it all about? says Mario.

'It is the work of devils,' she repeated. 'Something that she ought never to have listened to,' cried Joanna, still in a fury. 'I will not have her trouble the mistress. Do you hear?'

Mario's face changed; he seemed to understand her as he too marched off. Joanna, who was in a downright passion, went on violently tying and shaking the big sacks, but more than once she stopped to stamp off her fury, and to shake her conical hat in anger at someone outside in the street.

Joanna was a character—a loyal rebel belonging to the dynasty of Sarti. Fortunata seemed to be the object of her blind devotion, the others the victims of it. She was a handsome girl; her teeth were like milk, her fair hair was pinned up like her mistress's, but she wore three or four little short sprays or frizzes over her forehead and cheeks, and I hardly ever saw her without her hat. There was a melancholy look in her blue eyes, which contrasted oddly with her broad smiles and childish gapes. She was curious and clumsy. She asked me endless questions about myself, my family. She would give a certain solemn shake of the head when she was puzzled, as if there were profundities unexplored into which she did not choose to enquire: such as the countries beyond Germany, the railways, the strangers who were beginning to come over the mountains to the valleys, where they came from, and their watches, what was to be done to procure them butcher's meat. Joanna looked stupid, but she was really full of cleverness. She could have thought and reasoned if she had chosen, and she had real flashes of genius at times, when anything came to stir her from her usual clumsy apathy. But as she was also extremely pig-headed and superstitious, her flashes of genius used to die out very often without making much impression upon herself or anyone else.

'Ah!' said she, calming down at last, preparing to shoulder her sack, and wiping some tears out of her eyes, 'it's a cruel world, that poisons the sweetest and dearest, that respects neither innocence nor youth.'

There was a pathetic emotion in her voice that surprised and touched me.

'What is it?' I asked.

'Eh! who can tell?' said the girl. 'There are three devils, three washer-women, opposite, who say wicked things of us, and La Jacoma repeats them to me. But I think she will not dare to do so again,' cried Joanna, 'or to disquiet the padrona any more with her tales.'

'But can't it be stopped?' said I.

'What can one say? what can one do?' cried Joanna. 'I am only a servant. Mario he is the master, he is. And he comes to put all right,—Hé! I know that he will make it all wrong. But who is to keep clear of error? Not masters, any more than servants. Mine will not listen to reason, and they will sacrifice a dove to their pride.'

Italian women are eloquent when they are excited.

This girl whisked up the sacks, her blue eyes sparkled, then dimmed, and there, like enchantment, was a gaping, wide-mouthed stupid Joanna again standing before me with her load.   I remember the look of the queer cellar-like place, with its bars, and the round iron scrolled windows, and green vine-stems outside.

Madame Sarti's voice was heard calling overhead, ' Beppo ! Beppo ! '

' She wants him to stir the polenta,' said Joanna.   ' It is no good to dwell upon evil.   We know how to make good polenta in our house.   Will you come and taste ? '

<hr />

VI.

JOANNA walked carefully upstairs into the kitchen, where a great wood flame was leaping on the high stone hearth, and a comfortable incantation in a huge cauldron already begun—water and Indian corn meal, which the padrona shook in, while Beppo, in his shirt-sleeves, stood by with a wonderful serious face.   Then he began working the mass round and round with a stick ; then he got excited, and worked harder and harder as the difficulty increased; then he finally leapt on the fireplace, and stood above them all, pounding and pushing and poking away with all his might. At last, after some five minutes, when the steam has carried away the water, and the mass is hardened enough, the fire begins to fail: just when Beppo seems. exhausted, Joanna brings a great wooden platter, and on to this board they cleverly roll out a polenta—an avalanche—a huge smoking, steaming mass. Then Tonina rushes forward and cuts the mass into two halves with a string, one for the servants—one for the master's table— and Beppo wipes his brow as he leaps down triumphantly from the stone hearth.

The widow still stood in the fireplace making up the fire. Joanna was bearing off one of the great smoking hemispheres on its platter; and Jacoma, the maid, was yawning in a chair, and resting from her morning's labour. It was a common enough scene of family life. A woman peeping in through the doorway, with a great pile of flax upon her head; for colour, take a blue gleam of sky, black beams and rafters, shining coppers, and white walls, against one of which stands the tall black crucifix, and just beside it Fortunata in her coral necklace and auburn locks. At this moment, as if he had been conjured up somewhere out of the great boiling copper, the Count's tall figure suddenly appeared. There was a hush and silence as he looked in.

'I shall want a room to-night,' he said, abruptly, 'and supper at eight. Here is some game; more than I shall want.' Little Fortunata, with her face all alight, seemed to awake first, and she sprang forward and took it from him. 'Thank you,' said he, smiling, and then he was gone. He was running upstairs four steps at a time. Madame Sarti had turned pale, and looked at her son. Antonina drew herself up very primly. Joanna flushed, and gave one quick glance at Fortunata. I began to guess the state of the case when, as I walked out into the street to join my sister-in-law, I saw the three heads nodding and straining from the opposite window.

In these friendly villages the people come crowding round the strangers, and staring with wondering brown eyes, like the little calves do on the mountains. H——, whom I had left alone safe installed in the shade of a hay *châlet*, with a penknife, a pencil, a church spire, a range of low mountains, india-rubber, and all the materials for a sketch,—I now found surrounded by a large family, on its way to the fields after the midday meal : there was a bald good-humoured woman, with false plaits ; a row of little boys and girls, pretty, as all the children are in these parts. Poor H—— was finishing her sketch to the usual catechism. 'Married? Where is the husband? How many boys and how many girls? Does our country please you?' (Pause for a compliment.) 'Are you Germans or Italians? English? Under what rule is England?—Across the sea?' —a whistle. Then a hurried dialogue among one another. 'They are not Christians.' 'No.' 'Yes: look at their rings.' Then a kind smile, and a genuine friendly 'Happy journey' at parting. The bald woman was unusually cheerful and talkative. She too was married, and these were five of her children. 'Were we staying at the inn? So the soldier had returned? It was as well perhaps. Eh? It is always well to have a man in a family; women are apt to be silly and indiscreet. Of course Madama Sarti and her daughters were far above her, but she loved them (our friend did); only there were enemies in the valley. Hé, they say terrible things. They say Fortunata looks too high, and are jealous, in short; but she is a pretty creature, and has no malice in her ways,' says our inform- ant, preparing to resume her trudge. 'Deh! come along, little ones,' and off she goes with her brood scrambling after her up the steep rocky pass.

'So that is the key to the poor mother's anxieties,' said I. 'That dear pretty little creature — can anyone be so cruel as to talk spitefully of her? It is too sad, H——.

' The padrona should be careful of appearances,' said H——, gravely, ' for the girl's own sake.'

Then, as we had already agreed, we walked on a little way to call upon our friend. It was a curious lovely old garden, at the back of the low white house in the village street, with great closed gates, and balconies, and little buttresses, and clothes hanging to dry upon the terrace. Here the two old ladies had lived for I don't know how many tranquil years. The grass was green, but long and straggling, and the paths were rough, so that, to our Eng lish eyes, there was a certain sadness about the place. But there was a real wealth of wonders;. and precious plants and trees and shrubs for those like H—— who know something of such things. Under a little wooden umbrella, darting up, green, and with delicate lace-work branches, was a slender Norfolk pine-tree; there an aloe in flower; here one or another learned fragrant shrub, and great oleander-trees with the flames bursting through the green, and pumpkins, common enough, but always splendid, along the wall, and strange, deep-coloured scent-less flowers in close serried rows along the beds, and trees, with unknown fragrant blossoms tossing. It was under one of these that Signora della Santa met us with a friendly welcome. 'Will you come in, or stay here?' she asked. ' The Marchesa desires her best compliments. She is not

yet up, or she would have the pleasure of receiving you.'
Then, after our usual little talk of journey and recollec-
tions, &c., H—— began to praise the garden, and exclaim
in admiration at the treasures she had seen there.

'To tell the truth, we deserve small credit,' said
Signora della Santa, much gratified. 'Saverio de Pavis,
who is a botanist, a nephew of my Marchesa, has the
garden planted, and conspires with the gardener to carry
out his experiments. He lives at Agordo, but often comes
over to see his aunt and his trees here. He is away just
now.' (H. and I looked at each other.) 'I am glad he is
keeping away,' the signora said : 'for, to tell the truth, there
has been some gossip in the town, and people said he was
paying great attention to your hostess's little daughter. I
happen to know that no such thought has ever crossed his
mind ; he thinks of his plants only, and doesn't live in the
world around him.'

Our friend was clever and reasonable, and I thought
it better to confess that I had seen her hero that very
morning.

'I am sorry to hear it,' said she. 'It was but the last
time I saw him that he was complaining of the inn, the
bad attendance, and indifferent cooking there. I regret
that people should make remarks. The Sartis are too

good and respectable to allow themselves to be attacked
by evil tongues.'

I could quite imagine her to be right.　We had a little
more talk, and from what she told us it seemed indeed as
if the Count lived in a world different from that which we
inhabited.　A world in which there were changes, but
they took thousands and thousands of years to effect; in
which there were kingdoms, and dynasties, and conquests
perhaps, but silent conquests undisputed.　If one flower
perished, another succeeded in its turn.　Laws could not
be broken in this tranquil realm, its state secrets might
be disclosed without fear of ill.　For this mystic silent
existence Saverio had given up the cares and turmoils of
quick daily life.　At one time the philosopher had been
ambitious and keen enough for the cause he loved, and had
been heart and soul on the Italian side, although a captain
in the Austrian army.　This was in his youth, and he had
been remarked and called to account.　He had been
taxed by the Austrians until his fortune was completely
ruined, and now Saverio was a poor man.　He had worked,
waited, and hoped, but when the Italian rule was established, the recognition he had expected never came.　And
then it was that, indignant and disappointed, he turned
his back upon Europe, upon kings, and court intrigue, and
favour.　He felt that he was by nature too hasty, too ner-

vous a man to keep pace with the rest of the rout. And
so he shut himself up in his old palace, and watched the
growth of the dandelions, and speculated upon the forma-
tion of the rocks about his home (his theory was that they
were coral rocks), and he wandered from peak to peak and
from pass to pass, and came home and wrote philosophical
treatises. ' His sisters are in despair, and think he has
gone mad, to shut himself up with his books and avoid all
human society,' said the old companion; ' but he is not
mad. He is moderately happy in his own way.'

VII.

WE did not think, when we left her waving farewells
at the great gate, how soon matters were to come to a
crisis. We were to go on the next day; and talking over
our plans and schemes, we had almost forgotten the existence of the Sartis. I walked up by the back way. As I
opened my door I found, as usual, someone in my room
(the whole family used to invade it unscrupulously),—a
pile of linen on the floor, two great copper pots full of
water, Joanna standing by a huge open press, with her
back turned. As I entered in there came from the sitting-

room beyond a great burst of voices. The girl turned round quick, and then I saw that her face was all working, flushed and agitated.

' It is my fault, all my fault!' she said, wringing her hands in an agony of despair. ' Ah, signora, go in. You may stop Mario. He is trying to make a quarrel with the Count.'

Mario had most certainly succeeded in his endeavour. I opened the door. There they all stood round the table, where the well-known green vasculum was lying—Mario flaming, Tonina smoothing her apron, Fortunata crying bitterly.

' Why do you stay here to be insulted? Why don't you go?' cried Mario to his sisters. ' What can you want with the Count's dried herbs? What does his Excellency mean by speaking to you in such an impatient and inso- lent fashion, and suspecting you honest girls of stealing them?' Then, turning round upon the Count again, who was looking very haughty and puzzled,—'I tell you that my sisters are not the common drudges that you seem to imagine. My sisters are not to be spoken to as if they were servants. They were well born, and respected by all.'

' Who ever doubted it?' said the Count, containing himself with difficulty, seizing his hat and his stick, and hastily crushing and doubling up a map, which he twisted round and round, and stuffed into the vasculum. 'I asked for a missing specimen and was vexed that it should have been destroyed. Who talks of stealing?'

'They are well born,' persisted Mario, who was in a tremendous passion, and evidently anxious to impress the fact of a quarrel; 'and I, too, although your Excellency may not choose to acknowledge it, am not of those who will endure the insults of the rich.'

'I have never given your existence one moment's consideration,' said his Excellency, now fairly in a passion too. Then seeing my open door, he hurried past me into the bedroom, where he stopped short with all his para-phernalia, while Joanna sprang forward.

'I—I only am to blame,' she cried, and would have caught his arm.

'Silence,' roared Mario from the next room, while the Count shook her off.

I thought it as well Saverio should not encounter the fierce champion Mario any more, and I silently pointed to the second door upon the balcony, which was open, and through which, with a haughty salutation, the Count strode away. I saw him marching down the village street, and disappearing in the distance—a grey-linen, grey-hatted figure. The peasants saluted him respectfully as he went along, but he, flying by at his usual pace, paid no attention to any of their greetings: on he went past the wine-shop—past the black arched entrance to the old brown house. He was gone.

But the scene was not over yet. A cry from Tonina called us hastily into the next room. Poor little Fortunata had fallen back fainting into her sister's arms. Dead, pale, dishevelled, with the silver pins falling loose from her hair, Tonina had dragged her to the carnation window. Mario, looking at once sulky, sorry and pacified, was pouring himself out a glass of black wine.' Joanna had run for one of the great copper pails of water, and with angry, blue glances at the corporal, for all his uniform and moustaches, began dashing the water with both hands into Fortunata's face. 'Go and fetch mamma, Mario,' said Tonina, severely; and then mamma came back, followed by the irrepressible Mario. He had evidently given his own version of the story. Poor mamma! troubled, puzzled, she alternated from the tenderest expressions of pity and sympathy to no less affectionate, but less sympathetic, maternal snubbings. 'For shame, Fortunata! Here is the lady. They will all see you down the street. Would Tonina do such a thing as faint for a caprice? Mario is right. Let the Count go his way. He is an original; nobody can predict from one day to another what he may do or say. His Excellency's state is too high for us. Thou art not born to be a countess, my little Fortunata—my dearest.' (Very sharp:) 'Mario, go, for the love of heaven! It will vex her to see thee when she recovers herself.'

Mario, doggedly, and calming down, with both hands up in the air and his fingers together,—' I am her true friend for all that; you women are ignorant, short-sighted, talkative, ambitious. You care not for the censure of the neighbours—for the insults that nobleman heaps upon the family of Sarti. But I—I tell you that I have saved you from the most imminent peril, and that you are ingrate all of you.'

So saying, Mario marched off, opening wide his ten fingers, clanking downstairs, and the padrona, who was evidently struck by his eloquence, again snubbed little Fortunata, who had quietly come round with her head on her sister's shoulder, and who was staring through the window and between the straggling branches of the carnations, with a sad far-away look, inexpressibly sorrowful and affecting.

' Eh! it is a bad day's work,' said Joanna, shrugging her shoulders. ' Mario has made an uproar and sacrificed his sister's happiness. She might have been a countess but for his stupidity.'

'I never thought he would have said so much,' sighed Tonina.

'Be quiet,' said Signora Sarti. 'Joanna, go to thy linen. Mario is justified. The Count has retired, and it would never do to allow the neighbours to talk with disrespect of Fortunata, and to look upon us with evil eyes. Mario says that the Count is sporting with the affections of an innocent. He is an original, and no one, not Mario nor any other, shall understand him.'

Fortunata was led off by Tonina, who was very kind and, as I thought, compunctious. Joanna began storing away the linen in the great closet in my room, but her tears dribbled on the pillow-cases with the frills, and the folded linen. 'To think it was all for that bit of grass, that little nasty flower,' poor sobbing Joanna burst out at last. 'To think that I—I, who would give my life for Fortunata, should have been the one to bring all this upon her. It was a little lilac flower of nothing at all. I have never seen any like it,' said the girl. This plant, it seemed, the Count had brought out of his tin case and examined during supper the night before, and then Fortunata had come in and talked to him and asked him to tell her the names of the stars (for the Count could tell everything by name—stars, flowers, animals, languages, medicines, printed books, it was all the same to him),

and while they were out on the balcony, Joanna had
cleared away the supper and found the flower lying on
the lid of the green case. For a little joke, after the
Count had gone to bed, she had given it to Fortunata,
saying it was a flower of good luck his Excellency had
sent her. Fortunata teased Joanna half the night to
know if this were true. It was a foolish joke, and when
Joanna saw how deeply her young mistress took it to
heart, she had confessed that it was but a joke. And
then Fortunata, half laughing half weeping, said all
the same she should keep it, and next morning she
showed Joanna a tiny crystal locket, into which she had
put the lilac bell. It would not hold the leaves, so she
had cut them away. And then came the Count, hunting
everywhere and in a state of excitement about his lost
flower, and Joanna, laughing, asked him if it was a
magical charm, and said it was safe, and when he
exclaimed eagerly, at last showed him the crystal locket
shyly, not knowing if he would be angry. And then the
Count said they had undone him, that he had picked
it at the risk of his life, that there was no other like it.
And while he was scolding, and Fortunata crying, Mario
came in.

'He meant to quarrel,' said Joanna, 'at the first

opportunity, and now they have quarrelled, and our poor Fortunata is the victim!'

'But, Joanna,' I said, 'the Count never has been serious in his intentions.'

'That is it. They will not believe it; but Fortunata felt, and I, too, felt, that at one time he meant to marry her, and she would have been his countess. He is hasty in temper, but true in heart. Now all is over. That flower has done it. I, too, am to blame. Who is not? Eh!'

A shake of the head—clink, clank—a great sob—exit Joanna, swinging her brazen pails.

VIII.

THE result of this painful little scene could not yet be known, as far as the Count was concerned. It seemed not unlikely that he would come no more. 'Perbacco! That is exactly what I wish,' said Mario. 'If it were an honest fellow who loved our Nata, and wished to make her his wife, that would be another matter; but the

Count only amuses himself, and the neighbours laugh in their sleeves.'

' It is to be hoped he will come no more,' said Tonina, placidly. ' Fortunata will forget him. She is young and has been silly. She must marry in' her own station, to her credit, like me, and then she can continue the business of the inn.'

H. said she felt inclined to box Tonina's ears, she spoke so complacently.

' Wait, wait, only wait,' cried Joanna, with a sapient shrug. ' Do you think our misfortunes are completed ? No ; Nata will die before long, and that will break my heart and the padrona's. She will die, I tell you, if the Count abandons her.' (Then a shake of the hat, then a mysterious mutter.) ' I think he might return when that blockhead of a Mario is gone. . . .'

Mario, whose leave was almost up, seemed to have some notion of the sort. He decreed in his decided way that Nata was to depart immediately, the farther the better. There was their cousin Hofer who would receive her at R——, in German Tyrol, and he would pass that way and see her on his return to Innsprück, where his regiment was quartered. Mario was in the Austrian service. That young man was a born autocrat. He would allow no excuse, grant no delay. I think, perhaps,

under the circumstances, he was right, for he heard more
of the universal gossip of the place than the poor women
had dreamt of.   So Mario declared that Nata wanted no
new clothes for her journey.   Escort!   Joanna could take
her; or, if she cared for company, there were the English
ladies going that very way.

'But, Mario, it is such a long way,' said poor Signora.
Sarti, who was not herself without a lingering hope that
all might yet come right.

'All the better,' cries Mario, magniloquent. 'I myself
will tell those who dare speak of us that she is gone.
Then let them say what they choose.   They will see that
our family is uncompromising in its self-respect, and will
allow no interference where its honour is concerned. - I
had rather you put a poniard into my heart than allowed
my sister's name to be lightly spoken of.'

'My poor little Nata,' sighed the poor mother,
taking the girl's hand and stroking it. 'My poor, poor
child!'

'If it were I,' cries Joanna, cocking her hat fiercely,
'do you think I would go? No, not for empires. Hi!
you might offer me gold and diamonds in vain; if I
loved truly, it is not I who would conceal my passion.
Struggle not against thy nature, my Nata, or thou wilt
die.   I know thy delicacy and tenderness of heart.   How

can Mario, who has no more sentiment than an ox, understand?'

'Will you be silent, you girl of nothing at all?' in a shriek of indignation from Tonina.

'I have a heart impassioned, but noble and self-sacrificing,' exclaims Mario, very angry, and looking as red as a turkey-cock. 'Why am I accused? I am acting for mamma, and upholding her wishes. Is it not so?' cries the young man. And he turned round upon the poor padrona, who only began to cry, so worried and troubled was she.

Little Nata was kissing her mother's withered cheeks again and again. 'Don't believe La Joanna. I am not going to die, my mamma,' she said. 'I suffer a little, but only a little. Mario is right. It is fitter that I should go, for how can I venture to believe the Count when he tells me he prefers me to all others? Yes, I will go, if it will stop people from blaming us.' And then she ran out of the kitchen, and went and sat on her little low chair in the corner by the window, at the far end of the passage, with her face hidden in her hands. There she sat, poor little soul. Over her head the great brown carnations were hanging; outside all the busy voices were echoing; the squares of light were travelling along the wooden floor. She never moved till she heard her mother's step upon the stairs; then she pulled out her work from her pocket, and began to sing a little song as she stuck the stitches.

When dinner was over, H. and I, and Tom and his pipe, generally went out together for a sociable little quartet upon the bridge. That evening, seeing Nata in the doorway, I called her to come with us. I thought it as well she should be seen with us; we two followed, and H. walked slowly a-head, leaning upon her son's arm. We left the *pallone*-players beginning their game; we went along the narrow street. In every doorway the little white children were clustering on the step nibbling their suppers,—lumps of polenta, little bowls of milk; the parents ate within, or stood leaning over the little balconies where the flax was hanging to dry. We caught glimpses of copper and wood and fire interiors; in the air was a tinkling of coming flocks, a murmuring chorus of voices, and then the thud of some late carding-pin, still falling upon the flax. Old women, past other work, were sitting spinning at the doors and nodding their white locks at us as we passed. The attention we generally excited was rather diverted on this occasion by the passage of two pedlars with huge green umbrellas slipped down into the little rings along the side of the packs. I saw a group as we passed standing round some drawers opened out to display the glittering tinsel.

treasures that dazzle the peasant-girls in wonder; and then, beyond the village, we came to the little bridge across the stream, and we sat down upon a log that happened to be felled and lying on the bank.

So Tom smoked his pipe in the glow of the evening; the stream washing by reflected yellow and crimson, and the emerald lights from the broad leaves of Indian corn, among which the country people were strolling. Presently another echo reached us, an Alpine chaunt, at once cheerful and melancholy; then came a hurried procession of little goats, followed by the deliberate steps of the grey cows coming down from the mountains; then more women plodding home with their loads of flax, and little children running bare-legged, and dragging implements of labour bigger than themselves, or carrying small heaps in little baskets fitted to their backs. Then came the cheerful company of country youths, walking six of a row, shirt-sleeves gleaming, arm-in-arm, hats well cocked, like Joanna's; they struck up again with all their lungs as they entered the village. After a little while we saw another group of people advancing, with a hum of voices that sounded both softer and shriller than the peasants' queer falsettos. 'It is all the gentry of the town,' Nata said; 'a great party went out this morning to camp in the woods.'

The gentry seemed to have been enjoying their picnic thoroughly; they advanced in a long line, two and two, young men and pretty young women with dark heads all uncovered, except one, who, I think, wore a black veil flung over her white dress and glossy black locks. They, too, were walking arm in arm, laughing, and whispering, and talking gaily, and coming in a sort of step.

'That first lady is to be married on Monday,' said Nata. 'That is her "sposo" she is walking with: he is engaged in the mines at Agordo.' They swept by quite close, their garments touching ours as they passed. One young girl nodded gravely to Fortunata, the others were too happy or too absorbed to notice her. There was something almost bacchanalian in the little procession: the white dresses, the garlands and flowers they were bringing back, the subdued happy excitement as they swept on through the calm of the evening. As the last of the file went by, I saw Fortunata flush and start: There was the Count with a lady on his arm walking on with the rest. I thought he saw us, for he stopped, imperceptibly almost, never looking, but he passed on without a sign, and disappeared with the rest down the village street.

A minute after, Nata quietly said she must go home to see to the supper; would I please not disturb myself to come with her? And she got up and walked very quickly,

in a sort of zigzag way at first, but afterwards straightly
as usual.

Later in the evening we also got up to go. Tom's
pipe was smoked out. It was getting chilly, and H. was
wrapping her Indian shawl more and more closely round
her shoulders. On our way we met the padrona, standing
with the little group that was still gazing at the pedlar's
wondrous wares.

'Why, Signora, have you been buying some of those
little saints?' said Tom.

'These are silver pins for Nata,' said the padrona,
joining us, showing us her little parcel. 'I ran after the
pedlar,' she explained, coming along. 'My little Nata
came home so pale, so sad, that I thought I would try and
give her one moment's pleasure. Mario is right. I have
been foolish and ambitious; but Fortunata is so good, so
dear, that is my excuse,' said the poor, proud mother. 'I
thought my child was deserving of any fate, or never
would I have encouraged the Count; but oh; they must
not dare say things against her fair fame. It is as if one
of these sharp pins was piercing my breast when I think
of it all. But when she is gone, people will see that
we are proud and will not suffer a breath against our
honour.' Then she began to tell me that 'Cousin Hofer'
was a lady like herself, a widow in German Tyrol, keeping,

as she did, an inn partly for pleasure—for the advantage of society. The Hofer's house was only habitable in the summer. If we really intended crossing the Seisser Alp on our way to Bolsano, we should pass very near it, 'and,' said Signora Sarti, 'I know not how to thank the gentry for their offer to look after the girls. I shall keep Mario three days longer, and it will be better,' she said, 'for us all; and Joanna will be a companion to Nata. The two are faithful friends.'

Fortunata met us pale but smiling when we came in. She had laid out the supper, she had brought a lamp to light us. All that evening she was coming and going, nervously busy, and more than once I heard her laugh. It was a sad musical laugh, very near to tears, but not bitter. There was nothing bitter in her nature. My nephew, Tom, who had had a sentiment early crushed in the bud, he told us, was much interested when we spoke to him. He willingly agreed, at his mother's request, to the extra infliction of two more women to escort. 'Four was no worse than two,' Tom remarked; 'and it was not for long.'

IX.

THAT evening I went to bed to toss and turn, and hear voices and see lights and faces suddenly flashed upon the darkness. Long after midnight I heard the padrona silently creeping upstairs. I lay starting at the striking of clocks, at the melancholy cry of the watchman. 'The hour is one,' he said; 'The hour is two;' and his voice echoed all along the silent village. At last I got up, and, putting on a dressing-gown, I opened the door upon the wooden gallery, and I saw that I was not alone to watch and wake; another figure was standing leaning against the banister. I guessed who it was when I saw the dark shade of a conical hat.

'Who is it?' whispered Joanna; 'ah, the Signora frightened me!' Then, for a minute, we stood together looking at the burning sky above the black roofs of the houses. 'Look at the stars how they shine! Is it not a beautiful silence?' said Joanna. 'The Count can tell the name of every one, big and little. He is learned, too learned,' said Joanna, bitterly, with a shrug. 'He has bewitched her. Ah, signora! Fortunata is asleep at last! She restrains her complaints not to vex her mother; but when we are alone it is as if she would be broken by her sorrow. She has told me how he passed her without a look. I suffered so in her sorrow I could not rest, and I thought the stars would do me good.'

Joanna had something of her great namesake's nature —a simple enthusiasm and courage, and deep-hearted devotion. To her, the kingdom to be conquered was Fortunata's happiness; her dear Fortunata who lay crying herself to sleep upon her straw mattress with all her gleaming hair twisted over the pillow, and her white beautiful face hidden. The padrona's white linen was not whiter than Fortunata's skin. A lady! she was sweet enough to be a lady all the rest of her life if it so pleased her, and sit with her hands before her for ever and ever. Tonina, so Joanna thought, was no better than herself, except in being the padrona's daughter and wearing an alpaca dress; but Nata! It was to Nata that all Joanna's gratitude and love for the shelter and home-love the widow had given her was bestowed. So she whispered on in the darkness. It was then, as she looked up over the housetops at the clear burning night, that she vowed a vow to the bright stars that if she could do anything, anything in the whole world, to make Nata happy she would do it, and suddenly the thought came to her of replacing the flower. Nata's mother was asleep after her long day's work; for a time, poor soul, her anxieties were calmed. Nata's sister was dreaming warm and placid in her bed by the window.

What would I not have given afterwards to have been quietly asleep in my bed, instead of waking, and making cruel mischief by my thoughtless words! Is it an excuse that, at that minute, dreams seemed so vivid, commonplace and realities so far away? 'Signora,' Joanna said to me in mysterious whispers, 'shall I tell you what I think? I think the Count makes magic with his flowers, and that the purple bell-flower poor Nata destroyed was a magic herb, and has worked all this ill. He spoke strangely. He said that alone was wanting to complete his work, and he could find no other in its place. He was angry, so angry! Signora, do the English believe in magic?'

'No one believes in charms, Joanna,' I said; 'only poets, not practical people. My nephew burns a magic leaf, and a smoke rises and rises, and those who practise the incantation say that it cures ill-humour. And I, too, have a precious little herb in a tin box in my portmanteau. It looks brown and dry; but, if I pour water on it, a delicious fragrance comes, and if I am tired and sad it cheers me. Some people might call these wonderful things tea-leaves and tobacco. . . . '

'Eh!' says Joanna, 'who can tell! If the Signora only knew of precious herbs that would bring honourable love as well as peace of mind, *that* would be well for all.'

I thought she was laughing, that she understood me. It was so dark I could not see her face; but I make no excuses, for I was punished after, and blamed myself when it was too late.

'There was a great enchanter once in England, Joanna. His name was Gulielmo. He could summon fairies at his will, and once he sent his messengers flying, and bade them bring a purple flower, of which the juice divided lovers strangely, and made much mischief; and then, when all seemed hopeless,' I said, getting sleepy by degrees, 'the fairies flew at his command, and upon the wild thymy bank another flower was growing, and all was well again, and the lovers united. But that was hundreds of years ago, and the great enchanter is dead. Good-night, Joanna. It is time for you to go to sleep, instead of looking at the stars.' And so I went back to peaceful dreams, all unconscious of the ill I had done.

X.

THE village turned out to see our start on the morning of our departure for C——. The Austrian soldiers lent a hand, knots were tied with immense exertion, chairs and steps placed in convenient positions for the ascent of gigantic mules. Windows were noisily opened, advice was given, pieces of string were freely distributed; an hour must have passed in tying and untying every part of the apparatus of four bags and a knapsack and three sheepskin saddles: the very tails of the mules seemed to me fastened on with string. At last we clattered off cheerfully through the village street with our heads over our shoulders responding to the signora's farewell wavings and blessings. I can see the slim anxious figure before me now standing by the fountain and watching us go. Mario cried out that he should follow on Monday, and flourished his cap. The three hateful washerwomen burst out into shrill laughter. Then we passed Signora della Santa's door; then the house of our talkative friend with all the children. Five or six of them rushed out frantic into the street. Tom trudged ahead with his great axe, then came Bruno, who had bustled to the front with his pan-

niers full of hand-bags; then H. and I on our sheepskins
highly perched; and Nata last with Joanna walking by
the side of her mule. She was very pale and silent, and
Joanna spoke not a word at starting. More than once I
saw her looking back at the familiar sight. The ridges
of the mountains, with the well-known dents and clefts,
the piled roofs of the village, the steeple. There was
Signora della Santa's gate, looking now quite small, like a
doll's house; there was the chimney of the ' Black Eagle,'
and the smoke from the kitchen where the pot was boiling. I could imagine how those lines and shadows must
look to Joanna, like the lines and marks on a familiar
face. Nata never turned her head, but rode on drooping
and thoughtful all through the golden hours of that great
day.

How can one write it down? A flowing melody of
mountain, and valley, and rushing water, and green
things drifting and creeping everywhere; flowers white,
and gold, and violet, as it were, striking sweet notes.
High and solemn ridges dominating green valleys, and
limpid streams rippling with a sweet impetuous dash.
Now we follow Bruno along a narrow gorge of dazzling
shadow and solemn lights. They come flowing from the
towering heights overhead. We ride through a dell of
moss and of lawn folded against the rocks, and round the

tall stems of the cedar-trees. They stand keeping watch like sentinels at the gate of the pass. Then higher still the open world shines round us, snow-peaks heave, the blue heaven comes down, the mules climb step by step, the sun begins to burn; we pass crosses casting a slender line of shade across the rocks that pave our way; we scale smooth fragrant alps, where the goats and cows come from over the horizon tinkling down to meet us, and to gaze at us with wild brown eyes. The people at work up in the faint green heights seem to look down at us too. Time passes; the lights grow more clear, the colours more light. We cross a wide green alp, where a few satyrs, and shepherds in goat-skins, and brown-faced children are keeping the flocks; and then at last we stop in a scooped, green, silent valley, where the procession comes to a halt, and Bruno quietly begins to browse, and the mules, seeing Bruno stop, stop too, and Peter and Luigi, the mulemen, light their pipes afresh. We are at the summit of the pass.

Peter was a great big fellow, a German Tyrolese, with this constant pipe in his mouth (it was painted with a cottage and a rural view). He seemed much taken by Joanna, and tried to make conversation all along the road. He now came to offer assistance; but she treated his advances in a very lofty fashion, and

turning her back, began unpacking for herself the
basket of provisions we had brought—ripe figs, hard
eggs, and rolls, and a little wine. The guides went to
a wooden châlet close by, and came back with a pail
of milk. They were followed by some children, and a
girl of about fifteen, and a calf that instantly trotted
up to Bruno and moo'd. High up the father and
mother were at work reaping the grass, and one little
girl was toiling up the long burning slope with their
mid-day meal. I was going to begin my lunch when
H. called me.

'Come here for one minute,' she said. She was
standing on a little eminence. I hardly know now what
we saw at that hour as we stood there together. Our
hearts and eyes were opened suddenly, for the sky was
so purple blue, the rocks at hand tinted, dented,
modelled with tender inscrutable transitions, beautiful,
tremulous, with blue and brown; the world beyond was
snow and light and rocky ridge. The ice-bound Marmolata rose before us: we saw peak beyond peak, an infinity not too infinite. At our feet the soft brushwood
all flowered and tangled with tendrils and leaves. There
were great soft grey star-thistles, blue-bells, leaves tongue-
shaped, streaked with red veins, argentine, and bronze,
and silver. . . .

When we came back I was surprised to find Joanna talking very confidentially to the tall guide, Peter of the shirt-sleeves. Her haughty reserve seemed to have melted, and she was asking him questions, one after another, about the country, the ways, the guides, the travellers, and the rocks. Had he ever been up the Marmolata? What was it like up there? And the Schlern—that was where we were going; was it green? were there any flowers? was it very difficult to ascend?

'It was not easy for women,' the guide said. 'The Count de Pavis had been up last year, and this year again; but he had alert legs, they said.'

'I should like to go?' said Joanna, thoughtfully.

'Shall I take you?' said the guide, gallantly.

Joanna looked at me, and did not answer.

That night we slept at a little inn in a lonely, desolate, place, with ragged, gentle people, wooden houses falling to decay, and foaming waters rushing through many streams and troughs. Fortunata dined with us in a great bedroom, where our dinner was served, by a crucifix. Joanna waited,—nothing would induce her to sit down.

On the second day's journey we came to a desolate pass, where rocks, rounded and massed in strange un- natural shapes, were piled along the road. There was something human, and, to me, most horrible about them: they were not ragged, and rugged, and wild, like those we had passed before; but they looked as if they had been modelled by some terrible hands, rounded, smoothed, and kneaded for some strange purpose, and poised one on the other in awful-looking heaps of lumps and balls and columns, upon which no flowers could spring, no green things could grow.

'There! Nata is crushed by a load like one of those,' said Joanna; 'and I, too, have one upon my heart.'

For some time past the clouds had been gathering, and a damp mist enclosed us closer and closer, parting to show black tossing waves of cloud beyond; there was an echo of thunder in the air.

Nata still rode on in her sad, listless way; she did not seem to care whether storm or sunshine fell upon her head.

'There is a storm coming,' said Tom, cheerfully.

'Don't be afraid,' cried the guide. 'We are close to a shelter.'

We pushed on, and, as he promised, we were able to reach a little lonely hut, standing at the edge of the great Seisser Alp, just before the storm broke. The old landlord came out to shake us by the hand and make us

welcome.   He was a strange old man, with leather-
breeches and grey stockings, and a hook nose and a lean
brown face.   He brought us into his room, smoke-stained
and wood-panelled, and bidding us be seated, he left us
hastily, to hurry down and put the animals under shelter;
and then the shadowy armies came rolling across the
mighty Alp, echoing, deafening, and breaking into falling
streams of water.

'It will soon be over,' the landlord said, coming up
with the guides, and putting places for us all at his tripod
table. 'I have got bread,' he said, 'and cheese, and
wine; plenty to make merry with for married and single.
Are you married?' he asked Fortunata, who blushed up
and shook her head smiling.

'Then,' said the old fellow, 'you have no sorrows
and no joys. The single have neither sorrows nor joys.
Will you stay with me and be my sennerinn? You
shall milk the cows, and learn to call my pigs by their
names.'

'That is more suitable for me,' said Joanna, laughing.
'I will stay and be your sennerinn.'

So we sat breaking the hard wooden biscuits, and
listening to the storms all trouping round the lonely
chalet. Tom stood outside the door, on the wooden
balcony, watching for a break in the clouds. The old

fellow busied himself waiting on us, talking, and serving us. He made his own cheese, he told us, and his butter; he did everything himself, and lived alone, except when travellers came, like ourselves, to visit him. He had various ingenious devices for lessening his labours. I remember, among other things, noticing a wooden pipe for pigs'-wash from the balcony straight into the trough below. The tall guide, who was used to storms, sat with his two arms on the table, gaping at Joanna, and philosophically smoking his great pipe. His companion went down to have a look at the beasts. Our old host, in his turn, produced a handsome silver pipe, with a top such as they use in those parts; and when H. said, smiling, that it was pretty, he pulled it out of his mouth and begged her to smoke it for him. Tom went off into convulsive chuckles at the notion of his mother smoking a pipe. The old fellow laughed, seeing us laugh, and then skipped off quickly to see to some household arrangement.

'The last visitors I had,' said he, clattering about among his pans, 'were English, like yourselves—two ladies and two gentlemen. The gentlemen had been up the Schlern. One of them was a botanist, and he told me that there was no such place, not in all his country, for flowers and grasses. He had white and blue, and red and violet—a box full. See, he left me some edelweiss,' said the old fellow, pointing to a great bunch stuck into his hat that was hanging on a peg.

'And this is the way to the Schlern?' said Joanna.

'This is one of the ways,' said the host. 'You cross the Alp by the Horses' Teeth—oh, it is nothing; and if I had my young legs—' here he slapped his leather gaiters. 'People sometimes sleep here before they start; look, I have a handsome guest-chamber.' And as he spoke he opened a door and showed us a wooden chamber with three beds in it. 'You ladies will be comfortable in there if you have to stay all night.'

'Confound the weather!' said Tom, coming in from the gallery, and shaking himself.

There were three rooms to the châlet: the dairy, the kitchen, and the guest-chamber, all opening into one another; underneath were the pigs' house and the hay stable. In another stable, separate from the house, the mules were safely housed, dry and warm, out of the pouring rain. It was falling in sheets of water, and hail came, we could scarcely tell from whence, so thick were the clouds and the vapours rolling along the ground. But the guides went on predicting fine weather, and about three o'clock the clouds broke and the vapours drifted away; a bright sun came out suddenly, a world was created out of the chaos, and once more we started on our journey. The old fellow bade us farewell, and then let us go our way. He stood in his gallery as we rode away; he never looked after us. I can hear him now calling his pigs by their names. They were his real friends and companions in his lonely châlet in the midst of that great Alp.

XI.

THE baths of R—— lie deep hidden among cool green woods, where the waters ripple through mosses. From the crest of the opposite mountain we could see the shining summits of fir-trees and a golden gloom among their stems. An old ruined castle on the hill stood solitary and radiant. Some black rooks were floating over it in a crescent, but I could see no sign of a dwelling-place for human people. As we stumbled along we passed some peasants, who stared, and smiled, and marched on. One woman looked earnestly at Fortunata riding by, and suddenly emptied half the pears in her basket into the girl's lap. But it was Joanna who nodded

'Thank you,' and began to crunch the ripe fruit. All day long she had come with even steps, never hurrying, rarely lagging behind; and yet she talked to every passerby, told them with pride that we were travelling together, asked questions all along the road, shook hands freely, and made the holy sign by every wayside cross. As for Nata, she hardly looked up or spoke, but jogged on quietly, drooping a little with sad eyes that scarcely brightened. She did not care for the beauty of sights we passed. People in far worse trouble than Nata's can perhaps feel with living people and animate happiness, and find comfort in it; but it is in vain to ask them to be glad because we have taken them to a high pass, and because the sun is shining on a heap of earth and trees, and the flowers are luxuriant. It is only when the first bitterness of the spirit is past that the voice of nature can reach sad ears. Her call is too still, too gentle, to be heard when a tumult is in the heart.

'This is now the last ascent,' said the guide, as we reached the woods: 'this path leads straight to the baths.'

Where had we come to? Did gods bathe in the waters above? had they passed before us, leaving the radiance of their footsteps behind them? Now that we had entered the gloom we found it changed to a delight, a mystery, a shimmer. Golden twigs and stems, and creeping sprays hid the radiating sky: everywhere hung veils of moss, so wild, so soft, that it seemed as if they must have come gently blown by the wind; we passed a crystal pool reflecting these sweet wonders; there was a faint fragrant essence in the air, glistering pine-cones were piled along the grass, and flowers and wild straw-berries sparkled like rubies. It was the last golden minute of this long day: suddenly the evening came upon us, and the enchantment was over.

We were not yet at our journey's end, for Peter lighted a fresh pipe. When we asked where the house could be, the men nodded and pointed, and strode on by the stumbling mules. We were utterly tired out, and the way seemed very long; but at last the path opened wider, and a woman came strolling along knitting in the twi-light. She signed to the men and passed on; then we saw four people walking arm-in-arm, who stood to let us pass, but said nothing; and at last, at a turn, we came upon an open space, in the midst of which were two dusky wooden houses. Shadowy groups were standing round about in the twilight, and overhead silent dusky figures were watching from a wooden gallery.

So here, in the very heart of this fairy land, the country people had built their little bath-house, and would come to drink the waters. They were big, gentle, ox-eyed people, with solemn ways and calm faces. Even the children played in a sober fashion in their little conical hats. Frau Hofer came half-way down the wooden stairs to meet us, and gravely kissed her cousin; she was followed by a sort of Audrey,—a big peasant-woman,—who strode before us along the gallery, and silently flung wide open the doors of our room. The gallery crossed one great window dimly lighted, and as I passed I saw that this was the altar window of a little chapel, and the lights were burning on the altar. At the end of the gallery was an open balcony, where two old men were sitting on a bench close to my door, smoking their silver-topped pipes and listening to the chorus coming from the dusk below. It was a quaint mystical place that we had come to. I thought of the woods through which we had passed rustling in the twilight, now that the tide of light had ebbed away; of sleeping birds, of torpid insects, and closed chalices of flowers, of the little snakes lying drowsy in the mossy rocks, and squirrels, and all the harmless woodland life, while here was this strange silent company, wakeful still, and assembled round the little chapel. Was it all fairy work? were these stately people courtiers in disguise? was Rosalind among them, and melancholy Jaques? or was this the wood in which poor Hermia wandered, and Titania hid her Indian boy? Had Shakspeare been here in a dream one night?

The bed-rooms were little rooms with wooden doors and floors and windows, and little straw beds; Joanna and Nata had one together, and my room came next. 'Come quick and rest, Nata,' I heard the sturdy Joanna saying. She had speedily made friends with the landlady, and I presently met her hurrying along the passage carrying some supper for herself and Nata on a little tray: some fish, two glasses of sparkling water, and a piece of bread.

'She is tired, poor little thing. I am taking this to her,' said Joanna. 'The gentry are served in the dining-room—they will find the priest there and our guides.'

There was a tall crucifix at the end of the long bare dining-room, where the priest was supping with his candle before him, and a table was set opposite with another that was lighted for us. Peter and the other man were also sitting drinking and munching the hard seed-biscuit of the country with their enormous mouths, a few peasants looked in at us and went away, the little waitress came and went, like Nata and her sister used to do, with her pouch of office hanging from her waist. In the middle of his supper the old priest rose from table, and stood with folded hands and reverently said a prayer, and then sat down again. Joanna, who had come in, crossed herself devoutly, and then went up and entered into conversation with him. He listened and ate, and responded with benevolent nods. Did many gentry come to the place ? Not many, Joanna imagined ; it was not to compare for furniture to their own 'Black Eagle,' at C——.

'But it is pretty here in the forest in summer-time,' said the old priest.

'Eh! summer is better than winter,' says Joanna; 'everything looks so green, and there is plenty of food for the cattle, and flowers grow by the cart-full.'

The old priest told her, as he helped himself to prunes, that this was the country for flowers. 'Collectors came from every part of Europe; up on the Schlern,' he said, 'there are many rare species I myself have gathered there.' We left her still plying him with questions, to go and sit out in the dusk of the wooden gallery until it was time to go to bed. Fragrant and cool came the air blowing in our faces, softly shone the stars and the great crescent moon beyond the ruined castle. One or two of the people spoke to us, as they, too, stood admiring and leaning against the wooden balustrade. One funny little girl, called Urse, came up and sat upon the bench beside me, and asked as usual if we were married, and showed H.

her silver ring that her father had given her, only it was too dark to see the little cross upon it and the letters beneath.

XII.

Fortunata came knocking at my door early next morning before I was quite ready. I had been listening for some time to the waking sounds, the voices in the chapel, the children calling to one another, the pump, the footsteps on the wooden gallery. I had heard little Urse chattering outside my door, and Fortunata and Madame Hofer calling Joanna once or twice.

'Is Joanna with you?' Fortunata said.

I answered through my door: 'I have not seen her; tell them to prepare our breakfast with buttered eggs.'

'Yes,' said Fortunata, going away.

Our breakfast was ready spread in the long room. There were three glasses, very brightly polished, to drink the coffee, three dry twisted horns of bread, and a great dish of eggs broken up, and smoking and cooked with pepper. We felt a little ashamed of our luxurious habits when we saw the peasant-women coming shyly to ask for their modest glasses of fresh water and dry half horns of bread. I was pouring H.'s coffee into her glass when Fortunata came again.

'Had we all we wished? could she get us anything?'
'Signora,' Fortunata said. 'I cannot imagine where Joanna can be. She was gone when I awoke this morning; she has not been to mass; she has had no breakfast; I cannot find her anywhere.'

'She has gone off for a ramble this lovely morning,' said H. 'My dear, ask Madame Hofer for some more hot milk.'

'Cousin Hofer says she may have gone up to the castle,' Fortunata cried, coming back with the milk; and then H. proposed we should all go there after breakfast.

Many of the women were only now coming out of the chapel and crowding through the doorway. The old fellows, whose devotions were shorter—naturally, at their age, they could not have so much to pray for—were already established on their wooden benches, and stiffly stretching their kneebreeches along the gallery and in front of the baths; they gravely nodded good mornings over their pipes. , Urse and her little brother were standing swinging two great baskets on the green in front of the houses, and we asked them to come with us. But they said no, they were going to pick strawberries with Peter; he had desired them to wait.

Peter came up at this minute, and I asked him if he had seen nothing of Joanna. We had missed her, and were a little anxious. The giant chuckled, as if it was a capital joke. 'Had she run away? She was a strong one, she had no timidity, and would come to no harm. She wishes to outrun you all,' Peter said. 'There are plenty on the Alp to help her if she loses her way; besides, I told her many things as we came along; and now she will see the world for herself.'

I could not help a disagreeable feeling that this great fellow knew more than he chose to tell. However, my suspicions were too vague to put into other people's heads. I watched him march off with swinging shirt-sleeves, and the two children scampering after with their baskets.

We had a charming stroll to the old castle, climbing step by step between the circling stems of the fir-trees, among grey stones and mosses, and under bright changing shadows. Fortunata cheered up a little, and told us a story on the way.

'Once,' she said, 'there was another castle belonging to a cruel knight, who ravaged all the country round, and when the owner of this castle had to go away for a long journey, he desired his lady if she loved him not to pass beyond the walls till his return, and he collected provisions for a year, and he left her with her maid to wait his return. And some time after he had left, a little baby was born to the lady, and she and the maid tended it and nursed it. But when the year was nearly at an end, the provisions began to fail.

'The knight did not return till a year and a day after he had left his home. Then he came hurrying up the hill, and he saw someone watching for him from the tower-window, and he spurred his horse and waved his hand. But when he entered the castle all was silent, and no one came to meet him. The lady was dead,' said Nata; 'she had died watching from the window, with her little baby in her arms. The provisions were all gone and they had starved to death; and the poor maid was dead, too,' said Nata, and as she said it she turned a little pale and stumbled over a stone. 'The villagers say the white lady sometimes watches still from the old tower-window with her infant in her arms,' she added. 'Look! was that any one? can Joanna be up there?'

We reached the mossy old castle, with its sweet wild woodland view, but we found no Joanna, only some goats browsing the grass among the ruins. I could see that Fortunata was getting very anxious, though she said little; she was weak and impressionable, and her languor seemed to have changed into a sort of fever; her cheeks burned. I scolded her for it and for being so silly as to be frightened, but in truth we too thought it strange when we got down to find no news of the girl. Our Audrey was cleaning her pails, and knew nothing of Joanna, except that she had not come back. And then Nata went away into the little chapel. I saw her kneeling there, poor little thing, with her face buried in her hands, as I passed the gallery window.

Joanna was a stout, hearty girl. Madame Hofer said, as Peter had done, that she had gone out for a walk and probably lost her way; but there were people at work on the Alps all about who would put her in the right road again. To quiet Fortunata, we determined to send round to the neighbouring châlets and ask if she had been seen, and this being settled, Madame Hofer went on with her cooking. All the peasant people were very kind and re-assuring; one or two of them volunteered to go off and look for her. The old fellows took their silver pipes out of their mouths to recount their own early exploits. 'Per-haps she has gone up the Schlern,' said one of the boys, open-mouthed; but he was peremptorily snubbed for the suggestion by his grandfather. 'The Schlern was not for little boys or women.' And so the time passed slowly as the shadows shifted, to the hum of the voices tranquilly discoursing, to the measured footsteps of the people cross-

ing the little gallery. The old men, who seemed per
manently established on the bench outside my door, made
their jokes as the younger women passed by; the housemaid, followed by her tame goat, clumped from the well
to the kitchen and back to the well again with her tubs.
It was all sunny and warm and sweet, and would have been
utterly peaceful to me if it had not been for the thought
of poor little Nata with her burning cheeks. Seeing her flit
past my window, I thought it best to lay hands upon her.

'Come in here, Nata,' I said, 'and keep still, my dear.
You will flurry yourself into a fever if you come and go in
the sun. We have sent some messengers to ask for news of
Joanna. Madame Hofer will send us word when they return.'

'Cousin Hofer only laughs,' Fortunata said, trying not
to cry. The troubles and agitations of the last few days
had told upon her nerves. I guessed that they had been
strained to the uttermost before. For herself, the girl had
plenty of spirit, and had done her best to bear the doubt,
vexation, and wretchedness from which she had suffered so
cruelly of late. She had been good, and uttered no word
of complaint; but who can say what cruel pangs that poor
little heart had endured? She had been foolish, perhaps, and
romantic; but Nata's was a deep sweet nature, and her
heart beat truly; and though she could struggle for herself, she broke down in nervous terror for Joanna.

'Oh, Signora,' she said, a little wildly, 'all this time I have tried not to feel, and to-day I am all like one who is dead. I don't feel, and yet I know that I am suffering. Yesterday was a terrible day, so beautiful, and yet so sad ; all I saw only seemed like beautiful pain, and Joanna walked beside me, saying, " Courage, courage ; " and now, if harm has come to her, if wild beasts—if——' Nata broke out into sobs.

'Listen, my dear,' I said. 'This is all nonsense; there are no wild beasts in these woods except little squirrels and rabbits, and when Joanna comes home we will give her the scolding she deserves for frightening us all. Now you must lie down and wait patiently till the messengers return. Don't, my child.' She was kissing my hand just like a child. She did not lie down, but sat on the straw chair beside the bed, resting her aching head on the dark cotton counterpane. The tears and the silence soothed her, and now that she had ceased to struggle against her terrors they seemed to harass her less. At last she was quiet, and I, sitting in the window, took up a book and tried to read. It was a pretty story, but I could not fix my mind upon it. I looked at Madame Hofer standing in the gallery and resting after her morning's work, and then at the fir-trees, and at the

bright azure beyond them ; and then I watched little Urse
and her brother running across the green. They ran straight
towards a peasant-woman who was knitting a stocking in
the sun. At first I thought they were at play, for they
clung to her skirt and the woman bent over them. I
fancied she might be their mother. She dropped her
knitting and caught little Urse's hand. Something in her
action disturbed me, and at the same time I saw Madame
Hofer lean forward over the low wooden gallery. It might
be a fancy, but my heart began to beat with a nervous
apprehension as I put down my book and went out
quickly. When I came out on the balcony I found that
it was indeed no play that was going on : the children
were sobbing, and their mother, with a scared face, was
hurrying towards the house.

'Frau Hofer !' she said, 'come you quick—here is
something happened in the wood!' We ran down the
steps together. I had left the door of my room open, and
at the cry the woman gave Nata came running out too.
She seemed to guess what had happened almost before the
children spoke.

'Joanna was lying at the foot of the Schlern,' they
said. 'The gentleman found her, and he called Hans,'
sobbed little Urse, 'when he was climbing for strawberries,

and I called Peter, and when Peter came he told us to stop, and ran away, and he did not come back, and she was lying quite still in her hat.'

'And there was blood upon it,' said Hans, 'and Urse said she was dead, and the gentleman got angry, and said, "Why did no one come?" and I was frightened. And Urse came too.'

'I could not stay alone with the stranger, he frightened me,' sobbed little Urse.

'You heartless children, to leave her!' cried Frau Hofer, striking at Hans. Nata caught her hand. 'It is well that they came to tell us; now we can go to her,' she said, quite calmly, and in a faint shrill voice. 'Hans will show the way. Will you tell someone to follow us, Cousin Hofer, with wine and a blanket to carry her home.' Nata was the calmest and most collected of us all.

The children led the way along the winding path, under the trees; on our way we met Peter, the carter, flying through the brushwood. He had been, I don't know where, to leave a message for the doctor. 'He is in these parts to-day,' he said breathless; 'he is curing Anton Burlis' mother of her fever. Courage,' said he, kindly, 'I guessed where she was gone. Joanna is not dead, don't fear. So I said to the man who found her,

" Ho! she will live. I gave myself just such another crack on the head, and I am none the worse." ' Madame Hofer shrugged her shoulders. ' *Your* head!' she said, expressively.

' The stranger is gone,' said Peter. ' Here she is by this great rock.'

She was not dead, poor dear child. She was lying senseless, alone, in her hat, as the children described her, in a still green nook, at the foot of the great Schlern mountain. Everywhere hung green veils of light, and of soft mosses spreading over every stone and path-way, and green misty depths showed beyond the stems of the fir-trees. Was this sweet silent valley the valley of the shadow of death? I wondered. Was this a death-bed? —this carpet, where gentians and harebells were shining and white petals blown by the wind, and insects gathering sweet juices out of silver stars. Even from the rocks green creepers were hanging ; those cruel massed rocks from which she must have fallen!

At the time I hardly saw anything but her pale lips. Now the whole scene rises up before me in its intense sadness and beauty. That still green dell with the sound of the crickets whistling, Madame Hofer's scared face, the children hanging back behind their mother's skirt, and Nata, tender and passionate, kneeling by the poor senseless body, raising the pale head in her arms, gently loosening the hat from the clotted plaits to which it had been fastened. If Joanna lived, this absurd hat had probably saved her life. Dear honest Joanna, surely there was no life so precious among us all; so useful, so kindly, so cheerful and contented. Soon some of the good people came from the bath-house, bringing a hay-cloth to carry her home. They laid her gently down upon it; they were all subdued by that mystery of inanition, and spoke below their breaths. Only Peter talked out as usual, and described 'his crack' to each new comer.

XIII.

SOMETHING now happened which seemed to add to the strangeness and unreality of this sad moment. For some minutes past a murmuring sound had reached us from the heights above, and we now saw a quaint procession—men and women—passing along the edge of the cliff overhead, in conical hats like poor Joanna's; the men wore flapping waistcoats like Peter's; they all held rosaries in their hands, and were praying aloud as they went. They did not see us, nor did they hear Peter when he called; their prayers drowned his voice. It is not the first time that such a thing has happened. As he cried 'Hola!' they walked on, and disappeared, but another voice, nearer at hand, and from a different direction, answered, and in a minute more a figure came leaping from rock to rock with quick awkward haste, and hurried towards us. . . . Did I not recognise it? Those long loose limbs, that nervous haste, that green vasculum swinging from its strap! I looked once, and then again bewildered, and then at Nata, who was gazing with a changing face. . . . Yes, she too recognised him: it was the Count, he was unmistakable. 'Ah, there he is come back,' said Peter, in a satisfied tone. 'He found her, but he did not know what to do till I came up.' Even at this moment, to my shame I confess, a thought of what the future might have in store came to me. Dear honest Joanna herself, would she not have been the first to share it? The load seemed lightened. All must be well for Nata, since Count Saverio had come to her. All well! Of what was I thinking? Here was De Pavis trembling and scared, Nata crying, and our poor Joanna lying senseless, still in her bearer's arms, with her fair hair clotted with blood.

'Thank heaven you are here! I thought you were never coming,' said the Count, coming straight towards us and not looking surprised to see us. 'I had gone a little way to look for you. We must get her home. I found her by the strangest, saddest chance. Don't cry, Nata; she *must* get well.' He was trembling. He seemed quite unnerved, and unlike himself; perhaps for the first time in his life he had come in contact with a real sorrow.

And so they carried her home, quickly and carefully, along the little winding paths, crossing the little brooks, stopping beneath the branches of the fir-trees. Peter was at Joanna's head, two stout peasant-women held the cloth at her feet, and Nata walked at her side. The first great burst of summer was over, and the life of this sylvan world seemed subdued to a gentler radiance. The year was ending in peaceful dissolution. But our Joanna's life was not yet at its end; nor had her warm heart ceased to beat for ever for those she loved. Many of the peasants from the bath-house had joined us, and came quietly along. More than one of these compassionate people fell down on their knees by the wayside cross to pray for Joanna's life, as she was carried by, with that silent face, and the heavy hand hanging over the side of the cloth.

All the way back Saverio never spoke, nor did Nata seem to heed his presence: her whole wistful heart seemed given to Joanna. But as they walked along, I saw him looking at her with a humble pitiful look that touched me and made me like him better than I had ever done. She was so changed, so thin, so sad. Even his return could not bring back her bloom all in one moment. What a mystery it is that the happiness, the light of one life, should be so often in the gift of another's will! Which of us is there that does not hold chords that may vibrate from the very hearts of those about us? Let us pray that with reverent and loving care we may use our power, half-unconscious as it is. . . .

I hurried on before them to make ready a room, and I had hardly prepared everything, with Audrey's help, when she said, looking from the gallery, 'Here they come, and there is the doctor.' The doctor came walking through the wood, and met the little procession as it reached the foot of the wooden stairs. Many brown hands were held out to greet him, and he nodded right and left as he followed Joanna's bearers up the creaking wooden flight. He was an old man with long white hair and a staff and silver pipe, which he gave me to hold while he helped to lay Joanna on the straw bed which had been made ready.

'There are too many here,' he said, motioning the people gently out of the room. 'She will soon revive.'

'That is as I told you,' said Peter, with a slap upon his knee. Then he jerked his chin. 'What is that she is holding in her hand?' he said.

Madame Hofer gently unclasped the poor fingers and took a tuft of crushed purple flowers from between them. 'It is only a flower!' she said.

'It is Moretti's Campanula,' said the doctor, taking it into his own hand. "She must have caught it as she fell, poor child. It grows high up on the rock.'

There was a moment's silence, then a sudden burst of new tears.

'Oh, my dear, my poor dear,' sobbed Nata, as she fell on her knees, and hiding her face in her hands. 'The flower, the lilac flower! Oh, Signora, do you remember?'

Did I remember!—my foolish words and nonsense,— talk of charms and magic, Joanna's wistful eyes and self-reproach that night upon the terrace. Only too well I remembered it all. Could it be that *I* had done all this mischief by my idle words? Ah me, the reproach was mine now, and I was too old to cry it away like Fortunata.

The Count seemed uneasy too; he turned very red, and I think he muttered something about the 'Devil take that infernal flower!' as he left the room; but he came back wistfully the next instant to say, 'Courage, Nata: don't cry!' And he put his arm round her and raised her up. She looked at him through her tears with a half-doubting trustful look, like some little wild animal that trembles yet knows no fear.

Then they all went away, and we undressed Joanna as well as we could. It seemed an age while the doctor examined her. She was cruelly bruised and cut and sprained on the side on which she had fallen; and there, besides, was the one deep cruel wound beneath her hair; but the skull was uninjured; the high hat had truly saved her life. Peter stood outside ready to go off again for medicine and bandages to the Alp where the doctor was staying; Nata's tears kept dropping— dropping on the counterpane, on the straw mattress, on the dear pale face. They were softer, happier tears, as Joanna's colour revived a little beneath this gentle rain; light came into her dim eyes, she stirred and whispered, 'Nata, here!' then she opened her soft lids wide and looked a little wildly from one to the other. The doctor nodded. 'All goes well,' he said; and then he wrote something against the wall, and he went to the door and gave it to Peter, who bounded down the gallery in two steps. There was a whisper outside amongst the peasants, while here inside Madame Hofer stood with a candle and a pair of scissors; and Nata was hanging over Joanna's bed silently, and yet with all her tenderest heart's signs and unspoken language welcoming her back to life after that awful journey from which she was returning.

. 'The Signora!' Joanna said, recognising me; then she began feeling about the bedclothes and faltered something about a flower.

'Hush—hush! It is safe, you are safe; all, all is well,' said Nata, clasping her hands. 'Lie still while we thank God for your deliverance from peril.'

Some minutes afterwards I saw the doctor looking about uneasily from one side to the other. ' Is anything amiss?' I asked, anxiously. 'I have mislaid my pipe,' he said, and then I discovered that I had been holding the pipe all the while in my hand.

The doctor had done his work, and sat chattering with the old oracles down below. Joanna was unconscious again, but this time it was only a quiet sleep after the pain and fatigue of having her hurts dressed and attended to. H., with her kind face beaming with sympathy, came gently stirring the door-handle to call me to supper.

'This morning it was Joanna. Now it is Fortunata who is lost, just when supper is ready too,' said Madame Hofer, meeting us, and speaking with some asperity.

XIV.

H. WAITED till she was gone, then she laid her hand on my arm and pointed to two dim figures on a seat beneath a tree. As we were looking at them they got up and came strolling towards the house. A minute or two after they came into the dining-room. They stood at the door, blinking their eyes in the dazzle of two candles and the soup-tureen. Perhaps I ought to have had more apprehensions, but somehow since Saverio's return I had felt none, and I went to meet them, saying, 'Come, here is the soup. Joanna is asleep, and Urse's mother is with her, and we are only waiting for you.'

'I am sorry to have detained you,' said the Count,

standing quite erect, with a look of such real happiness
in his face that it was not difficult to foresee what was
coming, while Nata took my hand and pressed it, with
a long soft thrill that told me all I wanted to know.
However, they said no more just then, and all supper-
time the Count was much as usual. Nata ate nothing,
but sat with innocent happy eyes, looking as I had
never seen her look before. I was struck, for the first
time, by her extreme beauty and dazzling brilliancy of
colour. It was like sunlight shining after a cloud had
passed away. During supper the Count told us that
he had been busy of late completing a collection, and
writing the last chapters of his work upon mountain
campanulas. There are no less than sixty different
species of these charming flowers, he informed us, of
which forty are to be found in the Alps alone. ' I
wished to give my whole mind to my work,' he said,
with an odd look as he ate his chicken. ' My book has
given me a great deal of trouble, and taken a long time
to write,' he added.

Almost too long a time for his happiness, I thought.
After supper I went out into the gallery again. Seeing
me standing a little apart, Nata came up, flung her
arms round me, and began whispering her happiness
in the twilight

' Oh, Signora, he loves me—he loves me—he is my betrothed.'

Afterwards I heard more, not from Nata nor from the Count, but from my old friend Della Santa ; she it was who had warned him of the cruel gossip of the place. ˉHe was greatly disturbed and shocked, and very indignant. He had never faced the matter fairly until then. In spite of his aunt's horrified warnings he started at once to follow Nata, and only once (so he confessed long afterwards) did he hesitate at the thought of the storm he should bring about his head by such a marriage. This was a minute before chance, or Providence, brought him to the rock where poor Joanna was lying.

How sweet the evening fell after that long toilsome day. The full moon came sliding up from behind the roof, the lights gleamed, the dark figures passed, and very very far away the echo of an evening hymn reached us from one of the Alps. The doctor and the priest passed us smoking their pipes. ' You may be quite at ease about your patient,' said the doctor, nodding as he went by.

It seemed too much almost. ' You will never be able to persuade Joanna that the purple flower is not a charm,' said H.

'I will try,' I said, feeling very much ashamed. 'I shall tell her that charms are not the things themselves, but are signs of the facts they represent. When I put my hand in yours, it is a sign that I love you, that I am thinking of you. When people love each other truly, anything, everything becomes a charm; and flowers, and bits of hair, and old ribbons, and rings, and all sorts of rubbish, become priceless.'

'I think I understand you,' said H. smiling; 'but I don't think Joanna will.' And I am afraid H. was right.

THE END.

LONDON : PRINTED BY
SPOTTISWOODE AND CO., NEW-STREET SQUARE
AND PARLIAMENT STREET

www.ingramcontent.com/pod-product-compliance
Lightning Source LLC
Chambersburg PA
CBHW050902130726
47900CB00015B/1752